July's Trials
A Larry Macklin Mystery-Book 9

A. E. Howe

Books in the Larry Macklin Mystery Series:

November's Past
(Book 1)

December's Secrets
(Book 2)

January's Betrayal
(Book 3)

February's Regrets
(Book 4)

March's Luck
(Book 5)

April's Desires
(Book 6)

May's Danger
(Book 7)

June's Troubles
(Book 8)

July's Trials
(Book 9)

ISBN: 0-9997968-1-X
ISBN-13: 978-0-9997968-1-8

DEDICATION

For the families of law enforcement officers everywhere.
May your loved ones always come home safe.

CHAPTER ONE

I awoke to the sound of the air conditioner cycling on. *Welcome to summer in north Florida,* I thought. The roar of the air was quickly drowned out by the thunder of little paws running through the house, accompanied by the occasional gruff bark or insistent meow.

"Time to get up," I said, rolling over and poking my girlfriend, Cara Laursen. "The kids are hungry."

"Is the sun up?" she asked, a pillow clutched firmly over her face.

"Define 'up.'"

"Big, sunny, happy face kind of thing in the eastern sky," came her muffled answer from under the pillow.

"Barely. But it's already hot enough for the air to be running."

Alvin, Cara's Pug, chose that moment to hop up on the bed. I left her to see to the dog while I stumbled to the bathroom and then on into the kitchen to put an end to the steady meowing that was coming from Ivy. The tabby never thought that my visit to the toilet should take precedence over her breakfast.

"If I didn't go to the bathroom first then the kitchen could get very wet," I explained to her as she waited impatiently for her food.

Half an hour later, Cara and I were sitting at the table together, eating our breakfast. As she finished her yogurt, I smiled at her apologetically.

"I'm sorry I have to go in on a Sunday, but it was the only day we could get this particular group of lawyers together." The Thompson drug case was finally coming to trial and I'd spent the better part of the past week in depositions.

"You meeting Matt?"

"Yep. Then we're taking his car to pick up Eddie."

Matt Greene was a DEA agent who had worked as a deputy with the Adams County Sherriff's Office until this past January. He and I had had some clashes when he worked for our department, but since he'd taken the job with the Drug Enforcement Agency our relationship had become more cordial. We'd had to work together a couple of times on cases that crossed jurisdictions.

"You all playing nice?"

"Actually, I kind of like working with him. Strange. I couldn't stand him when he was here, but now…"

"You're lucky he still talks to you. You *did* try to arrest him for murder." Cara gave me a wicked grin.

"Yeah, yeah. We've gotten past that," I said, smiling back at her. "Life can be very odd sometimes."

"You've both changed and grown," Cara said, channeling her hippy mother's New Age philosophy.

"I hate to say it, but you might have a point. Are you claiming that you've had a maturing effect on me?"

"You were old when I met you."

"Thanks a lot."

"Tell Matt hi for me. We should get together for dinner while he's here," Cara said, getting up and taking our bowls to the sink.

I clipped my holster and badge onto my belt and picked up my jacket. Even though we'd be spending the day in meetings with lawyers, I had no plans to actually wear it unless I had to. The temperature would be hovering near ninety-five with the humidity almost the same. July in Florida was simply brutal. I gave Cara a quick kiss and headed out into the heat.

Shortly before one o'clock, I finally walked out of the lawyer's office. It was in a building in downtown Calhoun that also housed other law firms and various professional offices.

"Eddie's a piece of work," Matt said. We were standing in the hallway, waiting for Eddie Thompson as he used the bathroom.

"He's… different."

"I have to admit it, though, he's getting the job done."

Matt was the DEA's lead agent on the Thompson task force. I was acting as the liaison from the sheriff's office, and I was also there to keep Eddie calm and on task. He'd been my confidential informant for months and the case against the Thompson family drug gang had come about through our "professional" relationship. The case had grown over the past couple of months to the point where there were dozens of lawyers, state attorneys and law enforcement agencies involved. Matt and I were tasked with escorting Eddie to his depositions. We'd been at it for several days. Today it had taken almost four hours before the lawyers had run out of questions.

"You want to grab something to eat on the way back to the safe house?" I asked.

"Tell you what. Let's turn Eddie over to the marshals at the safe house and go out afterward."

"Eddie's going to want something." Eddie always wanted to stop and eat when we took him anywhere. He'd actually put some weight on his skinny frame now that he was off of drugs and getting three or more square meals a day.

"We'll hit the Whataburger drive-thru on the way back. That'll make him happy."

The bathroom door opened and Eddie came out looking

nervous, which was not unusual. I couldn't blame him. Serving as the chief witness against his family's illicit drug operation was like putting on antlers and a brown suit and sneaking around in the woods during hunting season.

"Where are we going to eat? I'm starving."

"We'll stop at the Whataburger and you can get whatever you want to take back to the safe house," I told him.

"I'm starting to think you all don't like being seen with me," he said with a little pout.

"Honestly, it's not that much fun going into a restaurant wearing plate armor."

"You got a point there," Eddie agreed, awkwardly adjusting the heavy metal plates in the vest he wore that had "DEA" stenciled in large yellow letters on both sides. We all wore the vests anytime we were outside with Eddie. Not only did we have other members of his family to worry about, but there had recently been an ad on the dark web offering a fifty-thousand-dollar reward for anyone who could permanently silence Eddie.

We exited the building with Matt in front, Eddie in the middle and me bringing up the rear. As soon as I was out the door, sweat started to soak through my shirt.

Even though it was Sunday, there were quite a few people moving around downtown. Several churches near the square had only recently let out and folks were still lingering outside and socializing despite the heat. Matt and I kept our eyes open for anyone approaching Eddie as we walked toward Matt's car.

Eddie looked exhausted. This had been his third deposition detailing his father's and grandfather's various illegal activities. The Thompsons were a rot that had been poisoning Adams County for generations.

"You did good," I told him as we reached the car.

"They're going to kill me," he responded morosely.

"No they won't. They're going to be in jail for a long, long time," Matt said encouragingly.

He was reaching out to open the door when Eddie

started slapping his pockets.

"Crap!" he said, wheeling around and bumping into me. One of the steel plates in his vest banged into my hand.

"What the hell?" I muttered, shaking my hand and grabbing at Eddie as he tried to barge past me. His nervous personality caused him to act erratically on a good day, and the past week had not been made up of good days.

"I left my phone in the bathroom."

"Leave it!" I pushed him back toward the car. "I'll pick it up later."

"No. I need it."

"It's not like you can call anyone," I said reasonably.

"Music… games," he whined, acting like an eight-year-old. In his defense, he had been living under a microscope for days and being locked up in the safe house couldn't have been much fun. I sighed.

"Okay, okay. You and I will go back. Matt, do you mind keeping an eye out from here? And if you want to go ahead and get the air going inside the car, that wouldn't break my heart."

Matt looked around with a trained eye before answering. "Sure. You got your radio. Call before you come back out."

"10-4."

I walked Eddie back toward the building, keeping one hand on his arm to make sure he didn't get too far out in front of me. I kept my head on a swivel, looking right and left as we approached. Five feet from the glass door, Eddie and I were pushed hard from behind. As I fell to the ground, I saw the glass in front of me explode. Seconds later, my ears were assaulted by a deafening roar.

I rolled over and saw Matt's car engulfed in flames. Both of the front doors had been blown off and the roof was gone. I got to my hands and knees and crawled over to Eddie, who was clutching his head and whimpering softly.

"Are you okay?" I asked, patting him down swiftly and looking for injuries.

"They really did try to kill me," he said in a dazed voice.

"Are you hurt?" I said firmly.

"No," he answered slowly, staring at the burning car.

"Stay here!"

I got up and ran toward the car as my mind went on autopilot. I used my radio to call for backup and an ambulance, barely aware of what I was saying. Twenty feet from the car, I saw what remained of Matt and stopped and turned away.

I saw a middle-aged woman lying on the ground behind me, maybe forty feet from the car. There was blood on her face. That's when I became aware of other people standing on the sidewalks and staring at me. Cars were stopped in the street, their drivers gawking at the destruction.

"Don't get up," I told the woman as I hurried over to her. She looked at me with unfocused eyes. Kneeling beside her, I could see that most of the blood appeared to be coming from several superficial cuts.

"Are you okay?" she asked me.

"What?"

"There's blood…" She reached out and touched my forehead. Only then did I realize that I'd hit my head when I fell. I reached up and felt a large scrape bleeding freely above my eyebrow.

Finally I could hear sirens. "Stay here until the EMTs have seen you," I instructed the woman.

"What happened?" she asked as I stood up.

I ignored her. The initial rush of adrenaline was fading and my head was beginning to throb. Suddenly I remembered Eddie and started back toward the office building. Several of the lawyers we'd just met with were standing outside in shock. Lying on the ground in a pile of shattered glass was Eddie's ballistic vest. Only the vest.

My head was on fire now and downtown was erupting in total chaos. Half of our sheriff's deputies, the fire department and two ambulances were already on the scene. Pete Henley, my old partner, arrived and took charge, personally making sure that one of the EMTs dragged me over to an ambulance. I kept insisting that I needed to find Eddie, but Pete only nodded as he hurried away.

Dad arrived within minutes. As sheriff, he fully trusted his investigators to handle the details, but this case was going to require his direct involvement. While Pete saw to the immediate problems of securing the scene, coordinating traffic and treating the injured, Dad began coordinating with the various federal agencies involved and prepared for the onslaught of media.

Even as I tried to fight off the ministrations of the EMT, I knew that I wasn't thinking straight. Part of it was the throbbing pain of the headache, but I was also having a hard time processing what had happened. I couldn't believe that Matt had been killed in an instant. There was a voice inside my head telling me that I had to find Eddie… that I had to make all of this right.

The EMT was talking to me, but nothing he said made any sense. As if from a distance, I heard myself arguing with everyone that I was fine, but they obviously didn't believe me. We were headed to the hospital within twenty minutes of the explosion.

CHAPTER TWO

"Really, I'm okay," I told Cara, looking at my watch. Almost four hours had passed since the bomb had gone off.

"That's not what the doctor says."

"I'm not staying here overnight," I said, trying to look focused. I'd been given some pain medication—not too much, but enough to make me feel a little floaty. The doctor had said that I clearly had a concussion, but his main concern was that there could be bleeding inside my skull. Now we were waiting for him to review the results of the X-rays and scans to tell us how bad it was.

One advantage I'd noticed to being in law enforcement was that I often seemed to get more attentive service from medical professionals. After only half an hour of watching Cara pace around the exam room, the doctor returned.

"The good news is I couldn't see any bleeding or swelling." He then proceeded to ask me a series of questions about events and people in my life, sometimes checking with Cara to make sure that I was answering them correctly.

"Okay. As long as he doesn't have trouble walking or vision issues, then he's fine to sleep. If there are any signs of a problem, ask him some simple questions. If he seems off, bring him straight back here. Understood?"

"Absolutely," Cara told him, giving me a stern look that said she was going to be in charge for the next twenty-four hours.

"I'm not sure if I'll even be able to sleep," I said grimly. Despite the pain in my head, I wanted nothing more than to get caught up with the investigation.

"You need to take it easy. Rest is important. Another concussion in the next few weeks would not be good for you. It could lead to some serious long-term effects. Do I need to give you the full lecture?" The doctor fixed me with a hard stare.

"No, I hear you," I said, raising my hands in surrender.

As soon as the doctor left, I got out of bed and changed out of the flimsy hospital gown back into my ash-and-sweat-stained clothes. When I finished, Cara was staring at me.

"I'll physically take it easy, I promise," I told her. "But I'm going to find out who did this." I felt my jaw clench and the pounding in my head increased.

"There are a lot of people out looking for the person who planted that bomb. You heard the doctor. You need to rest."

I knew that Cara was just concerned for me, but I felt like she didn't know me at all if she thought I was going to see Matt murdered right in front of me and then not go on the hunt for his killer.

"I have to be a part of the investigation," I said, trying not to snap at her.

"I know. But let some of the others carry the bulk of the responsibility." She touched my arm lightly.

"Come on. Let's get out of here," I said, trying to smile and failing miserably.

Cara opened the door to find a large, middle-aged man wearing a suit standing in front of us. He fumbled in his pocket and pulled out a leather case to display a badge.

"Agent Harvey, Alcohol, Tobacco and Firearms. Deputy Larry Macklin?"

"I am."

"I need to ask you a few questions about the explosion."

"I guess we can talk in here," I said.

"Won't take long. I just want to get a few answers as we launch our investigation." He turned to Cara. "Would you mind waiting outside?"

Cara's eyes narrowed, but before she could tell him to shove off, I caught her eye and nodded. Reluctantly, she left the room.

"What type of bomb was it?" I asked before he had a chance to say a word.

"We don't know anything yet. You're the one with the answers right now," Harvey said, not unkindly. "First, tell me what you were doing, starting about thirty minutes before the event."

I told him everything I could remember up until the moment I found myself lying on the ground.

"Did you see Agent Greene open the car door?"

"No."

"Did you see him use a clicker to unlock the door?"

"Yes, I think so."

"So you and the witness, Eddie Thompson, were headed back toward the lawyer's office where Eddie said he'd left his phone. Did you hear Greene open or close the car door?"

"No. It was out on the street, and I was focusing my attention on the hundred and eighty degrees in front of us. I knew that Matt would have our backs."

"Don't you think he'd have been better able to perform his job if he hadn't gotten into the car?" Even though I couldn't detect any inflection in the question to make it sound accusatory, it was hard not to take it that way.

"Matt Greene was one of the most professional law enforcement officers I have ever met. If he got into the car then it was because he felt that the area was secure, and that he could perform his duty from inside the car." I paused as I remembered something, then said, my voice quiet, "I *did* ask him to start the air conditioner." For the first time, I realized that Matt might have died doing something that I had requested.

"Okay, did you hear him start the car?"

"No."

"Had you all turned on the radio or the air conditioner that morning when you rode to the lawyer's office?"

"We definitely did not have the radio on. I'm not sure whether the air was on or not. It wasn't too hot when we left the safe house." I tried to think. "I know that the temperature in the car wasn't uncomfortable."

"Do you think that Agent Greene might have turned on the radio when he got in the car?"

"I don't know. However, I will say that he wasn't someone to allow a lot of distractions while he was working. So I doubt it. Are you thinking that the bomb was hooked up to an electrical switch? Aren't most bombs these days detonated by phones or other wireless devices?"

"We don't have any opinions yet. I'm just gathering information that will be used later to make a determination." Agent Harvey paused for a moment, then relented a little on the I'm-a-federal-agent-robot routine. "If we assume that the bomb was intended to kill the witness, then it seems more likely that the person wasn't watching and using a remote detonator."

"Otherwise he'd have waited until Eddie was in the car. That makes sense."

I could hear voices from the other side of the door. I couldn't quite make out what they were saying, but it sounded heated. I could tell from the look on Agent Harvey's face that he was trying to listen too.

"That's all I need for the moment, but we'll be back in touch. We'll need a more detailed statement."

"Sure," I said, moving toward the door. When I opened it, I found Cara face to face with another man in a suit. I'd clearly interrupted an argument.

The man turned to me in relief. "Agent Devlin, DEA," he said, flipping his ID at me.

"I told you, he's answered questions for one of you

already. You don't need to badger him." Cara wasn't letting it go.

"And I told *you* that we need to find the witness in this case. Questioning Deputy Macklin is a priority," the man shot back at her.

"Eddie still hasn't been found?" I asked.

"No," Devlin said, glaring at Cara, who looked back at me and frowned. "Obviously we need to locate him as soon as possible. Do you think that he was abducted from the crime scene?"

I sighed and leaned against the door jam. "Knowing Eddie, I'd say he got spooked and took off. Two points. First, why would someone that wanted to silence him bother to abduct him when they could have just shot him... or both of us, for that matter? Second, if they *did* abduct him, then why would they take the time to take off his tactical vest?"

"Have you tried to get in contact with him?"

"No."

"He's been a little busy," Cara said angrily. Devlin had clearly pissed her off.

"The doctor said that you should be fine."

I wondered what the hell the doctor had been doing, telling some guy with the DEA what my condition was. "Look, if Eddie has gone to ground then it might take him a day or two to surface. Honestly, I can't say I blame him for running."

"Do you have any contact information for him that isn't in his witness protection file?"

"No," I lied.

Agent Harvey, who'd been listening patiently, decided that it was time to go and eased past us.

"I need to get home, but I'll talk to you tomorrow. Trust me. I'll find Eddie, and I plan on finding whoever did this to Matt."

"I didn't know Matt that long, but when one of our agents is murdered it becomes a top priority," Devlin said.

"I assumed that. And when one of my friends is

murdered, it becomes *my* top priority," I said, giving him my best stare. "Finding the murderer and finding Eddie are my jobs now." I just hoped that Dad would agree with me.

Devlin looked like he wanted to say something in response, but our faces must have been enough to discourage him.

"Fine. Tomorrow, then," he said and turned away.

Cara and I started to follow him down the hall when we saw another suit approaching. This time it was a woman with her FBI credentials hanging on her belt.

"No, absolutely not," Cara said to her as we got closer.

"I'm Special Agent—" the woman started, ignoring Cara.

"Sorry, can't talk right now," I said, nodding to Cara, who was giving the woman a dark scowl. "Doctor's orders. Call me in the morning."

"I don't think—"

"I gave Agents Harvey and Devlin what I could for now."

We were able to get around her and make our way out of the hospital without encountering any other federal agents.

Cara drove us home in silence. About halfway there, I couldn't take it anymore. It was unlike her to be so quiet. "What?" I asked.

"We don't need to talk about it right now," she said, staring out the windshield and squinting a little at the glare. The summer sun was still above the horizon as we headed west.

Of course, knowing that there was something she thought we needed to talk about made it impossible for me to think of anything else.

"What's wrong?" I asked, watching her purse her lips and stare out the window.

"Really, I…" She trailed off. Cara didn't play games, so I knew that something was really bothering her and she didn't know how to talk about it. That did nothing to make me feel better.

"Just tell me," I said, trying not to sound frustrated.

She sighed heavily and turned her head, looking at me for the first time since we got in the car. "It's complicated because I don't know how I feel about it. Well, that's not true. I know how I feel, I just don't know what you can do to make it better." She was weaving a complicated conversational thread.

"What's bothering you?"

"It's this!" She sounded exasperated, but I still didn't know what she was talking about.

"What?" I asked again, my voice rising a little.

"How many times have you been hurt or almost killed in the last six months?"

"A few. But I'm not trying to get hurt. It's part of the—" Then I realized why she'd been hesitant to bring it up. When we'd first gotten together, Cara had been uncomfortable with me being in law enforcement. It had been the biggest stumbling block to our relationship and it had taken us a while to overcome the issue.

"Exactly. I know I said that I'd come to terms with your job, and I really thought I had... But here I am taking you home from the hospital again. And Matt... I was really starting to like Matt..."

I watched as she lost the war against her tears. "Pull over."

Once it was safe, Cara pulled off to the side of the road. I touched her arm and she fell against me, giving in to her sobs. It was awkward with the seatbelts and bucket seats, but I managed to embrace her.

"I liked him too. And I'm going to find the person responsible for this." My voice sounded odd to me. Distant and angry. Not angry at Cara, just angry.

"I want you to catch them, but I couldn't stand losing you," she said into my shoulder.

"I'm not trying to get hurt, I swear. It wouldn't have been as bad today if I hadn't been wearing twenty pounds of steel plates. Which I was wearing so that I wouldn't get shot," I added, trying to joke.

"Just promise me you'll be careful," she said.

I kissed her gently and retrieved a napkin from the dash. Once her eyes were finally dry, we got moving again.

With Cara's attention focused back on the road, I pulled out my phone and called my partner, Darlene Marks. I'd texted her earlier to let her know I was okay, but we hadn't had a chance to talk about the explosion.

"I want to say something smartass, but nothing seems very funny today," she said.

"I know what you mean. Tell me Dad hasn't let the Feds take over."

"He's done the best he can. Pete is the lead investigator for our department, and your dad refused to let any of the Feds take evidence from the crime scene until we'd cataloged it. I thought it was going to turn into a knock-down, drag-out fight, but they relented. Your dad did have to agree to let an FBI team supervise."

"No sign of Eddie?"

"Not that I've seen, and Pete pulled me in to help, so I probably would have heard."

"I'll go looking for him tomorrow."

"Could someone have grabbed him after the bomb went off?"

"I've been trying to remember everything that happened, but I don't think so. I know it sounds like a set-up. Bomb goes off and everyone's attention is focused on the wreckage, allowing someone to grab the witness. But why would they take him? Like I told Agent Devlin at the hospital, they could have shot him right there."

"They didn't want to be seen?"

"They could have worn a mask. Besides, it would have been hard to get the vest off without Eddie's cooperation. Abducting him just doesn't make much sense."

"Maybe they thought it would go over better with a jury if Eddie just disappeared. If he's shot dead, it validates his information."

"Maybe. Still, without Eddie to cross-examine, the evidence won't get into court anyway. Even if he'd been shot in front of witnesses, that wouldn't be admissible in the drug and racketeering trials unless you could prove conclusively that his murder was tied to the other crimes. That would be a pretty tall order."

"I hope you're right."

"Me too. I kind of like the squirrelly little guy," I said.

"Are you sure that you'll be up to coming in tomorrow?" Darlene asked.

I looked over at Cara to see if she was listening. She gave me a look that was part *I wish you wouldn't* and part *I know you're going to anyway*.

"I just got a bump on the head. I'm fine."

I hung up with Darlene and called Pete next.

"It's all pretty grim," he said, sounding the way I felt.

"I don't think any of us are going to be having much fun any time soon."

"Matt's DEA supervisor notified his parents," Pete said.

I'd wondered who would take on that task. "I want to talk to them myself. I was the last person to see him. I know nothing will make them feel better, but maybe it will mean something to them. Losing any child is devastating, but losing a son like Matt… would be brutal."

There was an uncomfortable silence as we both thought about all the parents we'd had to notify of the death of a child. Then the image of Dad came to my mind. How would he have reacted if it had been me that was killed instead of Matt?

"What have you found out so far?" I asked Pete, breaking the silence.

"You haven't been cleared to work the case." Pete could be a stickler for some rules, but I didn't think he was going to be able to stonewall me on this one. We had too much water under the bridge for that.

"Don't make me remind you of past rule transgressions that one of us might have done to help out the other."

"Hush! The Feds are involved, so our phones are probably already bugged," he said with a small tinge of humor.

"We can do this over the phone, or you can meet me at my place. We'll be there in about twenty minutes."

"I'll come out there."

"You don't really think they're listening in, do you?"

"No, but Sarah wanted me to bring you some food. Besides, I want to question you."

"Are you going to be both good cop *and* bad cop?"

"I'll see you in half an hour," he responded, avoiding the question.

When Cara pulled into our driveway, I insisted on getting out and opening the gate. Back in the car, I felt odd riding up the drive through the twenty acres to our little doublewide. Everything seemed different. Maybe the concussion was worse than I thought.

CHAPTER THREE

I had just enough time to get a shower and change out of my ruined clothes before Pete showed up with the dinner that his wife, Sarah, had sent with him.

"She likes to feed people. Anything from a death in the family to a toothache, her answer is to send food. Honestly, she just likes feeding people. You've probably noticed," Pete said, showing off his round girth. "Seriously though, you have to stop getting hurt. Sarah's starting to think that law enforcement is dangerous work."

"I'm not doing this on purpose," I said, half joking, half exasperated and fully hoping that Cara hadn't heard him.

His face darkened. "I know. Jokes aren't very funny today. I can't believe that Matt's really dead."

We sat down at the kitchen table.

"He *is* dead, and I'm going to find out who's responsible. With some luck, we'll see the day they're strapped down to a gurney in Raiford." The death penalty was an imperfect system of justice, but there were times when I couldn't help but feel that it was justified. This was one of them. Whoever had planted that bomb did so with no concern for who they killed or injured.

"Matt and I were never friends and probably wouldn't

22

ever have been, but I respected him," Pete said. I appreciated him saying that. Matt and Pete had had a contentious history that went back to their early years with Adams County. Pete probably could have let it go, but Matt had never seemed able to.

"What do you know about the bomb?" I asked, wanting to focus on the task at hand.

"Not much. The ATF doesn't want to give out any preliminary findings, but I eavesdropped on them as much as I could. The bomb was fairly sophisticated. There appears to have been some sort of remote activation or detonation. They can't tell which yet."

"So we're looking for someone with bomb building experience."

"Or someone who can learn what they need to know from videos on the Internet."

"I guess, if you're willing to look in the dark corners," I mused, feeling my skin crawl at the idea that evil could network so easily these days.

"On the bright side, there should be evidence if we find the right suspect. Building a bomb is going to leave traces."

"Was it detonated by cell phone?"

"They don't know yet."

"I guess we'll have to leave all the forensic detective work to the ATF and FBI."

"Pretty much."

"I've been thinking… Were they after Eddie or not?"

"If they were, they failed. But…" Pete looked thoughtful.

"Exactly. If they detonated the bomb with a remote device that allowed them to be close enough to see the car, then they killed who they wanted to kill."

"Matt." Pete scrunched up his face in thought. "Could be. But wouldn't it be dangerous to do it when Matt was on such a high profile case? Plus, with a bomb you're going to bring in the full alphabet soup of federal agencies. Why not just kill him when he's on vacation or at home?"

"Because you want everyone to think that Eddie was the

intended target."

"Or for some reason this was the best time."

"Matt hasn't been in the area much since he went from working for our department to working for the DEA."

"On the other hand, if the bomb was wired to go off when someone started the car or turned on the radio or whatever, then we don't know for sure who the target was."

"True."

"It might have been you," Pete said almost offhand. "It could have been meant for you," he repeated more thoughtfully.

"Enough!" I said, immediately feeling the tension in the room. I looked over my shoulder to see Cara staring back at us from the microwave, where she was warming up the food that Sarah had sent. She quickly looked away.

"I'm the least likely target. It was Matt's car and Eddie has a big red circle on his back because of this drug case. No one has threatened me, and there was no reason for anyone to think that I'd be driving that car."

"But it had become the established pattern for you and Matt to pick up Eddie in Matt's car. Someone could easily assume that you would be in the car when it was started this afternoon. Except for a fluke, you would have been."

"It's possible that I was the target, but not very probable."

Pete thought about that. "I agree."

"Eddie was the most likely target, followed by Matt," I emphasized.

"And then you," Pete added at exactly the same moment that Cara came to the table with our food.

I caught another look from her. What could I tell her? Even I had begun to feel a little unease in the pit of my stomach. I had to admit that the explosion had rattled me. I looked down at my hand. It wasn't shaking, but it *felt* like it was shaking. *I just need to get some sleep*, I told myself.

"How are the witness interviews going?" I asked, hoping to change the subject.

"We've done over thirty so far, and we're gathering as much security camera footage as we can. Your dad had to intervene to keep the different agencies from fighting over the data, finally getting them to agree to let it all siphon through our department. He also scheduled a meeting in the morning to work out the turf issues. It looks like we're going to form a joint task force."

"What time?"

"That's probably not a good idea."

"I'm going to be there."

"You're a witness and a victim."

We'd started to eat the chicken and dumplings that Sarah had made. Cara had fixed herself a plate and sat down next to me. I could feel her staring daggers at me.

"I'm going to be involved in this investigation," I said firmly, feeling like they were both ganging up on me. I knew I was being unreasonable. Pete and Cara were only thinking about what was best for me and the investigation.

Pete looked down at his plate. "Maybe that can happen, but you're going to have to finish your debriefing and write your report first."

"I'll write my report tonight." I knew he had a point. I shouldn't have been talking to Pete at all yet, let alone sitting in on a broader discussion of the evidence. Anything I heard could alter my perception of the events as I had experienced them. Human memory is very pliable. We constantly alter our memories to match new information as we become aware of it, and there is no way for us to distinguish between our original perceptions and the altered ones.

"You should wait a couple days," Pete said.

"I'll write it tonight," I insisted.

Pete shrugged. "Don't tell me. I'm not the one who has to make the decision on whether or not you'll take part in the meeting." I could tell he was irritated that I wasn't acting more reasonable.

"I'll deal with my dad."

"If you push this and he lets you into the meeting, then

others could use it as a way to take the investigation away from us," Pete said, looking me square in the eye.

"I won't push too hard. But I'm not going to be frozen out of this case," I said.

My head was beginning to ache again. I rubbed my temples and I felt a hand on my arm. I turned and looked at Cara. Her eyes were pleading with me.

"The investigation is important to all of us. I just think you need to stand back for a couple of days. Write your report. Be interviewed by the FBI, ATF and DEA, *then* start working your way into the investigation," Pete said.

I thought about this. "There is one thing I can do right now. I can search for Eddie," I told them.

"Now that makes sense. The DEA has taken the lead on it, but they don't have anyone who knows the area or even where to start looking. He was your CI. You have every right to try and establish whether or not he's okay." Pete sounded upbeat now that I'd hit on an idea he could back.

We talked for a few more minutes before Pete said he had to head back to the office. It was after dark and Pete had already worked a twelve-hour day, but that didn't matter. No one was going to rest easy until we had some answers.

"What about my car?" I asked Pete at the door.

"We thought it should be gone over by the bomb squad and the crime scene guys, just to be safe."

"Great. I hope you told them to detail it afterward." Nothing like having the interior of your car covered in fingerprint powder.

"Yeah, right," Pete said as he walked to his car.

Later, I looked up from my laptop and watched as Cara walked aimlessly from one room to the next.

"I'm the one that should be unsettled." I tried to make a joke of it, but the truth was, she was getting on my nerves. What I really wanted was to be left alone to think things through.

"I just can't seem to relax," she said, not meeting my eyes.

"You don't have to worry about me. I got a bad bump on the head, but I'm fine."

"I know you want to get right back to work, but is that really a good idea?"

I could tell that she was upset, but I just felt irritated at her mothering.

"I don't know what else to do. You want me to relax? Well, the best way for that to happen is if I feel like I'm doing something to catch the son of a bitch that killed Matt and almost killed Eddie and me!" I realized that I was almost yelling. Even though I knew I'd overreacted, I couldn't bring myself to apologize. My head hurt.

"Whatever. Do what you want," Cara said and went into the bedroom, closing the door behind her.

I knew she was scared and worried, but a strange anxiety was beating an agitated rhythm inside my head that left me without the ability to show her the compassion she deserved. I felt both helpless to reach out to her and a sense of relief that I would be alone.

Well, sort of alone. Both Ivy and Alvin seemed to sense that something wasn't right. The Pug lay on the floor snoring, instead of curled up next to me on the couch as he often was. Ivy, normally as clingy as the vine she was named for, spent the evening curled up on the back of the couch, watching me closely.

I texted Eddie on his regular phone as well as an old burner he'd used in the past, but I wasn't surprised when I received no response. Without access to the current files on the bombing, the best I could do that night was review old case files for me and Matt on my laptop. I kept digging deeper and running down rabbit holes until pain and exhaustion took over.

CHAPTER FOUR

When morning came, I was lying on the couch with a blanket over me. My laptop was still open on the coffee table. I stumbled into the bathroom where Cara was getting ready for work at the veterinary clinic, dressed in animal-print scrubs that seemed far cheerier than either of our moods.

"How are you feeling?"

"Better. Thanks for the blanket."

"I'd have carried you to bed, but you're a little too heavy," she said with half a smile.

"I needed the sleep."

"Are you going in to work?"

The question was asked tentatively and I knew that she didn't mean to upset me. Still, I had to push down my sense of irritation. Hadn't we been over this already?

"I have to start searching for Eddie." *And find a way to involve myself in the investigation*, I thought.

"I know." She came over and pulled me into a hug. "I love you."

I tensed up against my will. I knew that she could feel it, but she didn't react. I wanted to be able to really return the hug, but every nerve in my body felt like it was charged with electricity.

"I love you too," I finally answered, hoping it sounded natural.

"I guess you'll need me to drop you off at the office, huh?"

"If you would. I don't know how long they'll be with my car."

We managed to make small talk over breakfast, but the ride to work was uncomfortably quiet. When Cara pulled up outside the sheriff's office, I whistled. "Good thing I *don't* have my car."

The lot was filled to bursting, with some cars double parked. Two large RVs were taking up all of the spots at the back of the lot. One had "FBI Command Center" printed on the side while the other had "ATF Mobile Crime Lab" plastered across its side in four-foot-high letters. I couldn't see where the DEA had set up shop. Adding to the congestion were the various news trucks and vans clustered around the building, their satellite dishes pointing skyward.

Walking through the camera crews, I was glad that I'd taken off the bandages and cleaned the cut on my forehead. No one recognized me as I made my way to the front door and I worked hard not to make eye contact with anyone.

As soon as I walked through the doors, I saw Dad and a group of suits gathered in the hallway. I recognized the three agents that had accosted me at the hospital. All of them turned and looked at me.

"Good morning," I said.

They stared for another second before Agent Devlin stepped toward me. "Thanks for coming in, Deputy. We need to prioritize the search for our witness."

"I want to be brought up to speed on the investigation first."

"We can't do that until you have been completely debriefed and cleared as a suspect," said the female FBI agent, whose name I couldn't remember.

I bristled to think that they could be considering me a

suspect, even though I understood the rationale. "My friend and colleague was killed," I said through clenched teeth.

"And you have to be considered a suspect," the woman said.

"What we need Deputy Macklin to do right now is to assist us in finding our witness," Agent Devlin said, glaring at the FBI agent. Apparently there was a little interagency friction going on.

"Your witness has gone to ground. What *we* need right now is to gather all the information we can, particularly from a key witness who, because of his close ties to the sheriff's office, could hear or see things that could contaminate the evidence," she lectured Devlin. They stared at each other so hard that I thought guns might get drawn.

Dad finally stepped in. "My deputy will give you a full statement now and then he'll assist Agent Devlin in the search for the witness," he said in a firm, slightly-louder-than-indoor voice.

"We can use our interrogation room," I told the FBI agent. *Padilla, that's her name*, I thought, reading her badge as she continued to stare at Devlin.

She finally broke eye contact and turned to me. "We'll do it out in our command center. We have a room set up with cameras." Her voice was cold as steel.

"We have cameras too, but whatever," I said, drawing a disdainful glance from her as she breezed past me.

I didn't want to waste time with this right now, but I couldn't see any way around it. If it got me one step closer to coming to grips with the investigation, I was all for it.

I followed her into the tricked-out RV. There were a couple of other agents sitting around inside, drinking coffee and working off of laptops. She led me into a small room with three chairs and a table fully outfitted with steel loops for handcuffs.

"You get all the toys," I said stupidly. Pissing her off wasn't going to get this over with any quicker, but I just couldn't seem to shake my anger.

"Sit down. Like I told you, we're going to be recording this…" She gave the date, time, her name, my name and the case information in a clear monotone meant for the microphones.

"How long had you known the deceased?"

"His name is Matt Greene, and I met him when I joined the sheriff's department seven years ago."

"You and Agent Greene got along as fellow deputies?" Padilla was clearly trying to get me to say that we were friends so that she could catch me in a lie.

"Back then? No. I didn't like him and I don't think he liked me very much either," I said honestly. I didn't like the fact that we were wasting time on this crap, but I knew that any sign of anger on my part now would be seen as evidence that I had something to hide.

"Why didn't you like him?"

"I didn't like his attitude. He acted like he was better than the rest of us. What I came to appreciate was that he *did* work harder than most of the other investigators, including me. Eventually, I realized that the competition between us made me a better investigator. His detective work was exemplary."

"But at the time would it be fair to say you butted heads?"

"Yes."

"You were happy when he took the job as a DEA agent and moved away?"

"By that time I had mixed feelings."

"You said you saw him as competition. Did that ever extend into other areas of your life?" Her voice was flat, but my blood pressure started to rise.

"What do you mean by that?"

"For example, did you all ever compete for the attention of a woman?" Padilla was staring at me, no doubt hoping to see me flinch. I didn't, but I'm pretty sure that she could see my face flush in anger.

"Never," I said tightly.

"You weren't angry that he had come back to town on this assignment?" she asked, lifting her eyebrows as though she knew better.

"No," I responded, meeting her stare for stare. What I really wanted to do was call her out and make it clear that I knew she was throwing random darts in the hope they'd stick. I also wanted to tell her that I thought she was being an ass. It was a struggle to hold my tongue.

"Don't you think it was convenient that you didn't get into the car yesterday?" This hit hard.

"If we knew why the car blew up when Matt was the only one in it, that would go a long way toward figuring out who committed this crime," I said in what I hoped was a logical and emotionless tone.

"You look like a good suspect," she said, leaning back in her chair. Did I see a little smirk on her face? "After all, the only other witness to what happened has disappeared. Maybe the witness left his phone in the bathroom and maybe he didn't. Did anyone see you and the witness reenter the building to retrieve the phone?"

"Of course not. We never made it back inside the building."

"Which leaves us with just your word that any of that happened. Maybe you pretended that the witness left his phone inside so that Matt would be alone when the bomb went off," she said, trying to make it sound like a reasonable explanation.

"We had reached the car when Eddie informed me that he'd left his phone in the bathroom. After a brief exchange with Matt, it was agreed that I'd take Eddie back in to get his phone while Matt waited outside and kept watch," I said evenly.

"According to your statement to the ATF, you asked Matt to turn on the air conditioner. Why would you do that?"

"Because it's summer in Florida. We were wearing twenty pounds of plate armor and it was fuckin' hot!" I yelled, finally losing control. I leaned forward, my eyes wide and teeth clenched in anger. It must have looked great on the video footage.

Padilla gave me a wide smile. "Not as hot as it was for Matt."

It took everything I had not to launch myself across the table and slap that smug smile off of her face. I leaped out of my chair, but managed to channel my anger into my fist, slamming it down so hard on the table that the whole RV rocked. I heard the other agents get up and head our way.

"I'm fine!" Padilla shouted to the agents knocking at the door. "Sit down!" she ordered me.

Slowly, I eased back into the chair. "This is a waste of time," I said, fighting to get my breathing under control.

"I'll decide how I investigate this crime." Padilla was clearly enjoying the fact that she'd gotten a rise out of me. "Why did you leave the witness alone?"

"I needed to check on Agent Greene."

"It should have been obvious that he'd been killed instantly."

"I needed to check on him," I repeated. I was suddenly exhausted and unwilling to play her games.

"So you left the man you were responsible for protecting *unprotected* to go check on a man you knew couldn't possibly be alive." She sounded like a prosecutor with a courtroom full of spectators.

"I had sustained a serious blow to the head," I said, hating myself for making excuses for my decisions.

"The doctor said that you didn't suffer any internal bleeding." She looked at me as though she pitied anyone who was as stupid and derelict in his duties as I was.

The silence stretched out, but I refused to fill it.

"Do you know where the witness, Eddie Thompson, is now?"

"No."

"Have you been in contact with him since he left the scene of the explosion yesterday?"

"No."

"Do you know how to contact him?"

This was a little trickier. I had some thoughts on how to find him, but I didn't know if they'd work. "No."

"But you have some ideas," Padilla said as though reading my mind.

"As soon as you get done questioning me, I'm going to try to find him. And, yes, I know him well enough that I've got an idea where to start."

"Did you and Eddie plan the explosion together?"

"I had nothing to do with the explosion, and I doubt that Eddie did."

"Why don't you think he could have been involved in the murder of Agent Greene?"

"For one thing, Eddie doesn't have a motive. Why would he want to escape protective custody, an arrangement that he bargained for? Also, he was under pretty constant surveillance."

"He had a phone," she said as though I was dense. "Do *you* know who planted the bomb?"

"No."

"Did you see anyone approach the car at any time?"

The transition to practical questions almost threw me off balance. I had to stop and think about what she was asking. Had I seen anyone near the car yesterday?

"No. I met Matt at his motel and left my car there. Then we went and picked up Eddie from the safe house."

"Why did you go to Agent Greene's motel instead of having him meet you at your office?"

"From my house, his motel was on the way to Tallahassee and the safe house."

"Whose idea was it to meet at the motel?" she asked and I had to stop and think about it.

"We came up with the plan together. Matt knew the area as well as I did, so it just seemed like the best way to do it for both of us."

"Where was his car parked when you arrived at the motel

yesterday morning?"

It wasn't easy to go back and remember details that had been mundane a second before the bomb went off, but were now possible clues in the investigation. Of course, I asked witnesses to do it all the time. I didn't enjoy being on the other side of the table.

"His room was on the back side of the motel. His car was three or four spaces to the east of the door to his room. I parked right next to him on the east side of his car."

"Can you describe any other cars that were in the parking lot at the time?"

"The one to the east of my car was a blue or bluish silver van. A Dodge, maybe. Older model. I don't remember any other cars."

"Was the lot crowded?"

"No. Though there seemed to be a cluster of cars on that side of the motel. I thought it was odd at the time that most of the cars and trucks in the lot were in the back of the motel."

Padilla walked me through a lot of other details. Some seemed unimportant, like what sort of clothes Matt had been wearing. Others pointed toward the FBI already having specific information, like whether I'd noticed any tools or loose screws lying on the ground near Matt's car.

"That will be enough for now," she finally said. "I'll need you to sign a written statement and I may have additional questions."

"Nice working with you," I said as sarcastically as I could. She took no notice.

My watch said that it was only nine-thirty, though I felt like I'd already put in a full day's work. As I exited the RV, two agents stood outside drinking coffee. The man was leaning against the side of the RV.

"You survived the meat grinder," he said, raising his cup in salute.

The woman with him smiled just a little.

"Padilla worked in internal affairs for years. I've seen

twenty-year veterans come out of an interview with her with tears running down their faces and hunks of hair in their fists," she said casually. "Don't take it personally."

"Thanks," I said, not sounding at all grateful. I headed back into the office.

CHAPTER FIVE

I found Pete and Darlene at their desks discussing a small pile of reports from the night before. Patrol took the reports on their laptops, but for some reason they were still printed out. Once the reports were printed, our supervisor in criminal investigations, Lt. Johnson, would go through them. Most of the time he would assign them to particular investigators, but some days he just dumped them in a box and we were free to mix, match and trade them any way we wanted. This had apparently been one of those days.

"We've got dibs on this pile. Go find your own," Darlene said with a kindly smile. "How you feeling?"

"Like someone hit me in the head with a two-by-four." The words were my usual attempt at good humor, but my voice didn't sound right. "Haven't they cleared your calendars for the bombing?"

"Darlene is going to handle any serious cases and Johnson said we could give the minor stuff to Julio. He wants in CID so bad, he's practically been begging us to give him some hard cases."

I smiled in spite of myself, thinking of eager young Deputy Julio Ortiz. He'd come to my assistance more than once in the past few months.

"When's that meeting this morning?" I asked, in case Pete thought that I'd forgotten about it.

Pete looked down at his desk and didn't answer.

"Pete?"

"I did bring it up with your dad. But you can't be a part of this investigation. At least not right now." Pete still wouldn't meet my eyes.

"This is bullshit!" I said as the blood rushed to my face.

"We've got so many eyes on us right now. You need…" Pete hesitated.

"To let it go? I need to step back when someone blew up a colleague and almost killed me? Hell, no! I'll find this son of a bitch. I swear to God—" I realized I was yelling and noticed that everyone in the office had managed to find something more interesting to look at. "We'll see about this," I said in a more controlled voice.

I turned and hurried down the hall to my father's office, grinding my teeth the whole way. I put out my hand and pushed the glass door stenciled with the Adams County seal and "Sheriff Ted Macklin" so hard that it rattled in its frame. Dad's assistant didn't even try to slow me down when she saw me.

Once inside Dad's inner sanctum, I found him talking with Lt. Johnson. They both looked surprised at the interruption, but not at who was doing the interrupting. Dad turned to Johnson. "Give us a few minutes."

Johnson gave me a long stare as he walked past me. There was something about his gaze that made me uncomfortable.

"You aren't going to be involved with the investigation into Greene's murder right now," Dad said once Johnson had left. His face was set in stone and the look in his steely green eyes told me there was little point in arguing. But I did it anyway.

"You can't seriously think I'm a suspect, and I didn't witness that much," I said through clenched teeth.

"Calm down. You're being ridiculous. How's your

head?"

"I'm fine. Don't change the subject."

"Sit down."

"Where's Mauser?" I said, doing as I was told. Strangely, I was almost disappointed that my dad's monster Great Dane wasn't lurking around the office.

"I left him with Jamie today. Figured he wouldn't get his beauty sleep with all the strangers around the office."

"You can't freeze me out of the investigation."

"Nobody is freezing you out. Finding your CI is important. That's your job. Find him and we'll go from there," Dad said.

"I understand that. But I need to know that the rest of the investigation is on track. I hope it's not in the hands of that crazy FBI agent who just questioned me."

Dad smiled a little. "They said she was tough."

I had to bite back my thoughts on her.

"You trust Pete, don't you?" Dad asked after a minute.

"Of course."

"He's heading up the investigation from our end. Besides, don't you think I care about finding who killed Matt? He worked for me, for God's sake! You know I'll be riding herd over this case. Neither you nor Pete can go toe to toe with these federal agents alone. I spent most of yesterday afternoon and this morning on the phone with one group or the other." Dad was getting worked up.

I hadn't thought about his side of the equation. "Maybe…"

"Do your job and find Eddie. Get him back and all the focus can go to finding the person who planted that bomb."

With no other argument left to make, I stood up and walked out. Lt. Johnson was chatting with Dad's assistant outside the door.

"I want you in my office in half an hour," Johnson said to me as he went back in with Dad.

"Great," I mumbled to myself.

I went to my desk and tried to focus on Eddie. I looked

through all the notes I had on him, which included past residences, parole officers, known associates and a dozen different possible phone numbers. I dialed and texted all of the numbers, but the only call to receive an answer turned out to be a cousin who told me that he hoped Eddie was roasting in hell for turning on his family. I decided I would go out and drive around Eddie's old haunts after my talk with Lt. Johnson.

I had no idea what that would be about. The man was our supervisor, but he was the best kind. He gave us assignments, passed down information from the top and cleared up bureaucratic hurdles when we needed him to. Beyond that, he let us do our work without interference.

When I knocked on his door, he shouted "Come in!" in his best drill sergeant's voice. He was ex-military and the rumor was that he'd gone in as a private and come out as a captain. Not an easy feat. His office reflected a life of discipline. Everything in its place and a place for everything. I almost saluted as I approached his desk.

"Sit down."

That alone was a surprise. Usually, if you were called into Johnson's office, he transacted business so fast that there was no point in taking a seat. I sat.

Johnson locked eyes with me and gave me the same piercing gaze that had made me so uneasy earlier. "You've had a rough couple of months."

Without thinking, I rubbed the spot on my side where I'd been stabbed almost three months ago. "I'm fine," I said, hoping that he wasn't going to try and put me on some sort of light duty.

"I spent twenty years in the Army. I don't bullshit. I know that most of the time I'm your supervisor in name only. Your father's the sheriff. I knew how it would be when you became an investigator. But your father's a fair man, and you aren't a complete fool, so I work with it. Besides, my wife told me when I got out of the Army that I was going to have to learn to take things easy."

I had no idea where this was going. Was he just irritated because I went straight to Dad's office so often? "I'm sorry if I go around you sometimes. Okay, most of the time. I'll try and do better," I said, starting to get up. He waved me back down in the chair.

"I couldn't care less about that. I just told you I knew it would be part of the deal when you were assigned to CID."

"Then what's this all about?" I asked impatiently.

"My point is that you're assigned to my unit so I have a responsibility to you. And maybe I'm seeing something right now that your father can't see."

"I still don't—"

"Just shut up and listen to me." He pulled out the drill sergeant voice again. "You've been through a series of physical altercations over the last six months, then yesterday you were almost killed by a bomb that murdered a colleague in your presence. I served three tours in war zones, one as an NCO and two as a company officer. I'm not saying I know what you're going through. Everybody's different and everybody's experience is unique, but I can see that it's taking a toll on you."

"No offense, but I'm fine. I just need to find the bastard who did this. That's my only problem right now," I said as I pushed down my anger... An anger that just wouldn't go away.

"I never met a good soldier who didn't want to get back in the fight, but I met a lot who shouldn't."

"If you think for one minute you're going to keep me—"

He raised his hand. "I'm not going to keep you from doing what you need to do. I couldn't. I think we've established the fact that your father has the last word on that. What I'm telling you is, you need to attend to yourself. I'm also trying to let you know that I'm here for you. You can't stop your emotions. What you have to do is control your actions.

"It'd be best for you to back off and let others handle this. However, I know that's not going to happen. But I've seen men and women on the edge the way you are right now. There's no shame in it. But if you don't acknowledge the reality of your situation and find a way to control your actions, you could end up in a place you don't want to be."

Coming from a lot of other people, this speech wouldn't have made an impression on me. But hearing it from a man who seldom spoke more than a sentence, and sitting in his office surrounded by pictures of him with his unit in desert landscapes, I listened. I didn't know how to respond, but there was no doubting the sincerity and honesty in his words.

"Also, there's something about an explosion. I think it's the suddenness… or maybe the way it rips everything apart." Johnson was looking past me now, seeing something in his past.

We were silent for a moment, then I stood up. "I appreciate it. But you don't have to worry about me. I just need to get back to work."

"I'll be here," Johnson said as I left.

"Any word on my car?" I asked Pete when I got back to my desk.

"The techs haven't gotten to it yet."

"You can take my car. I'll check one out from patrol," Darlene said, digging in her pocket for her keys and holding them out to me. She followed me out to the car so she could get her stuff. "The unmarked will be a little less conspicuous."

"It'll help, though in the neighborhoods I'm going into, they're almost as good at spotting our unmarkeds as they are the patrol cars," I said as she retrieved her laptop and other gear.

"They should be done with yours by tomorrow." Darlene paused. "We're still partners. Let me know if you need backup."

"Knowing Eddie, he's probably burrowed in pretty deep. Right now, I'm just going to talk to folks and let the word get down to him that I'm looking for him."

"I don't envy the guy."

"He has every right to be scared."

I went searching for a woman who I knew to be one of Eddie's occasional hook-ups. He'd been spending less time with her now that he was off the drugs, but I figured desperate times called for desperate measures.

When I got to her apartment complex, there were no cars parked in front of her unit. While I was knocking on the door, an older woman stuck her head out of the office across the parking lot.

"Who you lookin' for?" she shouted. Rather than answering her by yelling back, I walked over to the office.

"Mrs. Holland?"

I was familiar with the complex from the years when I'd worked patrol. Most of the residents received Section 8 rental assistance, and with a low income population came frequent calls for service. It was a decently-run apartment complex with plenty of good people living in it, but it also tended to attract people with lots of problems in their lives.

"This have something to do with that explosion?" Mrs. Holland asked. "Come on in. Don't want to let all the cold air out."

"Thanks. I'm looking for Ella Shaw."

"Nice girl, but I had to send her on her way," Mrs. Holland said, shaking her head. "She kept falling behind on her rent. She'd lost her job. I learned long ago that I can't let someone keep sliding. If you keep lettin' 'em dig the hole, eventually it's so deep they can't ever get out." She sounded genuinely sorry.

"Has anyone else come looking for her?"

"I've seen a couple of odd ducks hanging around that block of apartments, but every time I've tried to find out who they are, they make a quick excuse and hop in their cars."

"When was this?"

"Last couple of weeks mostly, but there was a car last

night too."

"What happened last night?"

"I was locking up the laundry room at ten, and I saw a car with its brake lights on parked in front of Ella's old apartment. You know, like someone was sitting in the car with their foot on the brake, waitin' for someone. Didn't recognize the car, so I went to check it out."

"That's pretty dangerous."

"I had my smock on. Mace in the right pocket, gun in the left," she said. "Most of the folks around here, particularly the old folks, watch out for me. But I don't take chances. Been here ten years and maced four people and had to show my gun to a dozen more."

Internally, I shook my head. Her job couldn't possibly pay enough. "Who was in the car?"

"Two men. Windows were tinted. With the streetlights and all, I couldn't get a good look. When they realized I was coming straight for their car, they left fast enough."

The men had to have been looking for Eddie. I showed Mrs. Holland a picture of Eddie that I had on my phone. "Have you ever seen him?"

"Eddie? Sure. He hung out with Ella for a while. Nice boy. He'd do her laundry sometimes and come in and talk to me while he was waiting. He did drugs, but he seemed to keep it pretty much under control."

"Have you seen him lately?"

"Not since Ella moved. That was a month ago."

Mrs. Holland was able to give me a forwarding address for Ella, which turned out to be a trailer set back on a couple of acres about two miles from the apartment. A woman in her early sixties opened the door.

"I'm Jennie Thompson, Ella's grandmother," she said after looking long and hard at my ID. "Come on in." She backed away from the door to let me through.

The trailer was clean and tidy. Jennie walked over to the dining room table with difficulty. Her legs moved in an awkward shuffle.

She dropped into a chair and pointed at the one across from her. "Sit. And I'll prove I'm a mind reader by answering your top two questions. Yes, I was married to one of the Thompsons, and I was pretty much crippled in a car accident twenty years ago. The fault of another one of the Thompsons." She paused. "Guess that's three answers."

"Which Thompson are you married to?"

"Was married to. He was one of the good ones, but not too smart. He was killed in the accident."

The Thompson clan was a study in the dichotomy of human nature. One half were first responders, municipal employees and businessmen, while the other half dealt in drugs, stolen cars and the sex trade.

"So Ella is related to the Thompsons?" This was news to me.

"Yep."

"She and Eddie are cousins?"

"I guess so. Pretty distant though."

"But you all don't have anything to do with the… criminal element?"

"Eddie's the first Thompson I've let into my house since the accident. See, they caused it. My husband Van and I had been to a family get-together. A tailgate party. We were going home, and Van's brother, Andy—that'd be Justin Thompson's uncle—"

I held up my hand to stop her. "Back up a bit. I'm trying to get the relationships straight. So your husband was Daniel Thompson's brother?"

"That's right. Van was the youngest of the three boys. Also the nicest, and the only one of them that you could turn your back on without being robbed. We were driving home and Andy came driving up behind us in his pickup, drunk as a skunk. Like I said, Van wasn't very bright and thought anything his brothers did was hilarious. They started driving too damn fast and playing stupid games. I begged him to stop, and just when I thought he was going to, we flew off the road into a tree. Killed him instantly. Took me six months before I could walk again. I thank God every day that Ella's mom wasn't with us that day."

"What happened to Andy?" It was odd that I hadn't heard about this brother.

"Nothin'. Charged with reckless driving, got probation and his license was suspended for a year. You'd think he'd have hung around. Most of those Thompsons have no shame. But people liked Van. I think somewhere, deep down in Andy's black soul, there must have been something like a conscience, 'cause he moved away. About a year later he died from a heroin overdose." She didn't sound sorry at all about Andy's untimely end. "So you can see that me and the Thompsons aren't exactly best buds. Daniel's come right out and said he blames me for Andy's death."

"But you got along with Eddie?"

"Eddie reminds me a lot of Van. Sometimes even the bitterest apple tree can bear a sweet one."

"I guess you heard about the arrests and the trials."

"I was really proud of Eddie. That's where he's better than Van. Van couldn't admit that his brothers were scum."

"Eddie's missing and I'm trying to find him. Do you think he could be with Ella?"

She looked thoughtful. "I don't know. You'd have to ask her. They've stayed friends, so it's possible."

"Have you seen Eddie in the last couple of days?"

"No."

"Would you tell me if you had?"

"Only if Eddie wanted me to."

"You realize that Eddie is in danger?"

"He's a Thompson. He's been in danger since the day his mother gave birth to him. Eddie's not stupid."

"Okay. Where can I find Ella?"

"She's living with a friend of hers." I could hear the air quotes around the word "friend."

"You don't approve?"

"No. She dances for a living. Most likely does drugs. Drugs! I've tried everything I could to keep Ella from going into that pit. That's how I lost her mother."

"Her mother's dead?"

"I don't know. She moved up to Atlanta when she was twenty, two years after Ella was born. Ella would get a card from her off and on for a couple years, then they stopped. I tried to find her when Ella became a teenager, but the trail was too cold by then. It was the accident and me being crippled that did it. She just got too wild for me. Just another thing I owe the Thompsons for."

CHAPTER SIX

Jennie gave me directions to where I could find Ella. She was living on the north side of Calhoun in a rough area with run-down houses and trailers on large lots. Most yards were decorated with inoperable cars, trucks and toys.

Ella was staying in a wood-frame house raised up on concrete blocks. Paint was peeling off the walls and the screen on the front porch had so many holes and tears that it served no functional purpose. There was a red Toyota in the driveway that was registered to Ella. I walked across the rickety porch to the front door and knocked loudly. Waited and knocked some more. I was getting ready to walk around the house when the door finally opened.

"What?" Ella Shaw asked, sounding annoyed.

I'd never met her, but I recognized her from all the times Eddie had insisted on showing me pictures when he was hanging out with her. I figured he'd done it because he was insecure about the fact that I knew he liked dressing up in women's clothes. He seemed to constantly be trying to prove to the world that he wasn't gay. As if I cared.

"Ella, I'm Deputy Macklin with the sheriff's office."

"Shit!" she said, suddenly wide awake and looking as nervous as a squirrel crossing an eight-lane highway.

"Is Eddie here?" I asked, alerted by her panic.

"No. No! I don't know where he is." She sounded very sincere.

"I'd like to ask you some questions."

"Yeah, sure. Out here, though," she said, stepping onto the porch. She was obviously hiding something in the house. My curiosity was piqued and I wasn't in the mood for secrets.

"That's pretty stupid," I said bluntly. "Now I know you have something in your house that you don't want me to see."

Her mouth opened and closed like the proverbial fish out of water. The heat on the porch was stifling, the air hot and thick with moisture. Even in her tank top and cut-offs, she was starting to sweat, though I figured it was more from fear than the weather.

"Look, all I care about is finding Eddie. The only other thing that would be of interest to me at this point would be a dead body. I'm guessing what you're hiding is drugs and I can't tell you how little I care about your habit or your roommate's drug addiction right now. So let's go inside so I know that's all you're hiding."

Of course, she was well within her rights to tell me to take a hike. I had zero probable cause for a search warrant, even if I wanted to go to a judge.

"I am really screwed if you, like, go all cop on me."

"I want to find Eddie. Period," I said, slowly and loudly.

Apparently she believed me. With a sigh and a small whimper of fear, she turned and went back into the house, leaving the door open for me to follow.

The house was a dump with trash everywhere, mold covering the walls and a musty, rotten smell that was only partially hidden by the stale cigarette and dope odor.

"I didn't have time to clean up," Ella tried to joke.

There were two couches in the living room and I swear I've seen nicer ones waiting to be picked up at the curb. A large coffee table was littered with every possible type of drug paraphernalia. Small plastic jewel bags were scattered on the couches and table. Candles, scorched glass pipes and spoons finished off the air of modern drug den chic. I wanted to put on a mask and gloves just standing in the room.

"This would break your grandmother's heart," I said, angry at the stupid kid.

She dropped down on the couch facing me and buried her face in her hands. "I know, I know."

"Where is Eddie?"

"I thought he was with you. Your kind, at least."

My kind? "He ran off yesterday after the explosion."

"Explosion?" Apparently the druggie lifestyle didn't leave much time for keeping up with local news.

"A bomb went off in a car that Eddie and I were supposed to get into yesterday. He got scared and ran off. Now I'm trying to find him before the Thompsons get ahold of him."

"Oh, my God! A bomb? He said they'd kill him if they could."

"The Thompsons?"

"Who else? They're batshit crazy anyway." She seemed genuinely stunned by the news. "So Eddie's really missing?"

"Have you heard from him in the last couple of days?"

"No."

"When did you talk to him last?"

"I guess it was about a month ago." She stared down at her feet and didn't elaborate.

"You all aren't seeing each other anymore?"

"No. I didn't want to break it off, but Eddie got clean— or, at least, cleaner—and didn't want to be around drugs. What was I gonna do? All of my friends do drugs. It's crazy." She fell over on the couch, looking helpless and lost.

"He wanted you to get clean too?"

"I guess. He just said he couldn't be around a bunch of drug stuff." Her eyes were closed.

"Open your eyes and sit up," I ordered.

Slowly, she obeyed.

"You consider Eddie your friend, right?"

"Yes."

"Where do you think he'd go if he wanted to hide out for a while?"

"From his family?"

"Yeah, and anyone else."

"I don't know. He doesn't have a car. What with going clean and all that crap with his family... I don't know." She dug her phone out of her back pocket and looked at it. "I think he'd call me."

Since he could probably guess that Ella was lost in a drug haze and shacked up with questionable individuals, I thought that Eddie was showing good judgment by not contacting her.

"Is there anyone else that he considers a friend?"

"Just that guy with the sheriff's office." She paused and a light bulb went off. "I guess that's you," she said, really looking at me for the first time.

I finally dredged up a few more names from Ella, but she said that Eddie had broken off contact with them too. It was one o'clock by the time I left her hovel. I thought about lunch, but I wasn't hungry.

I called to check in with Pete.

"They're almost done with your car. And I'm pressing for the Feds to exclude you from the suspect list and give you access to the case."

"And how's that going?"

"Honestly?"

"Yes, please."

"The suits just stared at me like I was an idiot when I said it."

"Sorry to be responsible for diminishing you in their eyes," I said dryly.

"No worries there. They pretty much act like I'm an idiot no matter what I say. There is one upside."

"What's that?"

"I think your dad's about done with them. He might just override them," Pete said hopefully.

As much as I liked the idea, I didn't think it would happen. With his reelection on the line in four months, Dad couldn't afford to take chances like that.

I thanked Pete for his help and set out to track down the other guys that Ella had mentioned. I managed to find one of them, but he gave me the same story she had. No contact from Eddie in over a month. The guy was trying, I had to give him that.

I found myself driving randomly through some of the poorest neighborhoods in the county. The odds of seeing Eddie were next to none, but I was feeling at loose ends. Hopeless. Especially since finding Eddie wasn't going to find the killer. I was sure that Eddie had gone to ground. He was probably safer in his own undisclosed location than at a safe house.

My mind kept going down dark holes, most of which ended with the explosion that tore Matt apart. I tried to think about what Johnson had said. Did I have PTSD? But thinking about it didn't help. It just pissed me off. It felt like I had an agonizing injury without a physical center of pain.

At some point I noticed that I'd driven out of town and found myself on the road out to Dad's place. I pulled into his gravel drive with no idea why I was there.

Jamie's car was parked next to the house. He babysat Mauser when he wasn't attending classes at the community college in Tallahassee. He'd been a godsend. He was a natural animal trainer and had managed to instill a little discipline into the two-and-a-half-year-old overgrown puppy. Dad was indulgent with the Dane and had never set boundaries, so until Jamie had come along, Mauser had been out of control, frequently tearing through the walls of the house and generally wreaking havoc wherever he went.

I heard the rumble of thunder off in the distance as I got out of the car. Mercifully, the clouds were moving in. Afternoon thunderstorms were the only thing that made summer afternoons in Florida tolerable. I knocked on the front door and then opened it, hearing a loud grumble that built into a window-rattling bark.

"Jamie, it's me, Larry!"

One-hundred-and-ninety pounds of black-and-white canine menace came trotting into the hallway and happily crashed into me.

"I'm out in the garage!" I heard Jamie shout.

With Mauser bumping into me every couple of steps, I made my way to the door from the kitchen that led to garage. Jamie was sorting his laundry. "One of the perks of the job," he said. Then he looked up at me and added, "Hey, I heard about what happened yesterday. That must have been awful."

"It was pretty bad. I just came by to pick up some papers for Dad," I lied. "But while I'm here, I'll take Mauser for a walk."

"Sure. But he won't like it. It's hot out there."

"It's clouding up a bit. Want to go for a walk, big guy?" I asked Mauser, ruffling his ears. He gave me his standard look of happy expectation, his mouth hanging open and his huge tongue flopping out.

I took Mauser out into the pasture. Thick clouds covered the summer sun. Rain was falling somewhere close by, cooling the air noticeably. It was a gentle reminder that time passed and fall would eventually return. I saw Dad's two American Quarter Horses, Finn and Mac, napping under a live oak tree. Their ears flicked toward me, but otherwise they were much too lazy to be bothered by me or Mauser. They knew they still had a while before feeding time

Mauser followed his nose carelessly throughout the pasture. A pile of horse manure would catch his attention, then the scent of a rabbit or fox. Occasionally he'd trot back to me, bumping against my leg before giving me a tongue-lolling head toss and returning to the chase. Dad liked to joke that he had a little bloodhound in him.

Eventually he came back to my side, panting heavily with

his tongue hanging impossibly far out of his mouth. Even with the sun muted and rain close by, a dog his size couldn't stand much of Florida's summer weather.

"All right, sport, let's head back to the barn." Tired now, he was willing to fall in step beside me in approximation of a well-trained heel.

"What the hell am I doing out here walking the pasture with you anyway?"

Mauser just looked up at me with raised eyebrows.

"I've got work to do, but here I am talking to you. Who's the big fool now?"

He continued to stare at me, his mouth open in a goofy grin.

"It's all about the moment with you, isn't it?"

Now his eyes became focused on the large plastic wading pool that Dad kept for him next to the barn. He jogged over to it and I watched him step, one big paw after another, into the water before letting gravity settle him down. He splashed and drank deeply from the pool.

I sat down in an old plastic lawn chair and watched Mauser wallow in the water. I smelled the air and felt the cool breeze laced with electricity from the nearby storm. A crack of thunder announced the storm's rapid approach.

I tried to understand my reaction to the explosion and Matt's death. But I couldn't get a grip on how I really felt, let alone understand it or figure out how to deal with it. *And how is navel gazing going to help?* I chastised myself.

Part of my mind kept telling me that I just had to catch the person who did it. If I did that, then all of my problems would be solved. But another part told me I was screwing up—that I was going to lose Cara, botch the case and make a total ass of myself.

There was more thunder. Mauser stood up in his pool, stepped out carefully and came over to stand right next to me before giving his body a hearty shake, sending smelly dog water all over me.

I reached out and cupped his damp head in my hands.

He perked his floppy ears forward and stared at me with his big, soft brown eyes. Reflected in those eyes was trust, love and appreciation for an hour of happiness. I felt like I was looking into a wishing well, seeing everything that I wanted out of life just close enough to touch, but somehow unreachable.

"You're the biggest goofball I've ever met," I told him as tears formed in the corners of my eyes and my throat clenched with emotion. "Come on. Let's go in before we both get hit by lightning."

I wiped my eyes as we trotted toward the house, the first heavy drops of rain splashing down across the landscape.

CHAPTER SEVEN

I called Cara on the way back to the office.

"How are you feeling?" she asked.

"You want the truth?"

"How are you feeling *physically*?"

"Okay. And I'm trying to deal with the other part." I tried to sound as upbeat as I could.

"Right now, I'll settle for that. Will you be home for dinner?"

"I can't see why I wouldn't be. They aren't letting me do much, and I've about run out of leads searching for Eddie."

"Do you want anything special? I can make whatever you want or pick something up."

"Anything. Nothing. I don't have much of an appetite."

"You've got... No, I'm not going to sound like a nagging wife. Seriously though, you have to eat something."

"You're right. Fix anything. It'll be fine." I didn't want to be talking about food right now. "I'm on the way back to the office. I'll check in and then head home."

I saw Pete walking back from the evidence room as I reached my desk.

"Got something?" I asked, half hoping he would forget that I wasn't supposed to be privy to the investigation's inner workings.

"I should tell you that I can't tell you anything, but since what I just checked out was a negative, then I guess I can honestly tell you that we don't have anything without compromising the investigation." He said all of this in one breath, then gave me a small smile. "Wish I had something that I couldn't tell you about."

"I hear that, brother," I said with a sigh.

"Any luck locating Eddie?"

"Shots in the dark. I talked to some of his known associates, but he cut ties with a lot of them when he came into the witness protection program and went clean."

"I didn't know the U.S. Marshals were doing rehab now."

"It was working that way for Eddie. More power to him. But it's making it hard to find him."

"He didn't have any money, right?"

"As long as I've known him, he's been broke. Begging me for money almost every time I saw him. So hotels are out. Long distance travel is out."

Pete shrugged. "He'll either show up or he won't. Hopefully he won't end up with a toe tag."

That image caused my stomach to lurch. Eddie had done his share of stupid things, but at heart he was a good person. Now that Pete had said it, I couldn't get rid of the image of Eddie lying on a slab under Dr. Darzi's scalpel.

"Are they done with my car?"

"Almost forgot." Pete pulled my keys out of his pocket and handed them to me.

I checked emails and did a full background check on Ella Shaw. I also dug up some information on the accident that had crippled Jennie Thompson and killed her husband. Her description was pretty much on the money.

Finally I looked at my watch. It was four-thirty and I had to admit that I was really just killing time. What could Ella and Jennie possibly have to do with any of this except for being acquainted with Eddie?

I called Darlene. "You can have your car back."

"Praise the Lord and pass the ammunition. I'd forgotten what a ragged old patrol car will do to your back. Meet me at the garage."

The county's garage was about a mile south of downtown in the old industrial park. Darlene was chatting with one of the mechanics when I drove up.

"I arrested the guy's wife when I was with the city," she explained as she got her stuff out of the patrol car.

"He's forgiven you?"

"Are you kiddin'? Every time I see him, he thanks me again. Told me that if he'd known I was checking out an old patrol car, he would have gotten me a better one. His wife was a meth addict and had pawned everything they'd ever owned and was working at robbing his parents blind when I arrested her. He managed to get a divorce while she was locked up."

"She out?"

"Four, five years ago. She went on her merry way to Atlanta, Tampa, Orlando… who knows. She was deep into it. Doubt she's alive, to be honest. But Anthony and his boy are doing okay. Win some, lose some."

I gave her the keys as we climbed into her car. We drove back to the office in silence, which was not Darlene's normal state.

"You're quiet," I said, not really wanting to talk, but being totally bugged by the fact that she wasn't.

"If I say something, I'm just going to blabber on about how it wasn't your fault and you've got to get past it, blah, blah, blah. Total bullshit that doesn't mean anything except that I like you and I want you to feel better. And P.S., I don't have a clue how to help you. Really, it's best if I just keep my big mouth shut. You got lots of friends. Me included. You aren't stupid. I know you're feeling like crap…" She shrugged.

"Thanks, Darlene," I said and meant it.

She parked next to my car and I got out and closed the door.

"Hey…"

I leaned back in the window.

"Get the scent of the son of a bitch who did this and let me help you track him back to his hole."

"Deal," I said, and she put her fist out. I bumped it.

My text alert went off as I was opening my car door. I stopped and looked at the screen. The message read: *b. 1845* and was from a number that I didn't recognize. *Junk of one kind or another*, I thought, putting the phone back in my pocket and climbing into the car. The seat was too far back. I fixed the seat and adjusted the mirrors, getting black fingerprint powder dust all over my hands. I cursed vividly, looking for something clean to wipe my hands on and realizing that there were already smudges all over my clothes from climbing into the car.

"Hell with it," I muttered, wiping my hands on my thighs.

I reached for the ignition, then stopped. That message. Something about it seemed familiar. I looked at my phone again. 1845 could've been a year. Small case "b" before a year. Born? Born 1845.

I started the car and headed for Rose Hill Cemetery. It had been the site of my first few clandestine meetings with Eddie, as it was unlikely to be under the observation of anyone in his family's drug trade. I'd driven through the cemetery earlier in the day, but hadn't given it any real consideration. While it was a good place to meet out of sight of the casual passer-by, it didn't provide much in the way of long-term hideaway possibilities.

I parked and headed for the north side where we'd met in the past. I remembered that Eddie had once been confused by an old obelisk monument. It had listed a birth year, but no month or day. Eddie had asked me why I thought they hadn't listed a specific date next to the year. I'd speculated that it had to do with the lack of records from the early nineteenth century. This part of Florida had still been a frontier, with almost everyone who died there being born somewhere else.

I found the stone. The pillar had poetic quotes on three sides and the fourth side read: *Roselyn Esther Maitland—b. 1845—Died May 6, 1932*. I looked around. There was no sign of Eddie, but something caught my eye near the base of the monument. Several square-cut pieces of granite surrounded the base. Wedged between two of the stones was a small piece of paper. I pulled it out and saw *10:00* scrawled across it.

I assumed that he meant ten o'clock tonight. This time of year, it would be about half an hour after it got completely dark. I thought about texting and telling him to get his butt over there right now, but I figured he was right to be careful. I took the note and headed home.

Over dinner, Cara and I discussed everything except the issues that we needed to deal with. I finally admitted as much.

"I know we need to talk, but I want to give it a little time. Right now it's all too raw," I told her, giving her a hug that was too quick.

"I'm not pushing," she said, touching my arm. "And part of me wants you to be out there hunting down whoever did this."

"Good. I have to go back out tonight. Eddie wants to meet."

Cara visibly flinched. "I want to go with you."

"You can't. I don't have a good handle yet on what's going on. It'd be crazy to take you with me. I'm still kicking myself for putting you in danger when Sandra went missing in May."

"It's just so frightening not knowing…"

I wanted to tell her that tonight was no different from any other night that I had to work. Bad things could happen at any time. But I didn't think now was a good time to bring that up.

"I'll tell you what. I've got my phone. I'll text you when I get there. If anything seems odd, I'll call you. As soon as I meet with Eddie, I'll let you know. When I'm done, I'll call you. I swear I'll keep in touch every step of the way. Fair?"

It seemed ridiculous to me, but I was trying to see things from her point of view. I'd almost been killed the day before, and I'd had several other close calls in the past few months. She had every right to be nervous. Besides, it couldn't hurt to have another person ready to call 911 if the meeting did go south. Leaving a bread trail is seldom a bad idea.

Cara thought about what I'd promised, then nodded her head slowly. "Okay. But swear you'll be careful."

I nodded, biting my tongue to keep from callously replying, "Obviously." My angst was like a physical disease, weighing me down and making me irritable and pissy. I desperately wanted to shake it off.

At eight-thirty, I headed back to town. It was only a fifteen-minute drive, but I wanted to stop by the office and pick up something before heading to the cemetery.

I managed to sneak a pair of night-vision goggles out of the equipment room without anyone on the night shift noticing. Dad would kill me if he knew I was taking the expensive optics out of inventory without authorization, but tonight I wanted them.

Once at the cemetery, I parked along the street and snuck in through a section of broken fencing. Using the goggles, I surveyed the cemetery from several different points before finding a spot where I could be concealed and still watch all the approaches to the meeting location. Overkill? Maybe, but I had promised to be careful.

I was twenty minutes early. I settled against a tree to wait, texting Cara that I had arrived and was safe. Five minutes before ten, I saw a figure creeping through the cemetery. After two minutes of watching the person bumble along in the sultry evening air with his hoodie pulled up over his head, I knew that it was Eddie. I watched for a couple more minutes to be sure that he wasn't being followed, then got up and made my way over to the rendezvous point.

"Shit, you scared the hell out of me!" Eddie said when I

appeared around the corner of the obelisk. "What are those?"

I handed him the goggles. "Look through them."

The way he stretched his hand out to take them, you would have thought I was giving him a live cobra. Eddie smelled rough, worse than some homeless guys I'd encountered.

Hesitantly, Eddie held the goggles to his eyes. "Wow! Excellent." He looked from right to left, then tried walking with them and almost fell on his face.

While Eddie played with the glasses, I texted Cara that everything was fine.

"Hey, who are you texting?" he demanded, jumpy again.

I explained about Cara.

"Whipped much?" he asked, making a cracking motion with his arm. He saw the expression on my face and his hand dropped to his side. "Just kidding. Geez."

He handed the goggles back to me and we got down to the matter at hand.

"I thought you all were going to protect me?"

"You're alive, aren't you? Matt isn't," I said pointedly.

"I didn't mean nothin'. I really liked him. I'm just terrified. If he can get blown up, then…"

"Where are you staying?"

"You don't want to know." He took a deep breath. "There's an abandoned house about a mile from here. It's on a big wooded lot. They threw up a chain-link fence around the property a couple of years ago and now the house is so rotten that I don't think even the crackheads would use it. There's a cargo container behind the house. I'm sleeping in there."

"What are you doing for food?" I was impressed that he'd had the good sense not to contact anyone.

"Let's just say I might owe some people living around there some money." He sounded upset at having to steal. For all of Eddie's faults, I'd never known him to be a thief. He'd been one of the lucky drug users who had some control over their habit, his addiction more emotional than physical or mental.

"Do you think you can hold up there for a little while longer?"

"What's going on?"

"We're trying to figure out who bombed the car."

"Whoever did it, you know my grandfather ordered it." His voice had started to rise, but he caught himself and went back to whispering. "You got to cut him off. Round up all of his creepy minions."

"Between the DEA and our office, we've arrested all of his and your father's known associates."

"But a bunch of them are still out walking around!" Eddie hissed.

"They make bail, then they get out. You know that. There isn't much we can do about it. Who do you think might have made and planted that bomb?"

"That's the crazy thing. Honestly, my family is more the shotgun-in-the-face type. A bomb is out of the ordinary. Gramps is crazy, but like a fox. He doesn't usually miss."

"You've got a point. And doing it now when you're testifying just paints a big red arrow aimed right at your family," I said, trying to think things through. If I knew what evidence had already been collected, that would help. I needed to get closer to the investigation.

"You have to find out who did this. Can you smell me? If this goes on any longer, I'm just going to have to leave."

That wasn't an option. "Come here." I took out my phone.

"Why?" he asked suspiciously.

"I've got an idea. We're going to take a selfie. Trust me," I told him. Holding my breath against his stench, I pulled him in close and raised the camera. I took two pictures to be sure, then gently pushed him away and breathed deeply. "You know, it's only been one day."

"It's the middle of summer and that steel box is only half shaded. I'll see if I can find some clean clothes."

"Don't get yourself picked up or shot for burglary," I said sternly. "I'll throw a bag with some supplies over the fence in the morning."

"My waist is thirty and my inseam is twenty-eight. I don't suppose I could get a pair of Cara's…" He saw me raise my hand and stopped. "…Yeah, no. Whatever you've got is fine."

"Damn straight," I told him. I gave him a few more stern warnings and he promised to keep out of sight.

CHAPTER EIGHT

I got up in the morning filled with purpose. I had a plan and, come hell or high water, I was going to follow through with it. It was amazing how having a plan, no matter how crazy or lame, made me feel better.

"You okay?" Cara asked over breakfast. I couldn't blame her. I was acting a bit manic.

"We'll see," I said, not wanting to tell her about my plan in case it went badly.

I texted Pete and asked him if the task force working the case planned to meet that morning. Knowing me, his response was a succinct: *Yes, why?*

I responded with: *See you soon.*

"Seriously…" Cara said, seeing the strange smile on my face while I texted Pete.

I really didn't want to mess with her mind, so I put down my phone and looked at her. "Don't worry. I've got an idea how to get on the task force. The worst that can happen is I'll be fired." That last was meant as a joke but, if I was being honest, it was a possibility.

"You scare me sometimes," Cara said, but the corners of her mouth turned up a little.

"I'm going to be fine." I stood up and took her hand

before leaning in and giving her a gentle kiss. "I'm a long way from it, but I'll get there."

"*We'll* get there," she said.

On the way to the office, I stopped at the address Eddie had given me and tossed a bag of supplies over the fence. Parking was no problem this morning. The news vans were gone, as well as the ATF's forensic RV. Everything would have been back to normal except for the FBI's mobile command bus still occupying ten parking spaces near the rear of the building. Once inside, I found Pete at his desk, working on a presentation.

"Whatcha doin'?" I asked coyly.

He looked at me suspiciously while partly closing his laptop so that I couldn't see the screen. "What are you up to?"

"Nothing. Just interested in your work," I said innocently.

"I don't trust you. Whatever you're planning to do, don't. From the look on your face, I'd say you're about to get yourself fired."

"Who's going to get fired?" Darlene asked, walking up behind us.

Pete jerked a finger at me. "Him. He's plotting something that's not going to go well."

"Don't get fired, snowflake, I don't have time to break in a new partner. Though lately having you as a partner is like having no partner at all. Luckily, it's been pretty slow. When are you going to come back and work cases like a normal investigator?"

"Sorry, but I'm going to be too busy working on the bombing. I'll get back with you once we hang the guy responsible up by his toenails."

"There! I told you he's up to something. You can't work this case without permission," Pete scolded.

"I have no intention of working a case I'm not assigned to." Now they were both looking at me skeptically.

My phone went off with a series of gunshots: my

distinctive ringtone for Dad.

"Your master's voice," Pete said.

Responding to Dad's request to come to his office, I was greeted at the door by Mauser. When I managed to push past the beast, I saw that there was someone else in the room, which explained why Mauser was up and moving about. The big dog went back to molesting Agent Devlin from the DEA, who was standing by Dad's desk.

"Go lie down," Dad told Mauser, who ignored him and chose to lean against me instead.

"You know Devlin," Dad said by way of greeting to me. I nodded at them both. *Maybe I won't have to execute my crazy plan after all*, I thought, hoping that Dad and the DEA wanted to bring me in on the case.

"I talked with the Greenes. They're coming into town tomorrow," Dad said solemnly. "You've already spoken with them?" He looked at Devlin.

"Yes. I notified them of Matt's death."

"I'd like you both to meet them at the airport and offer any assistance you can. Devlin, you aren't under my authority, so this is one hundred percent optional for you. I just think that they deserve that bit of respect. They'll want to hear what happened to their son and I want to give them all the information we can."

"Of course. I'll be honored to meet them when they get in," Devlin said.

"Thanks for including me," I told Dad sincerely. "I think we owe them as much help as we can give."

"Offer to bring them here if they want, and I'll meet them and answer any questions they have. I'm sure they'll want to take Matt home to Orlando as soon as possible. Larry, contact Darzi and find out when the body will be released and see if the Greenes need any help making funeral arrangements. Thank you both. I'll let you know what time to meet them."

We were being dismissed. I followed Devlin out the door. "Got a minute?" I called to him once we were in the hallway.

"What's up?" he asked, turning back to me.

"I'd appreciate your support," I said, not knowing exactly how to broach the subject now that I'd brought it up.

"With what? I'm not a very important guy." Devlin sounded as though he already had an idea where I was going.

"You know I didn't have anything to do with that bomb."

"I know. But there are those on the task force that think you should be kept at arm's length."

"I'm not much of a witness either. I didn't see anything. It's not going to hurt having me on the case," I said passionately.

"I don't even think it's that. They just don't see what value you can bring to the group." He threw up a hand. "That's not my opinion. I'm a more-the-merrier kind of guy."

"All I'm asking is, if there comes a point in time when the subject of letting me in on the investigation comes up, I'd like you to back me up."

"Sure. I know that you had a history with Matt, but that you'd managed to patch things up. This must mean a lot to you."

"It does. You knew Matt pretty well?"

"Just a little bit. He took over my old job and I got moved up."

"So you were his supervisor?"

"Not really. He was a field agent and I got moved up to a coordinator position, so we worked together. I wouldn't say I out-ranked him though. I just had seniority over him."

"Got it. Anyway, I'd appreciate your support."

"If it comes up, no problem," he said and walked away.

It's going to come up, my inner voice said, sounding a bit like a Bond villain in my brain.

I headed back to my desk so that I could keep an eye on Pete and would know when he left for the task force meeting. In my head, I went over my plan again and again, trying to see if there were any angles that I hadn't seen. When it was almost ten, I watched surreptitiously as Pete got up and headed toward the conference room.

I waited fifteen minutes, then got up and followed him. With my stomach in knots, I took a deep breath and opened the conference room door. Dad was addressing the group, but stopped talking when he saw me. Everyone else in the room turned and looked.

"I'm sorry to interrupt," I said, not sorry at all.

"He can't be in here," Agent Padilla said sternly.

"Deputy Macklin, if you have something to present to the task force, you can do that, but the decision to keep you at a distance from this investigation still stands," Dad said in an even tone.

Pete looked down at the table, while Agents Devlin and Harvey sat across from him wearing neutral expressions. I was glad to see that Shantel Williams was also in the room. She was one of our best crime scene techs and the head of her department, as well as one of my best friends at the office. It wouldn't hurt having her there.

"I do have some information that everyone might find interesting," I said, holding up my phone to display the picture of me and Eddie. "I met with Eddie Thompson last night."

Everyone in the room sat up a little straighter in their chairs.

"Is he ready to come back into protective custody?" Devlin asked.

"That depends," I said and let a dramatic pause draw out.

"On what?" Devlin finally asked.

"On what I'm able to tell him about the investigation."

"What is this?" Padilla asked, an edge to her voice.

"I'm just telling you the facts. He only trusts and is willing to communicate with me, and he's not coming back into the fold until he can be assured by me that it's safe."

"It *is* safe," Devlin said without a trace of irony in his voice. I noticed that Harvey, the ATF agent, was choosing to stay out of it.

"I think that, after current events, he's going to need a bit more proof. Maybe I should say that *I'll* need more proof."

"Wait a minute. I don't like your attitude. I know where you're heading with this and I say no way!" Padilla glared at me.

"All I'm saying is that I need to know what's going on with the investigation and to feel like it's on the right track before I'll tell Eddie that it's safe to entrust his life to us and the U.S. Marshals again."

I was working hard at not sounding too much like I was trying to blackmail my way onto the task force, even though that was exactly what I was doing. I looked around the room to assess my audience. Pete still wasn't meeting my eyes, but Shantel was smiling. Dad looked mildly irritated, but not hostile. The ATF agent was actually looking at his phone, while Devlin appeared to be trying to calculate all of the variables. Padilla, on the other hand, was giving me a look that could kill. *What did I ever do to her?* I wondered.

"You are a material witness," Padilla said. "If you are called upon later to give testimony, it wouldn't be valid or credible." She was trying to make a logical argument that just wasn't there.

"With all due respect," I said, managing not to sneer, "juries are always going to see a law enforcement officer as a biased witness. We testify all the time during trials for cases we've investigated. Besides, I've already been debriefed by several federal agents, as you know," I said pointedly. "And I've submitted my written report."

"He has a point," Devlin said. "I'm not opposed to him being part of the task force. We need Eddie Thompson's cooperation, and he made it clear at the start that the one officer he trusts is Macklin."

"I never understood why he wasn't in this group in the first place," Shantel said, giving me a wink.

"I could use the help," Pete said, finally looking up with a quick smile on his lips.

"Sure," Agent Harvey said.

Everybody was staring at Padilla, who looked like someone had crammed a lemon down her throat. "I disagree. But I won't stand in the way," she said, buckling to peer pressure.

"Fine," Dad said. "Is there anything else you can tell us about Eddie Thompson? Did you question him about the explosion?"

I filled them in on what Eddie had said and offered to take any questions they had to him, then took a seat at the table and tried very hard not to look smug about it.

"Where are we on the bomb analysis?" Dad looked at Agent Harvey.

"As you know, we sent our forensic team back to our lab in Atlanta with all of the evidence collected. We'll be getting results back as they come in. I'm going to stay here and help interpret the results, and I'll write up the final report, which will take months," Harvey said.

"And is there anything you can provide us with now?"

"Just what we already knew or suspected. The bomb contained C4, which is good, since that's not the easiest compound to acquire and might give us some leads. The lab will analyze the debris and try to determine where the C4 came from. The amounts used weren't large. We know that the bomb was placed above the skids that protected the gas tank. From this we can deduce that the intent was to destroy not just the driver of the car, but everyone in it. We often see bombs that are designed to be detonated by the driver placed directly under the driver's seat. That way, you're assured of killing the driver, but can use a much smaller bomb."

"What about the means of detonation?" Padilla asked.

"Like our preliminary analysis showed, it was a two-stage trigger. A remote device—my guess would be a garage door opener—was used to prime it from a distance of about a hundred feet, then it was detonated when Agent Greene turned on the air conditioner. I will say that the air conditioner is still a working theory. I saw some evidence that leads us to believe that's where it was wired to, but I won't feel comfortable saying for sure until the lab has had a chance to check out everything from the car."

"So what does that tell us about the bomb maker?" Pete asked. "Are we looking for someone who knows bombs or is this a first-time effort?"

"Definitely a person who's been around bombs. Possibly ex-military. This isn't dissimilar to an IED. The use of C4 also suggests a military connection. Of course, with this involving an important drug case, that opens things up considerably. I'm sure that Devlin can attest to the fact that drug operations have the connections to get ahold of whatever they want."

"Everything from submarines, airplanes, sub-machine guns and more," Devlin agreed.

"So it could be that our killer bought the bomb and received instructions on how to set it up from a third party," Pete said.

Each time they mentioned the bomb or talked about the explosion, I was assaulted with images of concrete inches from my face, or my last sight of Matt in the flaming car. I was immediately filled with anger and my head started to ache. But nothing was going to make me get up and walk out of that meeting.

"Let me get this straight," I said. "You're suggesting that, at some point while we were in the deposition, the killer—or someone doing their bidding—walked within a hundred feet of the car and activated the device."

"It's possible. We've collected all the local CCTV footage we could find, as well as put out a call for anyone that might have been taking pictures nearby. Four security cameras captured footage within a hundred-foot radius around the car, but there are gaps in the coverage both in time and space," Pete said.

"Of course, we can't be sure that it wasn't activated before you all left Matt's motel that morning, since you can't remember whether the air conditioner was on or not,"

Padilla said as though I was purposefully withholding information.

"I know we used it the day before," I said, beginning to see the difficulty in narrowing down the timeline.

"Which also opens up the question of who the intended victim or victims were. Depending on whether the bomb was activated at the motel, the safe house or downtown, it could have been any one or all of you," Dad said.

For the first time, I seriously considered the possibility that I was the one the killer had tried to blow up. But I just couldn't believe that.

"I think we should start with the assumption that the victim was supposed to be Eddie Thompson," Devlin said.

"It's not a good idea to narrow an investigation without evidence clearly pointing in that direction." Padilla sounded like a professor lecturing a class.

"So what's your suggestion?" Dad asked her.

"I think we need to put all of the potential victims at the center of the investigation and work out from there. We should come up with a list of suspects based on motive, then see if any one of them had both the means and opportunity. If we can narrow the list to a manageable half dozen or less, then we can look for any trace or photographic evidence that would tie them directly to the crime." She looked around at all of us as if to ask, "See how simple it is?" I was disappointed when I realized that I agreed with her.

"That makes the most sense," I said, not making eye contact with her.

"The Thompsons go to the front of the class," Pete said.

"Eddie is the obvious target, but Matt was the one who got killed. I think looking into anyone that might have wanted him dead should be the second highest priority," I offered.

"Is there anyone who wants you dead?" Shantel asked pointedly.

"I guess it's possible. But most of the folks who really hate me are locked up behind bars. Look, we've all put people in jail. The reason bad guys don't tend to seek revenge against law enforcement is that there are a hell of a lot of other people involved in putting a suspect behind bars—prosecutors, judges, juries, you name it. Plus, most of them have a lifetime of screwing up and being thrown in jail."

"Vengeance against law enforcement officers is rare," Padilla agreed, surprising me. "Do you have any pending cases where your eyewitness testimony would make the difference between a conviction or an acquittal?"

"Nothing serious. All of the murder cases that I've closed have relied on a long chain of evidence. Getting rid of me wouldn't make much of a difference."

"Still, you should review all your cases from the last couple of years and check out where the felons are now," Dad said. I nodded.

Shantel reported that they had scoured the crime scene, the area around Matt's motel parking space and the safe house for evidence. It would take a week just to sort, catalog and begin to eliminate all the items recovered.

To wrap up the meeting, Dad summarized the action plans for everyone present. Agent Harvey would continue to monitor the investigation into the bomb and relay that information to the rest of us. Agent Devlin would look into whether anyone in the drug trade could have assisted the Thompsons in the building and detonation of the bomb. Agent Padilla would liaison with the FBI crime lab, making sure they assisted Shantel and helped run down out-of-state suspects. This would include compiling a list of fugitives with a history in explosions. Lastly, Pete and I were charged with background searches on Matt and myself to see if there were any suspects who might have played a hand in the bombing.

I was almost back to my desk, looking forward to gulping a couple aspirin and digging into the reports on the case, when my phone rang.

"Hey, Darlene, what's up?"

"I could use another pair of eyes, if you have a minute," she said. "I've got a dead body here. Everything says suicide, but…"

I really wanted to focus on the bombing, but Darlene didn't ask for favors lightly. "Tell me where," I said.

CHAPTER NINE

I pulled up at the rear of a line of vehicles parked on the side of a dirt road, including Darlene's unmarked, our crime scene van and the coroner's van. I parked far enough back to leave them plenty of room to load the body.

We were about two miles outside of town, not far from one of the county's trash and recycling collection centers. The dirt road led onto a large, private hunting tract. I found Darlene talking to a couple of Dr. Darzi's assistants. They were sweating in the shade of a large live oak tree. The temperature and humidity were both fighting to reach one hundred together.

"Thank God you're here," said one of the techs, a young guy whose name I couldn't quite remember. "She wouldn't let us load the body and get out of here until you showed up."

"You aren't going to melt, snowflake," Darlene said good-naturedly to the tech who, with his hair soaking wet and shirt drenched in sweat, looked exactly like he was melting.

"Thanks for coming out," she said to me. "I heard you muscled your way onto the task force. Good for you. Come on." She started walking toward a clearing. "We're damn lucky that the body was found so fast. This is hunting property and the owner just happened to be out here checking on his corn plot."

The area looked well maintained, with several open and mowed areas surrounded by second-growth forest, and a few areas of old-growth forest farther back. It was perfect for hunting turkey, deer, hogs and quail.

The first thing I noticed was a newish Honda sedan parked in one of the cleared areas. It looked very much out of place in the woods.

"That the victim's car?"

"Yep. Not exactly a hunting vehicle."

"When was this mowed last?" I knew it couldn't have been very long. The grass grew fast in the summer with plenty of rain, and lately we'd been getting regular afternoon showers.

"A week ago. The owner wasn't planning on coming out for another week, but he wanted to check on the corn plot. He has some game cameras out too. I had him point them out to me so we could collect them."

About a hundred feet from the car, a body was lying up against the side of an old rusted harrow. It couldn't have been seen from the road. It was hard to tell the age of the man because his face was gone. He was wearing slacks, a nice pair of casual brown leather shoes and a grey polo. His shirt was covered in gore and a shotgun lay across his lap.

"Joel Weaver, age fifty-three, assuming the man and the wallet are a match. Darzi will have to make that determination," Darlene said, scrutinizing the gaping bloody mess where his face had been. The front teeth were broken. From the look of things, he must have put the shotgun in his mouth and pulled the trigger.

"Wow, he's messed up," was all I could come up with. I had never seen a face that badly damaged.

"The shotgun is double-barreled and, according to one of the techs whose father has one like it, it has a double trigger so you can fire off both barrels at the same time."

I looked more closely at the gun. It was old, but well maintained. I wasn't a shotgun guy, but I could see that it was a side-by-side with exposed hammers and a double trigger. It was a coach shotgun, like you'd see in a western movie. Short, so it wouldn't have been hard for him to put it into his mouth and pull the triggers.

"Guess he wanted to make sure," I said, wondering how long it was going to take to get the image of this almost-headless corpse out of my mind. "Thanks for sharing."

"There's something weird about this. Does this look like the kind of guy who'd want to die out in the woods?" Darlene asked.

I thought about the car and his clothes. "No, not really. But the first rule of suicides is to expect the unexpected. People do strange things before they kill themselves. They go to places they've never gone, they talk to strangers when they never would have before. Especially the older ones. Maybe he has… had a terminal disease. He might not have wanted his family to find him. Who knows."

"I know I'm only getting started, but I feel like something's just not right here. I wanted someone else to look at it in all of its three-dimensional glory," Darlene told me with a slight smile.

"It's different. I'll give you that. But I think every suicide I've investigated has been odd in some way."

We got a couple dozen suicides a year in the county. About half could have been accidents. Those were always tough because the family would usually push for an accidental death ruling. If there was any room for doubt, we almost always went with an accidental overdose or a single-car accident. There wasn't any point in rubbing the family's nose in it.

"The property owner doesn't know anyone by the name of Joel Weaver."

"Maybe Joel had a friend who hunted here or his family used to own the property or a piece nearby," I suggested. "What's the address on his ID?"

"Cardinal Creek subdivision, north side of town. That's odd too. I know that subdivision pretty well from when I worked for the city. We got quite a few calls out there. Starter homes and lots of young families—always some domestic violence calls on the weekend, or kids vandalizing during the week. He'd be on the older part of the bell curve for that neighborhood."

Darlene was clearly bothered by this scene, but I didn't know what to tell her. It was odd, yes, but not off-the-scales strange. My Spidey senses weren't making much of a fuss.

"So what do you think happened?" I asked her.

"That's what bugs me. I don't know." What seemed odd to me was that Darlene seemed so indecisive. She was normally focused like a laser.

"We've walked a pretty large circle," a voice behind me said. I turned to see Marcus Brown, Shantel's usual partner, standing there looking like he was just two steps from heat stroke. He held up a couple of sealed evidence bags. "We found a few things, but almost all the trash around here has been out here for months. Probably since hunting season."

"Thanks, Marcus," Darlene said. "I got water in my car if you need it."

"I'm good. This time of year we keep a cooler full of Gatorade with us," he said and half stumbled back toward the van.

I moved in closer to the body and looked at how the gun was lying across the man's lap. He was leaning against the old farm equipment, his legs closed and sticking straight out in front of him. His arms were at his side and the gun lay across his lap with its barrel touching the ground.

"He probably would have had to put the shotgun between his legs to get the barrel in his mouth. But then again it's short, only about three feet," I said.

"And now it's lying across his legs. We did gunpowder residue tests of his hands and they came up positive. Not that that proves much. Anyone who had a shotgun fired off that close to them would have residue all over them. And that's an older shotgun, so it probably isn't too tight. More like granny, less like a new bride," she said, staring with squinted eyes at the body.

The coroner's assistants were standing about twenty feet away in a small patch of shade, looking anxious to get the body into their van.

"We've got all the pictures we need," Darlene muttered and waved to them. "No sense letting the guy rot in the heat any longer."

"Not doing us any good either," the young tech chided her.

They came over with a stretcher and we watched as they placed the corpse in a body bag. Even they flinched at handling the hollowed-out shell of a face.

Darlene pulled out her phone. "Dr. Darzi, this is Deputy Marks with the Adams County Sheriff's Office. I'm sending you a body that I strongly believe is a homicide, though it was presented as a suicide. His ID says he's Joel Weaver, but you'll see from the body that a positive identification couldn't be made at the scene. Anyway, let me know when you schedule the autopsy. I'd like to be there." She rang off. "I hate voicemail."

"Sorry I can't be of more help."

"You've got your own fish to fry. I'll dig into his background. With luck there'll be some evidence in his house or maybe something in the car when Marcus goes over it that will tell us for sure what we're dealing with."

"I'd give it fifty-fifty odds of being a homicide. Or at least that someone else was present."

We'd seen a few assisted suicides. They usually involved old or terminally ill victims that had talked someone into helping them. I'd been lucky not to have to work directly on any of them, but Pete had grieved for two months over how to handle one of his cases. The victim had been going to die a painful, undignified death made only a little better through large amounts of morphine. She had asked everyone she knew to help end her suffering. Finally, a niece had found a website that described the most humane way to assist someone. Unfortunately, she hadn't followed all of the advice, so her help had actually constituted murder. Pete hadn't wanted to ruin her life, so he'd worked with the State Attorney for weeks to come up with a strategy that had let her serve a probationary term for illegal distribution of a narcotic.

"I'll let you know what I find out," Darlene said. "Go on. Get back to Matt's case. You know, I worked with him on some joint cases when I was with the police." She paused for moment. "I liked him 'cause he wasn't a bullshitter."

"I'm not surprised you all got along. He was an A-personality too," I said, giving her a little smile. "You all would be burning up this county if you'd been partners."

"I think you're right," she said with a wink. "Go find the SOB who killed him." She shooed me away.

Back at the office, I dove into all the reports from the day of the explosion. With the after-church crowd there had been plenty of witnesses, but unfortunately the day had been just like any normal summer day up until the car blew up. People don't tend to commit to memory events of a day that's just routine. A few witnesses mentioned seeing odd people or people acting strangely. These would be hard to deal with. In the absence of real memory, some people tend to embellish in an effort to help an investigation. Each of these witnesses would have to be followed up with. I made a list of anyone who reported seeing or hearing something they thought was important. When I was done, I had over thirty names.

I found Pete in the evidence room looking over items that had been bagged and tagged, either at the scene or in Matt's motel parking lot.

"Made a list of witnesses to interview," I said as Shantel handed him a bag with a scrap of what looked like a store receipt.

"We're going to need to bring in some other deputies to help with that. We need to focus on checking Matt's background." He set the bagged item in a box. "And yours too."

I just nodded, fascinated with all the trash that had been picked up at the scene.

"Has Matt's motel room been searched?" I asked.

"ATF went over it after the explosion to make sure no bombs were planted there. After that, it was sealed."

"Marcus and I are heading there this afternoon to go over it," Shantel said, handing Pete another bag with a Coke can inside. Pete looked at the label on the bag and compared it to a computer monitor showing a map of the area. The map had numbers on it that corresponded to the bagged evidence. "Fifty feet from the car," Shantel said.

"Needs to be fingerprinted and DNA pulled, but it's a low priority," Pete said, putting it in a stack.

"I'm surprised Agent Padilla isn't supervising the sorting of evidence," I said.

"She was down here earlier. Gave me instructions on how to prioritize everything and instructed me to supervise Marcus and Shantel." Pete gave me a sour look. "FBI—what you gonna do?"

"Pretty much told me I wasn't qualified to handle it," Shantel said, clearly still irritated.

"Look, this is stupid," Pete said. "Shantel, you and Marcus sort this into high and low priority. Just give me the list when you get done." Pete refused to take the next bag that Shantel held out to him and we walked out of the evidence room.

"You want to go over my witness list? There are only a couple interesting accounts that hold any real potential until we have some suspects," I said.

"Sounds good. We'll do that, then start going over Matt's background and see if we can come up with anyone that might have had a motive."

An hour later we were sitting in the small conference room, making up action plans for us and the two deputies that we hoped to pull off of patrol to help.

"It's weird. I don't even know if Matt had a girlfriend while he lived here," I said, looking over a list of people we wanted to have interviewed.

"It wasn't like we were good friends with him. He hated me because I almost let him get killed, and you tried to put him in jail for murder," Pete said, sounding remorseful.

"True. I've got Deputy Pelham on my list to talk to. I saw them together a few times. She'd ask him questions a lot."

"She working today?"

"Not sure. She was on day shift a couple of weeks ago."

I got out my phone and called Marti in dispatch, who confirmed that Pelham was on the road, but that things were quiet. He promised to radio her and let her know that we wanted to talk with her. Fifteen minutes later there was a soft knock at the door.

Teresa Pelham was 5'10" with wide shoulders and straight blonde hair. She was able to roughhouse with the bad guys as well as any of the deputies in the department. Her manner came off as professional almost to the point of being intimidating, which wasn't a bad thing for a law enforcement officer. She had started with the department a few years after I did, just about the time that I had moved into CID.

Without thinking about it, Pete and I rose out of our seats when she came in, Southern manners being hard to shake.

"Hi, Teresa. We have a few questions that we'd like to ask you." I indicated a chair.

Like everyone at the office, she wore a black ribbon across her star. A pall seemed to hang over her, even more than a lot of other people in the department. Every time I'd worked with her, Teresa had literally vibrated with energy and enthusiasm. Today it wasn't there.

"Is this about Matt?" she asked.

"You knew him pretty well, didn't you?" Pete asked kindly.

"He was my FTO."

"Really?" I was surprised because Matt would have already been in CID when she was a new recruit. "How did that happen?"

"My first field training officer took another job about two weeks into my probation period. Matt volunteered to do it for a few weeks until someone else was assigned. But all the other experienced patrol officers either already had a rookie they were working with, or were doing other assignments. Eventually, Matt just offered to keep doing it. I was on the night shift, so he could work CID and then work patrol with me."

I knew Matt was a workaholic, but being a field training officer was more work than just taking an occasional shift on patrol, which was hard enough to do while working investigations.

"That's pretty amazing," was all I could think to say.

"This went on for the full six months?" Pete asked, sounding just as amazed as I was.

"Pretty much. Sometimes he'd have me ride with my sergeant if he had to work a case… or just needed to rest."

A thought occurred to me that I didn't want to entertain, but I couldn't see how I could avoid it. "Don't take this the wrong way, but for a man to put in those kinds of hours, he must have been dedicated to helping you. Do you think he had an interest in you that went beyond the workplace?"

Teresa looked lost in thought, staring down at her hands that were clutching each other on the table. "It was complicated," she eventually answered.

"That sounds like yes," Pete said, not being accusatory or confrontational.

"No. I just want to be honest. Nothing happened while he was my FTO. I guess I might have had a crush on him, but I don't think he thought of me that way. I can usually tell when a guy is interested in me. I didn't get any of that from him. Probably a good thing, because I might have been tempted." She paused, then quickly added, "But I would have had to resist. I wouldn't have let something like that interfere with my training."

From a lot of people, this would have sounded like they were protesting too much, but not from Teresa. From her it sounded sincere.

"What about after your probation period?" I asked.

"We went out for drinks once and to dinner a couple of times."

"When was this?"

"About a year and a half after I joined. So about a year before he left."

"These were dates?" I asked, wanting to make sure we were clear.

"For my part, they were dates. I'm not sure about Matt."

"But he asked you out?"

She laughed nervously. "Actually, I asked him."

I was beginning to think that there was a lot about Matt that we hadn't known or understood.

"But he said yes?" Pete asked. I knew that Pete's wife, Sarah, had actually been the one to ask him out on their first date, so it wasn't hard to believe.

"He did." She sighed. "But why I'm hesitating is that I just don't know how he really felt. We went out for drinks after a meeting at FDLE in Tallahassee. You know, we don't really have a decent bar here in the county, but since we were over there I thought, 'Here's a chance to go have a drink with this guy I like.' I asked, and he said sure. But once we were there, I couldn't decide if he thought I was just, you know, asking him to stop for a drink like you would a pal at work. We talked, mostly about work, and when we got ready to go I told him I'd be glad to go out to dinner with him sometime. He said it sounded like fun, just give him a call. A couple weeks later I bumped into him at work, one thing lead to another, and we made a dinner date." She sounded glad to finally talk about it.

"And that date?" I asked.

"Like the drinks. We were more like pals than a girl and a guy on a date."

An odd thought occurred to me. "I know he'd been divorced before he came to work for us. Do you think Matt was gay?" Even as I asked it, I didn't think it was likely.

"No. I'd ridden around with him for months in a patrol car. He was always very professional with me and with every woman we interacted with, but I could tell that some of them sparked an interest in him. But…"

"What?"

"It was like he wouldn't go there. And with me, he seemed more reserved sometimes than with women he didn't know. Kinda like he *might* be interested in me and that was why he put up a wall between us. Does that make any sense?"

With most people it wouldn't have, but there had been something about Matt when it came to emotion. He sometimes showed irritation that could verge on anger, especially with Pete or me, but he seldom showed any other sort of emotion.

"I think it does," I said. "You said there were two dates?"

"The second one was worse. Partly because I was getting frustrated. Once it was over, I just dropped the idea that we would ever be anything more than casual friends. The worst part was that I didn't know if it was something about me or him." She shrugged. "But I couldn't be too mad with him, because he was always nice to me and a great teacher."

"Did you ever contact him after he went to the DEA?" Pete asked.

"I did. Of course, right before he left there was all that… trouble." She cast her eyes away from mine. I'd screwed that one up for sure, but I'd done my penance for it. "I felt really bad about what happened. I didn't get a chance to say anything before he left, so I sent him an email telling him how grateful I was for his help and wishing him well in his new job."

"Did he respond?"

"Just a short email, you know, 'Sure, thanks, no problem,' that kind of thing. Felt a little bit like he was blowing me off.

Knowing him, I didn't take it personally."

"Did he have anyone else at the department that he was close to?"

"Not really. He worked all the time."

That had been my impression too. Darlene also worked a lot, but not even her hours could compare with Matt's.

"Of course, his goal was to get in with the Feds. You have to be a bit of an A-personality for that."

"Can you think of anything else you could tell us that might help find the person who killed him?" I asked gently.

"I assumed the bomb was meant for the witness. But I guess I can see why you're looking into Matt's background. He was the one who got killed," she said, almost talking to herself. "Not really. He didn't make many friends, but, well…" She stopped and her face flushed.

"What?"

"I was going to say he didn't make enemies either. Except he kinda did. You two. He really didn't like either one of you," she said so softly that I almost had to ask her to speak up.

"It's okay. He and I settled our differences," I said.

"I figured so when I heard that you all were working together with the witness. I used to get the feeling that his anger at you was because he wasn't happy being here. You were kinda the focus for that frustration. If that makes sense…" She sighed. "Matt was really a good guy. I hope you catch the person who did this. If you need help, I'd be glad to volunteer."

"Thanks. We might take you up on that," Pete said.

We all stood up and shook hands, then she left the room.

"What do you think?" Pete asked me.

"I think Matt was focused on his job. One hundred percent. I'll be interested to see his motel room."

Pete took out his phone and called Shantel. After listening for a minute, he told her we'd be there in ten minutes. "They're just about done checking for prints. Let's go."

CHAPTER TEN

"Like old times," I said on our way to the motel. Pete and I had been partners for most of my time in CID.

"I miss you, pardner," he said in a bad attempt at a Texas drawl.

I was driving so Pete was texting with his family and checking his phone every other minute. He and Sarah had two daughters and the four of them were as close as a family could be. Pete managed to have a full life outside of work, which was not an easy accomplishment for all law enforcement officers. The long hours, stress and danger didn't make it easy to maintain relationships outside of the job. I thought about Matt. Maybe that's why he'd kept his distance from Teresa. Maybe experience had taught him that he couldn't have a successful relationship along with his addiction to his work.

Pete finally put his phone down and asked, "How's everything going with Cara?" It was almost as though he'd known I'd just been thinking about the difficulties of maintaining relationships.

"Fine."

"Bullshit. Don't try to kid a kidder. I've seen you doing the old hound dog routine."

"I really don't want to talk about it," I said honestly.

"Which is exactly why you *need* to talk about it. First thing you have to get through your head is that you aren't going through anything that thousands of law enforcement officers haven't gone through before you."

Pete was the same shape as a grizzly bear and he approached the world in much the same way a bear would. Like a bear, if he wanted something he'd paw at it until he got it. It made him a great investigator, but it could also make him an annoying friend. I didn't have much choice. If he wanted me to talk, I was going to have to talk.

"Cara is just worried about me, that's all," I said, hoping that I could throw him a fish and be done. No such luck.

"Not a surprise since you've tried to kill yourself half a dozen times since she's known you. Hell, last month they had to pull you out of the ocean," he said, exaggerating just a bit.

"This is a little different." I still hoped he'd leave it alone.

"I'll tell you why she's worried." He sounded so serious that I looked over at him. "It's because she can see the fear in your eyes."

The blood rushed to my face, making it burn. "Don't be stupid."

"Is it? Then why are you embarrassed? Anybody with half a brain would have been terrified. Not only did you almost get blown apart, but someone you knew *was* killed."

I wished we were closer to the motel. I wanted this conversation to be over.

"You don't have to talk to me, but you're going to have to talk to someone. And it sounds like Cara isn't going to be that person."

He was really ramming the knife into my gut. Only our friendship and past mutual support for each other kept my mouth clamped shut.

"You know I've had my ups and downs. You can't keep it all inside." He looked over at me. "I see. You're trying to be like your dad. All stoic. Men like your dad are rare critters.

Ordinary folks like you and me should not try to live like they do."

I saw a kernel of truth in what Pete was saying. "I'm not *trying* to be like Dad."

"A whole bunch of crap goes on in our heads that we aren't in control of. A doctor told me that when I was trying to get over almost letting Matt get killed. That was the truest statement I think I've ever heard a doctor say. There was all kinds of crazy stuff going on in my head. Most of it was telling me that I was a worthless cop and should quit the department. Sometimes things that happen to us stir up all kinds of emotions that just aren't healthy."

"We're almost at the motel," I said, trying to divert him. After Lt. Johnson, Cara, Darlene and Pete, was anyone else going to try and put me under a microscope? At this point, I was starting to think that all the attention was part of my problem.

"Fine. I'll let it go for now. But I'm not going to let you screw up your job or your relationship with Cara. She's the best you're going to get." He paused. "Of course, *she* could do better." The jab helped to take a little of the tension out of the air.

"Go ahead, run my life. Someone should," I said, managing to make it sound lighthearted.

"That's the spirit."

I parked the car next to the crime scene van in the motel's parking lot. Inside the room, Shantel was finishing up in the bathroom. Marcus was going along behind her and cleaning up some of the mess they had made. Normally they wouldn't have bothered.

"Decided to play maid?" I asked Marcus.

"We just thought we ought to leave the room presentable in case his parents want to come see it," he answered.

"That's a nice gesture," I said, putting my hand on the older man's shoulder. I should have thought of it. Loved ones often want to see the last places their family members were before they died. A wife who wanted to see the parking lot where her husband was beaten to death or a mother who needed to see the place where the car hit the tree. They all just wanted to have one last connection with the victim.

"You all need more help," Pete said.

I had to agree. I knew that Marcus had spent the morning at Darlene's murder/suicide and Shantel had been locked in the evidence room with all the detritus from the bombing. And now here they were, going over Matt's motel room.

"We have help. Just not anyone we'd trust to handle this case," Shantel said grimly. "When this goes to trial, I don't want us responsible for any problems with the evidence. No, sir!"

I started to look around the room.

"Don't bother looking for his laptop," Marcus said. "The DEA grabbed that first thing." That made sense since it was their property to begin with and might have contained information about ongoing investigations. "There really isn't much here."

Pete and I put on gloves and went over Matt's luggage, feeling for any pockets or something hidden away in the lining. Nothing. His clothes were modest, but high quality. I got on the floor and crawled around, looking for anything that the others might have missed, while Pete went through Matt's toiletries.

"I see how it is. Ya'll don't trust us. After all these years," Shantel joked. "Marcus and I are done here. You can crawl around this place all you want, but you aren't going to find anything we didn't."

We waved goodbye as they left and went back to picking the room apart. It was late afternoon by the time we finished. It had been a long shot anyway, but it still felt like a letdown that we hadn't been able to find anything worth following up on.

Back at the office, I ran into Dad on my way to my desk.

"Matt's parents are coming in at ten tomorrow. Would you get with Devlin and arrange to meet them at the airport?" Dad said, looking tired.

"Sure. What's going on?"

"I just got a call from Chief Maxwell. He wants to be brought up to date on the investigation. He's stuck in Boston until Sunday."

"Oh, yeah. Maxwell and Matt knew each other back in Orlando before they both came up here."

"He and his wife are in Boston this week for a national law enforcement conference. I talked to him the afternoon of the bombing and filled him in. He wanted to come back then, but he's presenting on a panel Sunday morning."

"I'm surprised he didn't want one of his men sitting in on the meetings."

"I offered, but he said none of them would be able to add much."

Calhoun was a small city and didn't have a large budget for its police department. Maxwell did the best he could with what he had, but we'd taken one of his best officers when Darlene came to work for us. I hadn't been that surprised when Maxwell had announced that he was running against Dad for sheriff.

"I'm not looking forward to him coming back and sticking his nose in a situation that's already got too many cooks," Dad said, shaking his head as he walked away.

Cara and I had a quiet evening. She spent it curled up on the couch with Alvin, catching up on a show about British midwifes, while I plugged through Matt's old cases on my laptop with Ivy occasionally walking across the keyboard. There wasn't a lot of detail about the cases that I could access online, but I could at least get a general idea.

That night, I had a hard time falling asleep. There was an uncomfortable emotional distance between Cara and me that made it feel like I was sleeping in a stranger's bed. When I finally did fall asleep, I had nightmares where I kept losing the people I cared about in a thick fog shaken by thunder and lightning.

I was glad when morning finally came, even though I was

nervous about spending part of the day with Matt's parents. I wanted to reach out to them and help them in any way that I could, but I knew there was nothing I could do for them that would bring them real comfort. Being helpless in the face of such a great loss was daunting. I didn't have an appetite, but I forced myself to take the time to have breakfast with Cara.

"When will the funeral be?" she asked gently.

"I checked with Dr. Darzi. He said that the FBI, ATF and DEA have all agreed that the body can be released. The Greenes can go ahead with the burial whenever they want. I assume they'll take him home to Orlando to be buried, though I feel like we should have some sort of memorial for him here too." I had a hard time thinking about Matt's body, knowing that it had been horribly mangled by the explosion. As much as I'd wanted to be in on the investigation from the beginning, I was glad that I hadn't had to go to the autopsy.

"Are you sure you're up to this?" Cara said very cautiously.

"I'll be fine. I need to do this. It will make me feel like I'm doing something for Matt." The truth was, I *wasn't* sure that I was up to meeting his parents. It surprised me that I was glad Agent Devlin would be there too.

Cara reached over and put her hand on mine. I was able to give her a small smile in return. "I better get going."

I was wearing my best suit and was careful not to get too many cat hairs on it as I gently moved Ivy off of my laptop bag, then headed out the door.

I met Devlin in Tallahassee. His motel was only five miles from the airport.

"Have you ever met his parents?" I asked, trying to break the uncomfortable tension in the car.

"No. Like I said, I didn't know him that well. When he took over my old job, I worked with him for about a week, bringing him up to speed on ongoing investigations. After that, we just passed emails back and forth and had a few calls and meetings to discuss cases."

"I met them once when they visited Matt in Calhoun. He and I were still on the outs then, so the introductions were… strained. How often do you lose DEA agents?"

"Almost never. A few dozen since the agency began as part of the Treasury Department in the 1920s. If it's okay with his parents, the director, or at least the assistant director, would like to speak at Matt's funeral. I'm supposed to ask them about that today."

He paused, shifting uncomfortably. "I'm not looking forward to this. I graduated from college, finished my academy training and was only on the street with the Nashville police for about a year before being recruited by the DEA. I've never had to do a death notification, let alone talk to parents about their son's funeral." Before this, Devlin had always come across as self-assured and professional, but now he seemed as scared as a boy who had to tell his father that he'd done something bad.

"Grieving families are just that—grieving. They're so focused on their loss and pain that they don't hardly notice the people around them. You have a duty to perform. Just do it. You won't be hurting them. You're asking questions that need to be asked."

When I looked over at him, he just nodded and kept staring out the window.

I used my LEO clout and parked in the loading area outside baggage claim. I explained to the Tallahassee police sergeant working security why we were there.

"Your car's fine. Rough business. The sooner you catch the guy, the better," he said and walked off to chat with a skycap.

The Tallahassee airport was small. The "International" in its name was more a marketing gimmick than reality. Most of the time there were no lines and no waiting. Today, only a couple of flights were expected in the next half hour. The puddle jumper from Orlando was on time. We managed to convince security that, even with handguns, we weren't a risk, and waited for the Greenes to arrive at airside.

There were less than fifty people on the plane. I knew Matt's parents as soon as I saw them. Mrs. Greene was wearing a black dress while her husband wore a very dark grey suit and a black tie. They stood out like a hearse at the beach among all the other passengers dressed for a Florida summer.

"Mr. Greene," I said, stepping up to meet him. "I'm Deputy Macklin and this is Agent Devlin."

"I'm Tony," he said in an odd, robotic manner. He put his hand out to shake in an automatic gesture. "I'm sorry," he said and closed his eyes. It threw me off since those were the very words I'd intended to say to him.

"My husband isn't feeling very well," Mrs. Greene said, looking lost. Her eyes were sunken with dark rings around them that even makeup couldn't conceal.

"Shut up," he told her harshly, causing all of us to flinch. "I don't need you reporting on my health." He opened his eyes. They were wet and distant. "We have to get our luggage."

"I…" Mrs. Greene seemed to be trying to find a way to bridge the painful strangeness of the situation. "He's right. Of course, we need to get our luggage."

"This way," I said, pointing and starting to walk in the direction of baggage claim.

"You'll have to excuse us," Tony Greene said as he walked behind me. "We really can't stand each other." The words were bitter and delivered through thin lips.

"Tony, now is not the time."

"First words out of your mouth when we heard about… was that it was my fault. We don't have anything to hide from these men."

"You're awful," she said, looking down at the ground as we headed toward baggage claim.

This wasn't the first time I'd seen people lash out at each other when their loved ones had been killed, but it was no less uncomfortable for its familiarity. I looked back and saw Devlin trying to pretend that he was somewhere else.

"I'm awful, you're awful, the whole damned world is awful. We just have to bury the last good thing we had in the world, then you can go bury your head in a bottle and I'll see if I can work myself to death." The words were muttered with soul-crushing honesty. Mrs. Greene was crying quietly now.

I turned to Tony Greene with the thought that I would try to say something that would make him stop the bitter recriminations, but when I did I saw that his face had gone grey while his mouth still tried to form words. He uttered something unintelligible, looking at me as though he didn't have any idea who I was.

I was already yelling "Catch him!" when Greene headed for the floor. Devlin and I managed to break his fall. I didn't even have to call for an ambulance. There was already one on the way before I was able to loosen his tie. If you're going to collapse, an airport isn't the worst place to do it these days.

"What's wrong with him?" Mrs. Greene asked repeatedly.

I unbuttoned his shirt and tilted his head. His throat seemed to be clear, which I'd been afraid of. From his expression and eye flutter, I figured it was some sort of cerebral event. Aneurysm? Stroke? I was soon pulled out of the way by the paramedics, and within minutes the Greenes were rushed off in an ambulance.

"I'll find someone with the airline and have them collect their luggage and hold it until we know where to have it sent," I told Devlin. "Then we'll follow them to the hospital."

CHAPTER ELEVEN

"They're operating on him now," Mrs. Greene said as we joined her in an ICU waiting room.

"I don't know what to say." I was being honest. I couldn't imagine how her life had been ripped apart in the last couple of days.

"They think it's a stroke. The doctor thinks there's been a lot of damage. I don't know what to do." She was standing in the waiting room, staring at the nurses' station where people were going about their business as though lives weren't being improved or destroyed all around them.

"Why don't you sit down? It's probably going to be a while. Can we get you something to eat?" I asked her.

"No, no. I couldn't eat anything. I need him." Her hands were clenched into fists and gently tapping on her hips. "It's crazy. We… we've been through so much together. It should have all been different." Her eyes looked glassy and I started to worry that she might collapse too.

"Come over here and sit down. Agent Devlin, could you get her some water?" I asked the DEA agent, who was standing to the side and being pretty much useless, clearly out of his depth. I guided Mrs. Greene over to a row of chairs and eased her into one.

"Mrs. Greene, I had the airline hold your luggage." I thought that bringing up a mundane subject might help her to focus.

"Pam," she said. "Call me Pam."

"Don't worry about anything, Pam. We're here to help you."

Devlin came over holding a paper cup filled with ice water. She took it, but only managed a couple of sips before putting it down.

"I can't be alone," she said.

"We'll stay here with you."

"No. I mean I can't lose Tony too. When we lost Carter, I thought we wouldn't survive that. But we had Matt. Matt was such a good boy. He tried sooo hard to make his dad proud of him. I thought that Tony and I might separate when Matt moved out, but I think we stayed together because we wanted to see Matt whenever we could. If we had separated, each of us would have had less time with him. Tony's not a bad man. Stubborn. Oh, yes, he's stubborn. Pig-headed, my mother would have said." She was talking without making eye contact, looking at something in the distance or maybe in the past.

"Who was Carter?" I couldn't stop myself from asking.

"Carter." A sad smile spread across her face and a tear formed in the corner of her eye. I didn't think she was going to say anything else, but then she went on. "Our other son. He was five years older than Matt."

"You don't have to tell me about him if you don't want to."

"Don't worry. The pain is all I have left now." She reached out and touched my arm as though she wanted to see if I was real. "He died of pneumonia. Ridiculous, isn't it? In this day and age. He was sick, we knew that, but he said he would be fine. He went to bed one night and by morning it had settled into his lungs. By the time we got him to the hospital, he was sinking too fast. Nothing anyone could do." She grew silent, lost in old pains. Was that better than facing the horrors in the present? "He was only seventeen. Imagine, seventeen years was all he got. All we got with him. Now Matt. Why us?" And she looked at me as though she really thought I could give her an answer.

There wasn't anything to talk about after that. Devlin and I just stayed close until Dad got to the hospital a couple of hours later.

"You two can go. I'll stay with her for a while. I called Kirby. He'll come later and can stay with her for as long as she needs him." Sergeant Dill Kirby was a partially retired deputy who came in and manned our front desk most days. He was gruff, but with a big heart.

"Lost their firstborn and now Matt. I can't imagine how she feels," Devlin said as we drove back to his motel.

"You have kids?"

"Two girls. To lose one would be devastating, but to lose both of your children…" He shook his head.

"It had to have been tough on Matt too," I said, thinking of what it must have been like for him to lose a brother. Watching the pain and suffering that his parents went through. No wonder he had become such an A-personality. It was probably that or diving into the deep end of the drug and alcohol pool of depression and self-destruction.

"We never know what the people around us are going through," Devlin said in a way that made me think he was talking about something unrelated to Matt and his family.

It was one o'clock by the time I got to the office. Pete was heading out the door.

"Your father told me what happened," Pete said. "How much can one family go through?"

"I'm going to dig through some of Matt's old cases more closely. There were a couple that might have left someone pretty pissed off at him."

"We've got an interview set up with both of the Thompsons tomorrow."

"I really think it has to be them." Matt's old case files might provide some other options, but even money was on the Thompsons.

"I'm with you. But thinking and proving are two different things. How's your cross-dressing CI doing?"

"I need to check on him," I said, putting that on my list of things that needed to done sooner rather than later.

When I got to my desk, I gave Dad a call to check on Mr. Greene.

"Definitely a major stroke. Hell of it is, Pam Greene said that his birthday is next week…" Dad went on talking, but I was overcome by a full panic attack. I remembered that Cara's birthday was that weekend. Before the explosion, I'd planned to make dinner reservations and pick up a gift, but it had completely left my mind. Now I'd have to do something fast.

"I'll talk to you later," I told Dad and hung up.

Just then, Darlene walked into the office, chewing on a toothpick.

"You look like you're in a long dark tunnel facing the headlight of a train," she said cheerily.

"I need your help."

"Anytime, cupcake."

"This is serious. I really need to talk to you."

"I just came in to grab some things. I'm on my way out to interview a couple people about that body. You're welcome to ride along."

Once we were in the car and moving, I told her the situation.

"You forgot Cara's birthday? Man, you *do* need help," she said, shaking her head.

"With everything else that's been going on, I just… It's Sunday."

"I'll cut you some slack. It's been a horrible week."

"I've never been good at getting gifts for women. A little help would be much appreciated," I groveled.

"Where are you taking her for dinner?"

I held up a finger and did a quick search on my phone. "Crap, they're closed on Sunday!"

"Who?"

"Bella Bella in Tallahassee. That's where we went for our first date."

"Nice and romantic."

"But they're closed."

"Take her on Saturday night. That way, you all don't have to get up and go to work the next day. She won't mind that you're taking her out a day early. Cara's a practical woman."

"Okay. Good. You're right," I said and started to put my phone away.

"But you better make reservations now. They'll be busy on a Saturday night."

"Right again." I called and made the reservations.

"You might want to get a little cake or something to give her on Sunday," Darlene continued. She seemed be enjoying her role of event planner.

"Good idea. Any ideas on a gift?" I asked.

She turned and looked at me with a smile. "I haven't given you enough credit. Most guys in your situation would have asked one of their male buddies for advice, which is like asking a clown for advice about formal dress. Let's think about this. I don't know Cara that well, but let me sum up what I think and you tell me if I'm wrong. She's folksy, likes the outdoors, has simple tastes, likes animals. How am I doing so far?"

"Nailed it."

"I take it you're not pushing toward marriage right now?"

"No." I felt my face grow warm.

"Then no rings. That would be too confusing. Simple jewelry. Gold or silver?"

"What?"

"Does she tend to wear gold or silver jewelry?

I had to stop and think. "Silver. Mostly."

"Makes sense. Lucky for you, there's lots of reasonably priced silver jewelry out there. I suggest you make time to go over to the Quarter Moon in Tallahassee. They have lots of nice, artsy, handmade silver jewelry. Ask one of the clerks and they'll help you pick something."

"You think that's something she'd like to get from me?" I wasn't too sure.

"Trust me. Even if you don't pick out exactly what she would, she'll be touched by the gesture and it'll become her favorite piece." Darlene said it with such assurance that I felt sure she was right.

"Thanks."

"No prob. Now you can help me with these interviews. I'll take the neighbor on the left, you take the one on the right, and we'll get done twice as fast," she said, pulling into Joel Weaver's driveway.

"Have you been through the house yet?"

"I planned on doing that after talking with the neighbors. I called ahead so they know we're coming. I've got a stay-at-home wife and you have a renter." She paused. "He's got a drug record too. Have fun."

"Any questions in particular?"

"Just the usual. Here's Joel Weaver's photo," she said, sending me a text. "This is from the DMV. Make sure we're talking about the right guy. Also, ask if they saw him on the day of his death, or anyone else around his house for that matter."

"I got it." We got out of the car and headed in different directions.

I could hear a TV from inside the house on the right. I knocked loudly. A couple more knocks and a press on the doorbell finally brought a guy in his thirties to the door. He was my height and thin, with a haunted look that I recognized immediately. When he saw me, his hand started to shake a little.

"Yeah? Thought it was going to be a lady cop," he said, his face emotionless.

"We aren't here to bust you. Today, I couldn't care less what drugs you're doing." I held up my hand, stopping his protest. "Save it. Not in the mood. If it makes you feel better, we can talk out here."

"That'd be good," he mumbled, coming out and closing the door behind him.

"I wanted to ask a few questions about your neighbor, Joel Weaver."

"Didn't even remember his name. Hey, is he really dead? That's what I heard."

"Who'd you hear that from?" I asked.

He looked puzzled by the question. "I don't know. I think the guy up at the Fast Mart. Yeah, he asked me if I knew that one of my neighbors was found dead out in the woods."

"When was this?"

"What? When he was found? I don't know." If the guy had ever had two brain cells to rub together, the drugs had killed at least one of them. Why did I always get the drugged-out stupid ones?

"No, when did the guy at the Fast Mart tell you that your neighbor was dead?" I spelled it out.

"Like, this morning. I went up for some beer."

Great, I thought. "You said you didn't remember your neighbor's name. Did you ever talk to him?"

"A couple times, I guess. He was pretty weird."

"How?"

"Look at his lawn, man."

I turned to look and had to give Drug Boy some credit. Weaver's yard was certainly out of sync with the rest of the neighborhood. Most of the yards held toys or other junk, and almost all of them looked like they could've used a little work with a mower and garden shears. In contrast, Weaver's yard was neat, very neat. The hose was curled up below the faucet on the side of the house. The driveway had been precisely edged and all of the bushes were trimmed. I looked at the house. The paint was fresh and even the shades in the windows were all at the same height. *OCD much?* I thought.

"I see your point."

"He was always giving me hell about stuff. My this or that was on his lawn. Or my crabgrass or some crap was getting in his yard. All kinds of crazy. I told him to eff off or else. I can't be worrying about all that."

No, I thought uncharitably, *you're too worried about where your next heroin fix is going to come from.*

"Did you all ever talk about anything else?"

"No, not really. The guy was just jonesing all the time. I'd have thought he was on something, but no. It was just something going on up here." He tapped his head.

"Did you notice any change in his behavior lately?"

"I think I saw him less. When I first moved in, he was in and out quite a bit. Lately, not so much. I was glad, 'cause every time we saw each other, he'd get all wound up about my yard. The guy was loony, if you ask me. Somebody kill him?"

"We haven't determined that. Did he get in any fights with his other neighbors?"

"I stay out of other people's business 'cause I want them to stay out of mine."

"And I know you don't want me up in your business, so just answer my questions." The guy was getting on my nerves.

"No. I really didn't see him get in no fights. The guy across the street talked to me about him once."

"What'd he say?"

"Ha! He asked if the guy was crazy. I guess he'd been over to his house asking him not to put his garbage cans out on the street until the garbage truck turned onto our road. Of course, the other guy blew him off. I mean, who's going to sit there waiting for the garbage truck to come and then run their cans out?" I had to admit that was over the top.

"Have you seen anyone else around his house?"

"Like who?"

That's what I'm asking you, you idiot. "Anyone," I added for clarification.

"No, I don't think so."

"When was the last time you talked to Weaver?"

"It's been about a month."

"If you think of anything else, call me." I handed him one of my cards while trying not to touch his hands. He ran his fingers through his hair, looking as puzzled and confused as he had when he answered the door.

I decided to cross the street and talk to the other neighbor that Weaver might or might not have had an altercation with. My knock was answered by an older, big-bodied woman wearing a smock from the Supersave.

"What?" she asked by way of a greeting.

I showed her my ID. "I'd like to ask you a few questions about your neighbor across the street."

"So he was the body they found in the woods. Wow. Hey, come on in. I've got to go to work in a few minutes." She turned and walked into the house and I followed, closing the door behind me.

The living room was clean, but lived-in. The overstuffed furniture was meant for two people who liked to prop their feet up in the evenings. Comforters hung over the arms of both recliners, which faced a large flat-screen TV mounted on the wall. Here and there, the walls were hung with FSU and UF football knick-knacks.

"We're a split family. I grew up in Fort White down by Gainesville and my husband went to FSU. But now both teams suck, so we don't have much to argue about. Sit down."

I sat on the edge of the sofa, not wanting to sink into the plush cushions. "Did you know Mr. Weaver very well?"

"Wouldn't say that. I knew he was a kook, but that's about all."

"Why do you say he was a kook?"

"'Cause he was. Okay, I guess that's not fair. It's just that, ever since he moved in, he's been acting crazy, telling everybody how to keep their houses and lawns. I don't know how the man kept a job. Of course, he didn't."

"How's that?"

"He worked in Tallahassee for one of the car dealerships. He said he was their manager of finances or financial manager or some such. Anyway, about two months ago I noticed that his car wasn't gone in the morning anymore. You see, most of the time I don't go in until two or three, so I noticed when he stopped going to work."

"You think he was fired?"

"Fired or quit. I've got some good-for-nothin' nephews and I know the look of a man who's out of work and not looking. Now, with this guy, his clothes were still perfect, but he had that hangdog look in the eye."

"You say he bothered folks about their houses and yards?"

"Oh, man, yeah. He came over here at least a dozen times telling us we needed to paint something or trim this. Crazy. Dale is too damn nice. He'd humor him. Or at least he did until the last time. The guy just wouldn't take no for an answer. Finally, Dale told him to piss off and not come back. About time too. I told Dale that if he'd told him that the first time, we'd have all been better off."

"Dale's your husband?"

"Thirty-one years in August."

"What was Weaver upset about that time?"

"You won't believe this. He was upset 'cause we'd changed the curtains in the guest room and they didn't match the ones in the living room anymore. Dale told him not to be looking over here anymore."

"How'd Weaver take that?"

"Just looked like we'd spilled his milk and stolen his cookies. That guy wasn't right in the head. Did he kill himself?" she asked.

"We don't know yet," I said, but I was beginning to think it was likely, Darlene's intuition aside. "Did he have any visitors in the last couple of weeks?"

"Maybe," she said, pausing and tilting her head to the side.

"What do you mean?"

"Funny, I didn't think it at the time, but now that you're asking, I'm not sure." More thoughtful expressions.

"What?" I prompted her.

"There was a car parked on our street for a few nights. I wondered whose car it was. It was odd, because all three times it was parked right in front of the property line between that guy's house and the Lewises' house. Why would you park there? There's a telephone pole and bushes. Most people, if they're going to someone's house, they either park in the driveway or on the street right in front of the house."

"What can you tell me about the car?"

"It was dark. Maybe black or blue. Not very big. You know, that streetlight is out too." I made a note to mention the light to the public works department.

"Was there anyone in the car?"

"I don't think so, but like I said, it was dark."

"When was the last time you all spoke to Weaver?"

"That day when Dale told him to mind his own business. Guess that was at least a month ago."

I asked a few more questions and got all negatives. "If you remember anything else, just give me a call," I said, giving her my card.

"I sure will," she said, taking the card and looking at it. "Hey, are you related to the sheriff?"

"I'm his son."

"Well, isn't that something? I'd heard his boy was working with him. You tell your dad that we're looking forward to voting for him in November. Chief Maxwell is kind of an ass. He's come to my register a number of times. Now your dad, he's always a gentleman."

I thanked her, making a note to tell Dad that he owed me for handling a political stop for him. Darlene was opening the door to Weaver's house as I crossed the street.

"Mixed bag," I told her. "The general consensus is that Weaver wasn't tied down real tight. The woman across the street even made the assumption that he'd killed himself. On the other hand, she also mentioned that a strange car had been hanging out in the neighborhood."

"Yeah, the young woman I talked to said he was the worst neighbor she'd ever had and that he was crazy as a bed bug. That last is a direct quote. I'm probably just spinning my wheels," she said as we entered the house.

The inside wasn't just neat: it was weirdly neat. Everything seemed paired up, with all the furniture in each room as symmetrical as possible. Even his closet was divided in half, and each half was identical. Overall, the house was sparsely furnished with the extra bedroom void of anything at all. There was no trash. We couldn't even find a trashcan. *How do you do that?* I thought. There was quite a bit of food in the house, but it consisted entirely of soup, noodles and crackers. Lots of soup. There must have been hundreds of cans of soup, but just four types—tomato, chicken noodle, New England clam chowder and chicken and rice.

"He definitely had issues," I said, shaking my head at the third cabinet filled with tomato soup.

"Doesn't mean he offed himself," Darlene responded, standing in the middle of the kitchen and slowly turning around. "This house is clean. Okay, give me your honest opinion. Does a man who lives like this go out into the woods and blow off most of his head with a shotgun?"

I sighed. "Looking at things rationally, it doesn't make any sense. But, and it's a big but, this guy wasn't thinking rationally."

"Yeah, I hear you. There's crazy and then there's crazy. My point is that Weaver was crazy in a certain way."

"And I hear you. But suicides are not predictable."

Darlene looked thoughtful, then shook her head sadly. "One good thing about a victim who keeps their house this neat, you can see pretty quickly if there's anything out of place. We're done here. Let's head back to the corral," she said, turning and walking out of the kitchen.

CHAPTER TWELVE

As we drove back, I looked at my watch and saw that it was almost four-thirty. A long way to go and a short time to get there. I checked my phone and saw I'd missed a call from Pete.

"Where have you been?" was the first thing out of his mouth.

"Helping Darlene. What now?"

"I got a call from Maxwell. He started grilling me about the investigation, so I turned it around on him and told him that we needed to interview him since he and Matt were friends. To my surprise, he agreed to Skype with us at six this evening."

I told Pete I'd meet him in the conference room at five-thirty, then called Cara. "I'm going to be late this evening."

"That's fine. I had lunch with Sarah today."

It took me a minute. "Sarah Henley?" Cara knew Pete's wife, of course, but as far as I knew, they'd never met except when we were all together.

"She called and invited me to Deep Pit," Cara said casually.

What was this about? My mind tried to figure out all the angles. "Any reason?" I asked, knowing I shouldn't sound so suspicious.

"Ummm, I don't really want to talk about it over the phone," Cara said cryptically, making me want to pound my head onto the dash of Darlene's car.

"You can't give me a hint?"

"Really, it's not that big of a deal." *If it's not a big deal, then why can't you tell me about it over the phone?* I wanted to ask. "I'll tell you all about it when you get home."

"I've got to check on Eddie after the call with Maxwell, but I'll be there as soon as I can."

Darlene had heard most of the conversation. "Phone calls like that make me glad I'm between relationships," she said.

"We need to find you a guy so you can suffer with the rest of us," I said in jest.

"All I want is a man who's rich, handsome and obedient. Is that too much to ask?" she said, parking the car.

"No problem. I'll see what I can do."

As I got out of the car, my eye landed on the FBI command center still taking up space in our parking lot. Something popped unbidden into my brain: a memory of Devlin seeming to have something else on his mind when we were talking earlier. I decided to go over and chat with the FBI, just to make sure they were crossing all the t's and dotting all the i's. "Good luck with the Weaver case," I said to Darlene.

"Good luck with the birthday," she said over her shoulder on the way to the office. No one with an ounce of sense stands around for long in a Florida parking lot in the middle of summer.

I could hear the command center's generator running as I got close. I knocked on the door and Agent Padilla opened it. *Damn the bad luck*, I thought.

"Look who came knocking on my door," she said, smiling at me. I wasn't sure how to take this. It seemed friendly, but nothing about our earlier interactions had suggested that we were on friendly terms. "Come on in, you're letting the cool air out." She moved aside to let me in, then offered me a seat and asked if I wanted something to drink.

"From that look on your face, I'd guess you're surprised that I'm being nice to you," she said as she sat down across from me at the small table.

"I *was* wondering if this was your good cop act."

"Look, I had to bust your balls the other day. I didn't really think you had anything to do with the bombing, but I had to know. I knew you were still in shock. If I hit you hard, you'd probably show a crack or two if you were guilty. Nothing personal."

The truth was, it had felt very personal on Monday. "Did you have to be such a—"

"Bitch? You can say it. I did. It's my thing, and it works… sometimes. You aren't dumb. You know that interrogation is more art than science. The best chance for getting a good confession is to hit hard and fast. The good cop thing is dangerous. Too easy to find yourself leading a suspect, especially if they're young or not very sophisticated. By the way, when I was researching you and your dad, I came across the job you all did last month. I appreciated the way you all got that young man off. You might like to hear that after reading about it, I dug a little deeper and recommended that we file a federal case against the sheriff for violating the man's civil rights."

I was shocked, but happy to hear that Will Duncan's life would get a little harder. "Thanks."

She leaned forward. "Look, I'm moving up in the FBI. It's not easy. Being called Iron Slacks doesn't hurt, but I'd never take advantage of someone who's vulnerable. Me hitting you like that was a compliment. I sized you up as a big boy who could take it." She leaned back and gave me a crooked smile.

"There's also the part where you didn't want to let me on the task force."

"I still don't think you should be on the task force. Two

reasons. One, you're a witness. We still don't know everything that you might have seen or heard, but that evidence is now compromised since you've seen the files and we can't separate what you really saw from what you've read about. Memory is a wicked tangle of what we experienced and what we think we experienced."

Of course, I knew she was right.

"Two, you got your head messed up with the explosion. I saw it in your demeanor. Still do. You aren't doing yourself any good by immersing yourself in this case. That's just tearing at the scab. And if you aren't a whole person, as an LEO in a dangerous situation, you could be a threat to me and everyone else working the case." She shrugged. I thought of how hearing them talk about the bomb had made me feel and I wondered if she wasn't right. "But I said my piece and the decision was made by others. I'm not going to butt heads over it. So, if we've put all that behind us, what did you want to talk about?"

"I was thinking about some of the agents close to the Thompson case."

"Anyone in particular?" she asked, her eyes probing mine.

"Well… Not wanting to cast aspersions… But it came up because I thought Devlin was acting a bit odd this morning," I said lamely.

"Federal agents have been known to cross over to the dark side. DEA has certainly had problems with it in the past. Hard to keep everyone straight when there's all that money and drugs flying around. First thing I did when we came in on the case was to review everyone's files. I also made some discreet inquiries with the DEA's internal affairs people. Everybody looks clean. Since Devlin was going to be the lead and liaising with us, I did a deep cleaning on him. He came out looking good. If you noticed anything odd in his manner or behavior, it probably has to do with some personal issues. If he wants to tell you about his personal life, that's up to him. I'm not going to do it," she said, looking smug.

I kept going back and forth on her. One minute I admired and almost liked her, but the next I thought she was a complete ass. "Good. I just thought I should mention it."

"I'm an equal opportunity snoop. It's my job. And I'm very, very good at my job."

I left the RV certain that she was.

I got to my desk in time to go through a few emails and make some notes before our Skype meeting with Maxwell. When I got to the conference room, Pete was already there with his laptop set up for the meeting. A comparison of our notes showed that we were on the same page as far as the questions that we wanted to ask the chief.

"Did you know that Sarah and Cara had lunch together?" I asked with a few minutes to kill before the call.

"Ah. No. Maybe." Pete looked down at his notes that we'd just gone over in detail.

"Why did Sarah invite Cara to lunch?" I asked, taking the direct approach.

"I'm sure she just wanted to talk." Pete realized that I wasn't satisfied with that answer and threw up his hands. "Believe me, I didn't have… much of a part in it. Plus, I don't think I should be the one to discuss it with you. Really, it's nothing. Sarah just wanted to have a heart-to-heart with Cara."

I thought about pressing, but what was the point? He was right. It would be better to get it directly from Cara. "Sure," I said, giving him one last dirty look before I let it go.

"I would be there if I could," Maxwell said when we connected.

Chief Charles Maxwell was capable of talking out of both sides of his mouth, but now he seemed sincere. With all of the bad stuff I'd heard people say about the chief, being disloyal was not one of them. I knew from Matt that they'd been good friends back in Orlando, and Maxwell had pointed him in the direction of the Adams County Sheriff's Office. He would have hired him on with the Calhoun Police

Department, but he hadn't had a position open. Besides, the pay wasn't great and the prospects of promotion there were nonexistent. Maxwell had only taken the position of chief because his wife had gotten a prestigious job at FSU, and the Calhoun Police Department had offered the only opportunity at the time where Maxwell could be the boss. He'd been the chief of a larger force down near Orlando and grown accustomed to being the man in charge. His ego was huge, but so was his intelligence.

"We are working it hard," Pete said.

"I know that." Maxwell almost seemed human. "Did his parents get there? I talked to them Monday."

I told him about what happened at the airport. Maxwell looked stunned.

"They lived two doors down from us in Orlando. I don't know if you all are aware, but they lost another son years ago. Now they've lost Matt and Tony's in the hospital." He shook his head and looked away from the camera. "Is there any word on how he's doing?"

"He's in critical condition in ICU. I'll let you know if I hear of any changes," I said solemnly.

"I'd appreciate that." Maxwell turned back to the camera and took a deep breath, all business now. "What do you need from me?"

"When was the last time you talked with Matt?"

"These days you should ask when was the last time we communicated." Maxwell always had a better way. "He texted me a couple weeks ago when the depositions were scheduled and he knew he'd be coming into town. I told him he could stay at our house if he wanted, but he said that the Feds were paying for a room. We agreed to get together for dinner and we did on Saturday night."

"When did you and your wife leave for Boston?"

"Early Sunday morning."

"You knew you were leaving on Sunday, yet you invited him to stay at your house?" Pete asked.

"I wouldn't have had any problem letting Matt stay at our

house while we were gone."

"Did he talk about any problems he was having?"

"No. He seemed relaxed and happy. Oddly, he did seem a little homesick for Adams County."

"Why was that odd?" I said.

"Oh, come on. You know he wanted to work for the Feds. He was smart and ambitious. Made for bigger things. I was surprised he had any regrets about leaving our country-fried surroundings."

"Did he mention having problems with anyone, professionally or personally?"

Maxwell didn't answer right away, seeming to think about the question. "No, though he did say that the job was not as exciting as he thought it would be. Also, he didn't think that he got much support or attention from his supervisors." He paused. "But, really, it wasn't anything more than the normal complaints everyone has about their jobs. His dissatisfaction seemed to mesh with his nostalgia for his time with the sheriff's office."

"Did he have a girlfriend that you know of?"

"No. In fact, I asked him specifically if he'd been dating anyone. Matt said that there were a lot of beautiful woman up in Columbus, but that most of them seemed to be interested in dating men from Fort Benning. He said the young women tended to go after the enlisted men while the older ones looked for officers."

"What about relationships when he was here in Adams County?" Pete asked.

"There were a couple of girls that he went on dates with. Nothing serious. Matt's dead and we all want to find his killer, so I'm going to be honest. Matt was not good at interpersonal relationships. Really, personal commitments of any type."

"But you all were friends?" I asked.

"I think that he and I were friends because I knew him before… before his brother died. He and Carter were close. Carter was the perfect big brother. His death devastated

Matt."

"How did you all meet?" Pete said.

"I was in school with Carter and the three of us used to hang out together. Matt was about twelve when his brother died. His parents... Look, I'm not blaming them, but they withdrew from each other, and from Matt. I just made sure that Matt had someone to talk to."

I could see that talking about Matt was taking a toll on Maxwell. A couple of times he had to grit his jaw to keep from breaking down. He'd obviously felt like a brother to Matt.

"Do you remember him having any problems when he worked in Adams County? Anyone that he had an issue with?" I asked, knowing full well where Maxwell would go with his answer. He didn't disappoint.

"Ha! You two! There were a couple of years when, every time we talked, he'd end up bending my ear about the fat-ass who almost let him get killed and the sheriff's son who should get the golden nepotism award." He smiled. "No offense intended." Right, sure.

"Thanks for that. Besides Pete and me, did he ever talk about anyone else that he had a problem with?"

Maxwell looked thoughtful. "Nothing specific. He got some of the usual threats. Angry wives, men who swore he was railroading them, some parents who either thought he wasn't working hard enough to find or help their kids, or thought that he was persecuting their little darlings who almost never brutally beat up and raped people. You know the routine." He waved his hand dismissively. "I don't remember any one case that stood out."

Maxwell knew what he was talking about. He was more than capable of sorting out real concerns from the day-to-day petty aggravations of being an LEO.

I wanted to end the conversation with something cutting or smartass, but looking at Maxwell, all I saw was a man grieving for his friend. My better nature took over. "Thank you. If you think of anything else, call us. We're going to find his killer. And when you get back, I'll be glad to sit down and go over the case with you."

"I know we give each other crap a lot of times, but this is personal," he said grimly, looking through the camera at us.

"I agree," I said.

"Damn straight." Pete nodded.

After we disconnected, Pete said, "I didn't expect much."

"Then you got what you expected. But it's strange how my image of Matt is changing."

"I know what you mean. The world's a mean place. We forget that the other guy is at the mercy of the same mercurial forces that we are."

"Mercurial. Big word for a big guy," I said, trying to lighten the mood.

He flipped me a bird and gave me a smile in return.

CHAPTER THIRTEEN

As soon as the call with Maxwell ended, my mind had gone back to Cara and her lunch with Sarah. I was cursed with curiosity, which probably helped to make me a decent investigator, but the urge to know things could drive me crazy at times.

I tried to put my need to know aside long enough to check in with Eddie before heading home. I sent my second text of the day to the number that Eddie had used to contact me, not even sure if it was a phone he had with him. It said: *b. 1845.* I hoped that would convey the message that I wanted another meeting. Still not receiving an answer, I drove past the property where he was staying. He'd picked up the package I'd tossed over the fence, but I didn't see any sign of him. Sighing, I headed home.

The sun was just heading for the horizon as I drove up to my house. I had to temper my need to know with patience. Bombarding Cara with questions as soon as I walked in the door wasn't going to help. I did great, giving her a kiss in greeting, which she returned. I took a shower and changed into clothes that weren't sticky with sweat. After giving both Ivy and Alvin a little attention, I sat down at the table across from Cara with some warmed-up pizza for dinner.

"So what did Sarah want?" I asked, shooing Ivy away from my pizza. But before she could answer, my phone buzzed. I glanced at it. Eddie was finally responding: *half an hour.*

Cara saw the look on my face. "Who's that?"

I told her I'd have to go and meet Eddie. "But I have a minute," I lied. "What did Sarah want?" I repeated, trying to make it sound like I wasn't being eaten up with curiosity.

"It's kind of a long story. I don't want to rush through it. You go on."

No way, I thought. "Look, why don't you come with me? We can go for a nice drive on a summer's evening," I said, trying not to grit my teeth.

She saw through me. "Really, it's not a big deal."

I stared at her.

"Okay, fine, I'll come," she laughed, which made everything a little better.

The western sky turned orange as I drove back toward town. "I'm at your mercy," I said.

"Okay, so I guess Pete must have said something to her about a conversation that he'd had with you. Whatever, it doesn't matter what prompted her. She called, I guess, sort of as one woman with a cop for a husband to another woman with a cop for a boyfriend."

"I didn't know there was a group."

"You kid, but I guess there's a bit of comradery amongst LEO spouses."

"I'd think the bigger group would be the one for ex-wives and ex-girlfriends of cops. That would be the one with all the juicy gossip."

"I hope I don't get invited to that one," she said and punched me on the arm.

"Me too." I smiled, but I still wasn't satisfied with the answer. "So she was welcoming you to the fold? That's kind of weird."

"Seriously, she told me some things that helped." Cara said this so earnestly that I turned and looked at her.

"What?"

"I was honest with her. The bombing and, well, all the other stuff that's happened lately has me upset and worried. I told you that."

"I know." My eyes were back on the road, but I stretched out my arm and put my hand on her knee.

"Sarah said that it's a blessing in disguise to be married to a law enforcement officer and to know that their job is dangerous. She said that when she realized that Pete could go out the door one day and not come back... Well, that was the day that she asked Pete to make a pact with her."

"This didn't involve cutting their palms with knives, did it?" It was a lame joke, but Cara was being so serious that it scared me.

"No, quit it. She made him promise that they would treat every minute they had together like it was the last time they would ever see each other. Because it could be. Pete agreed. Now whenever they get into an argument and it looks like it might get out of hand, one of them just says 'LT.' 'LT' for last time. They just remind each other how precious their time together is." Cara's voice cracked a little.

"You okay?" I looked over at Cara and she smiled a little, nodding her head. Her red hair glowed in the last light of the disappearing sun.

"She said we're blessed because, while it's obvious that deputies face danger, it's true for everyone. Any moment together can be your last. We're just forced to face it."

"I'm glad she talked with you. Any other words of encouragement?" I said gently.

"She said that what was really hard at first was seeing Pete get brought down by all the ugliness that you all have to face on a day-to-day basis. Learning how to help him transition, every day he comes home, from a world of criminals and victims to a world of family and friends, took her a long time. They had to work on it together." She put her hand on mine and squeezed it.

I thought about Pete, who handled that constant beat-down better than any cop I knew. "They did a good job of it," I said. "I guess the question for you is, am *I* worth all that work?"

"Sarah made it clear that the work isn't one-sided," Cara said, smiling gently at me.

"And let me guess. This isn't one of those things where you deal with it once and you're done."

"Bingo." My hand got another squeeze.

"Yeah, yeah," I said, my mood already lighter.

We were almost to the cemetery when I thought I saw a car behind us rush through a four-way stop to keep up with my car. My heart sped up. Was I being followed? I decided that I would circle around through some side roads to be sure. I put both hands on the steering wheel and gripped it tightly.

"Why are we turning?" Cara asked.

"Someone may be following us." My heart was racing and I felt like I was on the edge of a panic attack. Why had I brought Cara with me? Stupid, stupid! My fear was rising much too fast for the situation. *Calm down*, I told myself. I made several more random turns, keeping an eye on the rearview mirror.

"Are they still back there?" Cara asked, craning her neck to look through the side mirror.

"No," I said, sighing in relief. "I'm not even sure anyone was back there in the first place." I was alarmed by how quickly my mind had gone into panic mode, knowing that probably all I had seen was someone rushing through a stop sign because they were late for dinner or to pick up their kids.

Despite the detour, we pulled into the cemetery right on time. I looked around and didn't see anyone, then got out and walked toward our usual meeting place. The cemetery was dark. The moon wasn't up and the live oak trees blocked out much of the ambient light from town. A movement to my right made me jump.

"Hey!" Eddie hissed.

"What the hell?" I blurted, dropping my hand from where it had automatically risen to my holster.

"Who's in your car?" he asked suspiciously.

"It's Cara."

Eddie was holding the bag I'd thrown over the fence. "I see you got the supplies," I said, also noticing that he smelled marginally better.

"I can't stay there anymore."

"What's wrong?"

"I'm just going crazy. No electricity, which is why I didn't get your texts at first. No water, which is why I smell. And, finally, there isn't any air conditioning and it's the middle of freakin' July," he moaned.

He might have a point, I admitted to myself.

"You can't go to anyone you know," I told him emphatically.

"Duh, I know that. I don't want to die."

I tried to think of somewhere safe for Eddie to hide out. I didn't feel comfortable turning him back over to the U.S. Marshals yet. Pete's place was out for a number of reasons and I didn't want to saddle Darlene with him. Besides, she had to go to work and, while Eddie wasn't the most dishonest ex-addict I'd ever run into, I wouldn't want to give him too many temptations. It would need to be with someone who was off the drug scene radar, yet didn't have a job to go to. And someone who wouldn't mind having a strange person thrust upon them. An idea occurred to me.

I saw a car rounding the corner of the cemetery. It sped up as it approached us and I looked back toward my car where Cara was sitting. Again I felt panic beginning to settle in. But after a second, the car roared on past the gates of the cemetery and into the distance.

"Come on," I said, not wanting to leave Cara alone any longer.

"Cara, Eddie. Eddie, Cara," I said when we were standing beside the car. "I'm going to make a call. It's okay for you to talk to her," I told Eddie, "so long as you don't talk about bras or panties."

I took my phone and walked twenty feet away. I had to do a bit of explaining, but the person I called seemed excited by the idea of having a captive audience. When I disconnected, I could hear Cara and Eddie talking about women's clothes. I sighed.

"What did I tell you?" I asked Eddie sternly.

"We were talking about silk slips, nothing about bras or panties."

"Eddie also gave me a list of preferences for the next bag of supplies," Cara said with barely disguised amusement.

"Not that I wasn't grateful, but if you're going to go to all the trouble to bring me stuff, it ought to be what I like," Eddie said. "Like the peanut butter crackers. I really prefer the cheesy ones, not the malted ones."

"Shut up right now before I beat you to death," I told him with a straight face.

"Come on. You're not that kind of cop."

"Don't push me. Get in. I've got a place for you to stay."

"Great. Where?"

"It has air conditioning, electricity, running water and plenty of books to read."

As I drove, I kept the windows down and my eyes constantly alternated from the road to the rearview mirror. When we pulled up to the house, I turned off the interior lights of the car so they wouldn't come on when we opened the doors.

"Nice place," Eddie said, looking up at the old, two-story Victorian house. I led them around to the back door where I'd asked the man to wait for us. He opened the door as soon as we came up the steps to the small porch.

"Come in," he said in a conspiratorial whisper, waving us through the doorway. Albert Griffin was the unofficial historian of Adams County. The former head librarian had taken it upon himself to turn his house into an archive of the area's past. One whole room was filled with issues of the local paper dating back a hundred years.

"This is Albert Griffin. Mr. Griffin, this is the star witness in the Thompson trials, Eddie Thompson."

"Marvelous. Your family has a really interesting history, filled both with heroes and rogues. I can't wait to ask you some questions."

"One rule," I said, holding up a finger. "You can't discuss the pending drug cases."

"Understood. I've read enough crime stories to understand some of the rules."

"Big place you got here," Eddie said, marveling at the old house. "Beautiful woodwork." Eddie was walking out of the kitchen when he let out a blood-curdling scream. I thought he was going to faint, but instead he blurted out just one word: "Cat!"

Brutus, one of Albert Griffin's many feline roommates and the boldest and most aggressive housecat I'd ever met, came strolling right toward Eddie, who was back-pedaling as fast as he could.

"That's just Brutus," Mr. Griffin said dismissively.

"I'm scared to death of cats," Eddie said in a high, squeaky voice.

"Oh, I've got almost a dozen," Mr. Griffin said, not helping.

"I can't stay here." Eddie was hiding behind Cara now. For her part, Cara was having a hard time not bursting into laughter.

"This isn't negotiable." I wasn't going to spend all night trying to find him a suitable, cat-free hideout. "You'll just have to make up your mind whether you're more scared of cats or bombs," I said bluntly.

Meanwhile Brutus, having smelled fear, was stalking Eddie with slow, deliberate steps and eyes that glowed yellow with some demonic internal flame.

"Don't show fear, Mr. Thompson, that just emboldens them." Mr. Griffin smiled kindly. "If you like, I can shoo him into another room."

"God, yes, please!" Eddie said to Mr. Griffin. To me he

said, "I can't stay here."

"Cats or bombs. Your choice, because I think someone was following me earlier. If they are after you, you have a better chance hiding out here than in that lot. Or on the run. But it's your call," I said as if I didn't care. Truth was, I didn't want to lose him as a witness and I sort of liked the strange little guy. I didn't want to see him knocked off by his bad news relatives.

Eddie looked around. "I guess I'll stay. I *do* need a shower."

"That's the spirit. And, from personal experience, I can say that you are quite unlikely to run into a cat while taking a shower."

"So what is it about cats?" Cara asked.

"Long story. But trust me, I have my reasons for being scared of them," Eddie said solemnly.

"Look on the bright side. This will give you time to work on your phobia," I said cheerfully.

"They keep the rats from eating my books. And they really are great company," Mr. Griffin said. "Let's see, your father is Justin and your grandfather is Daniel. Very interesting. Daniel's father, Lester, was considered by some to be the laziest man in town. He was quite the character. There are several articles about him in the *Adams County Times* from the 1930s. I could dig them up if you'd like to see them?" he asked Eddie.

"Yeah, I guess."

"Remember, Eddie's in hiding. Don't buy anything at the store that you wouldn't normally buy. Someone could be watching. If Eddie needs anything, call me and I'll bring it over," I said to Mr. Griffin. Then I looked at Eddie. "Stay indoors and away from the windows. Call no one."

Cara and I finally got home around midnight.

"I've got to go to bed. Pete and I are interviewing the Thompsons tomorrow," I told Cara, giving her a hug.

"This still has you upset, doesn't it?" Cara asked, looking me in the eye as we held each other.

"I'd say rattled. I… Like when I thought someone might be following us this evening, I was unnerved. I learned long ago that I wasn't immortal, but now there's a heightened sense of vulnerability."

"Getting over it might take a while. You have to give yourself time."

"I'm not sure I have a while. I can't get frightened every time there's a minor threat," I said, exasperated. "I need to be at my best."

"Pete and Darlene have your back."

"I know that, but in return I have to have theirs."

Cara didn't answer, but hugged me tighter.

CHAPTER FOURTEEN

Morning came early. By nine o'clock, Pete and I were sitting in the conference room with Agents Devlin and Padilla, going over our strategies for the interviews with Daniel and Justin Thompson.

"We're interviewing the old man first at ten o'clock," Pete said.

"Are their lawyers going to be present?" Devlin asked

Pete chuckled. "These days, they don't go to the bathroom without a lawyer being present. Ever since the indictments, they've stayed lawyered up."

"Do you really think they'll talk to you?"

"There's a good chance. Both of them have enormous egos. Also, they want to find out everything that we know about their operations," I said.

"And they both have nothing but contempt for those of us that work for the local constabulary," Pete said. Constabulary? I wanted to ask him if he'd bought a dictionary, but it wouldn't be fair to rib him in front of the Feds.

"We'll be watching on CCTV," Devlin said.

"Yes. I think with these two, that's the best way to handle it. They would be more guarded if either of you were in the room," I said.

"I can see that," Padilla allowed. "How are you all going to play it?"

"Again, they've both been around the block a few times. They aren't going to fall for any games. We'll just have to go in there with a plan and hope that we can get some information," Pete said.

"I think we'll be lucky if we just get some kind of indication as to whether they were or weren't involved in the bombing," I added.

"So far we have no physical evidence to link them, or anyone for that matter, to the bomb. I talked to Agent Harvey this morning. Mind you, they don't have any of the detailed test results back and won't for at least a month," Padilla said.

"We just have to go in there and throw mud around and see if any of it sticks," I said. "Daniel has nothing to lose one way or the other. He's in his seventies and, with or without Eddie's testimony, we have enough charges against him to put him away for the rest of his life. Justin, on the other hand, has a chance of seeing the light of day sometime in the future."

"Which gives him the stronger motive for killing Eddie," Devlin said.

"That's true, but he's not the firebrand that his father is, and he's not quite as smart. Daniel beat a man almost to death when he was younger just because the man looked at his wife. He's got the personality of a water moccasin. Justin is more of a rattlesnake," Pete said.

"Okay, you're losing me with the snake analogies," Padilla said.

"Sorry. A rattlesnake will give you a warning, and generally, if given a choice, will move away from you. A moccasin, on the other hand, doesn't give you much of a warning and they've been known to charge at people."

"Yeah, okay, I get the idea," Padilla said. "So your best bet is Justin?"

Pete and I looked at each other and nodded. "That's the way we see it," he said.

"When you're interviewing them, feel free to get into the drug trafficking charges. Never hurts to have more statements from the defendants on the record," Devlin suggested.

At a quarter to ten, we all walked over to the county jail where the two Thompsons were being housed in an area that had been specially arranged for them. They couldn't communicate with each other or the general population. This was a burden on the sheriff's office since Dad had to put a couple extra deputies on duty at the jail, and give overtime to others, in order to support their isolation in a manner that also met all the requirements of humane treatment, including outdoor exercise.

The interview room at the jail was small. On a good day, it could hold five people my size, or three-and-a-half the size of Pete. So we had to move around a little to make room when the deputy brought Daniel inside.

The old man looked rough and angry. His eyes were hooded and so dark that I could hardly see the pupils. Unlike his son, Daniel had been released on bail after his original arrest in January and had gone back to running their local operations. But we'd been watching him closely and he had finally slipped up enough in the spring that we had been able to arrest him again and keep him this time. I could practically feel his resentment.

His lawyer was someone I'd never met before, which was odd. In a county this size, you get to know all of the regular lawyers working in the area.

"I'm representing Mr. Thompson," the tall, grey-haired man said with a slight accent. His complexion was dark and I suspected that he was being paid by someone higher up in the drug trafficking chain of command. This was the first major drug case I'd been involved in, but my understanding was that this was standard practice. The defendant got a high-priced lawyer so the drug lord would know exactly what the defendant was saying and doing to save his own skin.

"Mr. Thompson has instructed me to, quote, shut my mouth and let him handle this, unquote, so unless things get completely out of hand, I'm just here to observe," said his lawyer. And those were the last words out of his mouth. We didn't even get a goodbye at the end of the interview.

"What an honor," Daniel Thompson sneered as the deputy handcuffed him to the table. "You big boys afraid of an old man like me?" he said, rattling the cuffs against the ring.

"We want to ask you a few questions," Pete started, but Daniel wasn't going to let anything go without a smartass comment.

"I bet you do. My lawyer said you all had some car trouble the other day." Daniel laughed viciously. His hair was uncombed and he kept rubbing his hands together, rattling the cuffs. "Shame it didn't kill that faggot grandson of mine."

He stopped and stared at me. "Hey, you're Macklin. You were there too. Yeah, it's a shame you all weren't blow into a million burned-up pieces of shit."

I swallowed hard and worked at maintaining my composure.

"So you wanted to see Eddie Thompson, Agent Matt Greene and Deputy Larry Macklin dead?" Pete asked calmly.

"Oh, hell yeah. Especially that traitorous cow's ass of a grandson. I'd gladly strangle him with my arthritic old hands," he said, holding up his hands to show his gnarled knuckles. "Aren't you going to ask me where I was when the bomb went off? Go ahead, ask me," he goaded Pete. "I'll give you two guesses and the first one don't count. I was in your crapper of a jail. No phone and no contact with the outside world. So tell me how I'm involved."

Unfortunately, he had a point. Clearly he had motive and he had enough contacts and money to have the means, but the opportunity... That was going to be the leak that sunk the ship.

He saw us hesitate. "I thought so. Come back when you figure out how I could have arranged it from in here," he said dismissively.

"You have plenty of friends on the outside," I said, knowing that it didn't mean anything.

"That's right. And if they arranged for a little fireworks without me encouraging them, then that's on them, isn't it? Go to hell and don't call home, you stupid idiots. You comin' in here and botherin' me when you haven't got a shred of proof that I did anything. Get out of my sight."

Daniel wasn't a stupid man, but prison and isolation at his age was making him less stable and less coherent. However, he still knew how to hit below the belt. "I've owned better cops than you."

He'd managed to corrupt a number of law enforcement officers, which was part of what had landed his family in jail. One of the men he'd turned was someone I had always assumed was a good deputy, and it had almost cost Dad his life. Only Eddie's help had prevented events from turning out worse than they did.

We soldiered on with Daniel for another twenty minutes for no good purpose. Shaking our heads, we watched as the deputy led him back down the corridor to his own private prison.

The debriefing with Padilla and Devlin was, well, brief. There wasn't much to talk about except for what a waste of air the old man was. Pete and I discussed the coming interview with Justin. Neither of us had a clue as to how it would go.

"What's the plan?" Pete asked.

"We go in, be professional and hope he shows some weakness. If he does, we try and exploit it," I said with a shrug. "We knew this was going to be a long shot from the beginning."

"The odds of getting anything out of a couple of career criminals who are facing enough charges to put them away for a couple hundred years is slim at best."

"It's like the serial killers who are on death row. They have nothing to lose, but also nothing to gain. If they give you something, it's as likely to be some sick game as it is a real lead."

"You're right. Guess we should be glad that Daniel was upfront with his intent to give us nothing," Pete said.

We stayed outside the interview room this time so that the deputy had plenty of room to take Justin in and get him chained to the table. Justin looked to be doing better than his father. His hair was combed and his eyes were clear. He also lacked his father's sneer.

His lawyer introduced himself as John Gonzales. No accent this time, but he looked like he could have been the son of Daniel's lawyer.

"Mr. Thompson has chosen to speak to you," he said, and then sat back in his chair, his eyes going back and forth between all of us as if he was watching a tennis game.

"For what it's worth, I'm here." Justin looked around the small room, giving the camera in the corner of the ceiling a good stare. "At least I'm getting to see a different room."

"You get out for exercise every day," I said.

"That's right. By the law, I get my hour in the fresh air."

"I can't feel sorry for you."

"Whatever. I don't care. It's all going to come down to what my lawyers can do." He looked at Gonzales, whose expression never changed.

"Do you have any idea why we're here?" Pete asked.

"Let me guess. It probably has to do with one of the dozen or more crimes you've charged me with. Or have you all dredged up some other crap you think I've done?" He looked irritated now.

"You didn't hear about the car bombing?" I asked.

"How the hell would I hear about something like that? I'm isolated from everyone except the guards."

"You need a better lawyer. Your father knew about it," I said, sensing a small weakness. The question was, could it become a large weakness?

Justin's eyes narrowed. He glanced over at Gonzales, who showed no indication that he'd even heard what we'd said. What kind of a lawyer was he? Of course, the answer was that he was there to protect someone's interests, just not Justin's. Justin saw it too and his lips went tight.

"So tell me about this bomb," Justin said.

"It blew up a car. Killed a DEA agent. You knew him. Matt Greene."

"Greene. Oh, yeah, the deputy turned Fed. He was an ass," Justin said and then must have seen something in our faces. "Yeah, maybe he didn't deserve that," he allowed. That Justin wanted to be seen as a more sympathetic character than his father was obvious.

"There were three people who should have been in that car when it blew up. Matt, myself and your son," I said flatly.

Justin looked surprised. "No kidding." There was a hesitation before he asked his next question. "So only Greene was killed?" Did he have some concern for his son, or was he hoping that Eddie had been killed as well? I couldn't tell from his expression, but based on the things Eddie had told me, I doubted he'd ever lost much sleep over his son's welfare.

"There were only a few other minor injuries," I said and Justin visibly relaxed. "Of course, you would have been happy to see the chief witness testifying against you taken out of the way."

Justin leaned back and seemed to consider my statement. "If you're asking if I wanted Eddie dead, my answer would be no. Do I wish he wasn't a queer little shit who turned against his family and friends? My answer for that would be yes. But the truth is, he's a traitorous, panty-wearing rat and I've accepted that." He paused and we waited, giving him time. "You all have enough to put me in jail for a very long time, with or without his testimony. There wouldn't be any point in me killing him. Besides, how do you think I managed it from here?" He shook his chained wrists against the table.

"Maybe you just wanted to get a little revenge." I decided to stick with motive for now and leave opportunity for later.

"Not likely."

"Does it sound like something your father might do?" Pete asked and I saw a flash in Justin's eyes. Anger? Fear? Opportunity?

"Dad does have a temper."

"And he appears to still be pulling the strings."

"I don't see how. I assume he's under the same sort of confinement I am."

"He is. But there are plenty of your former employees out there running around. Even a couple we pulled in who are already out on bail," Pete said.

"I'm a little disappointed that I was denied bail."

"Come on. If you got out on bail, then you'd be out of the country before most of us could get through security at a regular airport," I said.

"You sure think I have a lot of power."

"Let's just say we believe you have former bosses who'd be glad to get you away from the American legal system. Speaking of which, this bomb thing is a big deal. Bombs, terrorism, all of that gets people very nervous. So nervous that the powers that be might be very grateful to someone who helped them round up a bad guy with bomb-making skills. You know, drop-charges kind of grateful," Pete said.

Now I could definitely see the wheels turning in Justin's head.

"I had nothing whatsoever to do with this," he said emphatically.

"That's the beauty of it. I believe you. But I think you might be able to give us some information that could be useful," I said.

"And…?" Now his eyes were calculating. And Gonzales was suddenly showing a keen interest in the conversation.

"There would need to be some negotiation," I said, looking up at the camera in the corner. Justin followed my eyes.

"I can't be sure that I actually know anything or not."

"And I can't be sure what we could do to help you out if you did. See, that's what I mean about negotiation. Sometimes the bargaining can go easier with fewer people involved." I nodded toward his lawyer, who sat up stiffly.

"I would not advise you to talk to the authorities without legal counsel," he said sternly.

"They all say that," I said with a smile. The humor was lost on Gonzales, who looked like he wanted to reach across the table and slap me.

"I think I'll need a little time to think about it," Thompson said slowly. "I would assume that we're talking about a significant shift in my status."

"I'm not sure exactly what would be acceptable. I can tell you that you definitely won't be walking out the door right away. On the other hand, you might have the chance of a few golden years on the outside," I told him and he pursed his lips in thought.

Gonzales looked like he desperately wanted to pull out his phone and call someone.

Pete looked over at the lawyer and spoke directly to Justin. "I wouldn't wait too long."

Justin took his drift. "Give me a day or two, tops."

"Works for me. While you're thinking, look around at the walls. Think about the difference between life without parole versus thirty years with a chance of parole in fifteen," Pete said lightly.

Pete and I stood up to leave.

"I'd like to speak with my client alone," Gonzales said.

"That's up to your client," I said, looking at Justin.

"Not today," he said. The lawyer stood to the side awkwardly while a deputy unchained Justin and led him out of the room.

"Good thing your client isn't in with the general jail population, otherwise one of the inmates might hurt him. Aren't you glad we're taking such good care of him?" I said, staring Gonzales in the eyes as he went to go around me. He looked at me like I was a vagrant on Wall Street.

We met up with Padilla and Devlin back at the office.

"Sorry we didn't dig more into some of the drug charges. Things just seemed to gravitate in one direction," I said.

"No. This could be good. If we get him to give us something on the bomb plot, then we might be able to completely flip him. He knows a ton more about the operation than Eddie does. With him as an informant, we can go down the line and back up. You saw the look on that lawyer's face," Devlin said.

"And the lawyer is certainly being paid by someone higher up for the sole purpose of making sure that Justin doesn't flip," Pete said.

"I'll run him, but they hire their lawyers through dummy corporations. The money trail usually dead-ends at a Cayman Islands's bank or somewhere in Switzerland."

"The question is, what does Justin know about the bomb?" Pete said.

"I'd guess he knows about similar bomb plots carried out below the border. Or he knows of someone who is capable of doing it. Someone who was attached to their operation."

"That would be my guess," I said.

"So how did Daniel get the word out?" Pete asked.

"His lawyer is a possible leak. We can't prevent them from talking, and we haven't had surveillance on the lawyers prior to this," Devlin said.

"One of the guards?" Padilla suggested.

"I'd never say never, but I know that Captain Bennett, who runs the jail, hand-picked the details that would be responsible for looking after Daniel and Justin," I said.

"We've seen maximum-security federal prisons leak information in and out," Padilla said.

"And drugs make for a powerful motivator when money doesn't," Devlin allowed. "These guys are connected to a powerful cartel. The drugs and money are the carrots. The cartel also has sticks. A lot of good people can stand up to temptation, but when it comes to threats to their families…"

He shrugged.

"So what I take from this is that it's possible Daniel got the word out," I said. "Still, it bothers me that it was Matt who was killed. If they wanted to take out Eddie, they had other opportunities before this. He wasn't even in protective custody until he began giving his depositions."

"But the whole reason we put witnesses in custody as the trial approaches is because it becomes increasingly likely that the defendant will reach out as they become more desperate. We've seen it in the past. The day that someone's going in to give testimony, they disappear or are murdered. Besides, proximity and visibility play a part. Until now, Eddie mostly stayed away from Adams County, or was lying low inside the county. But since the depositions started, he's been keeping a regular schedule."

"That makes sense," Pete said. "If we go with the assumption that Daniel Thompson played a role in the bombing, then making a list of the people who have had contact with him while he's been in jail would give us some new leads to follow up."

"If it's the lawyer, you won't crack him," Padilla said with assurance. "These guys know that keeping their mouths shut is a matter of life and death."

"But maybe it's not him," Pete said.

"Agreed."

"Right now, our best bet is if Justin will roll over on his father," I said.

"And he either will or he won't. Putting pressure on him wouldn't do any good," Pete said.

CHAPTER FIFTEEN

"Let's go get lunch," Pete suggested innocently once we'd left Devlin and Padilla.

I stopped in the parking lot and looked at him. "I know what you're thinking," I said.

"Come on, the food is really good."

"I hear you. I'm just not sure I'm ready," I said.

For twenty years, Calhoun's best place to eat and catch up on local gossip had been Winston's Grill. Not surprisingly, though, when the owner was discovered to be a serial killer the place had shut down. Eventually, Pete had taken it upon himself to encourage and help Winston's daughter, Mary, to open a new restaurant. This wasn't purely altruistic on Pete's part. He'd almost needed grief counseling when Winston's had closed. He'd spent nearly every weekday morning in the place eating and taking the pulse of the county. Now he was fighting an uphill battle to get people to accept Mary's new restaurant, the Palmetto.

"Come on, you big baby," Pete said cajolingly.

I remembered there was still something I needed to talk with him about. "Okay, Hulk, we'll go there for lunch, but you're going to explain to me why you and Sarah are interfering in my relationship with Cara."

Pete's face flushed. "Oh, that."

"Yes, that. Get in the car. Let's go to lunch," I said, trying to sound pissed off when I really wasn't.

Mary had wisely chosen to move to a new location, though looking around at the empty seats at noon on a workday didn't suggest that it had solved all of her problems. The Palmetto was well laid out with lots of booths and the dining room was open, bright and airy. You just had to get past the idea that the owner's father had butchered people when he wasn't serving up good food.

"Pete!" Mary said with a big smile. She looked good, all things considered. The few times I'd seen her shortly after her father's arrest, she'd had a sad and haunted look. She still hadn't gained back all of her weight, and there were more wrinkles at her eyes than I remembered. "Larry. Thank you," she said to me. Her eyes were moist and the depth of her gratitude made me feel guilty for not having come in sooner.

"It's good to see you, Mary. The place looks nice. Smells good too." This last wasn't a lie. Mary was a great cook and the odors coming from the kitchen were heavy with Mediterranean spices.

"The gyros are to die for," Pete said without a trace of irony. I cast my eyes to the ground, trying not to think about her father.

Mary led us to a booth by a window. Once our orders were in and large glasses of iced tea were sitting in front of us, we leaned back in the seats and relaxed.

"Ideas?" Pete said.

"All I know is that I don't want to put all my eggs in the Thompson basket."

"I agree. They're the obvious culprits, but… something just doesn't seem right."

"For one thing, Eddie isn't dead. You know Daniel Thompson isn't one to screw up. If he wanted Eddie targeted, I don't think he'd use a bomb."

"True, but Daniel is getting long in the tooth. Besides, this might be more about his bosses than him."

"Yeah, I thought of that. And a bomb fits right in with drug dealers who want to make a point about rats. To them, the operation wouldn't even look like a complete failure. They killed a federal agent. That's a BFD and sends the message that they mean business."

"Which would mean that our best bet is to run down people that the DEA says could have been involved, and suspects that the ATF says might have experience with bombs. So we coordinate between the two and focus the investigation there," Pete said.

We were halfway through our excellent gyro platters when Pete suddenly looked like he'd drank from a carton of sour milk. His eyes were focused on the parking lot and I followed his gaze.

"Great," I muttered sarcastically. Two Calhoun police cars were parked in the lot, and walking toward the door were two middle-aged cops—one white and one dark brown. Beyond the color of their hair and skin, they could have been twins.

"Salt and Pepper," Pete moaned. "Please don't let them come over to our table."

Nicknamed Salt and Pepper, Officer Gordon and Officer Robinson had been burnt out long before they came to the Calhoun Police Department. They'd both worked down in Hillsborough County, one for the sheriff's office and one for the Tampa police force, before retiring and coming north. They'd known each other before, but once they started working in Calhoun, they'd become inseparable. Salt and Pepper were two of their nicer nicknames. Darlene, who'd had to work with them during her time on the police force, said that the two spent most of their time trying to figure how to get out of work.

"We'll be over by Son-of-Sheriff and his big buddy," we heard Gordon tell Mary. Pete hit his head on the table.

"Look at you two. Regular suits," Robinson said, coming over to our table.

"One may be regular, but the other is definitely extra

large," Gordon quipped.

"Wow, do you cowboys even have time to come in and get lunch?" Pete asked.

"Hell yeah, we've caught all the bad guys. It's safe. You two can go back outside now," Gordon said.

"We appreciate all your hard work," I said, letting sarcasm drip off of the words. I saw their expressions change and I thought for a moment I might have made a dent in their armor of indifference. Not so. But they did prove that they had some human feelings.

"I'm really sorry about Matt," Gordon said with more sincerity than I'd ever heard him use.

"I can't believe that shit," Robinson agreed. "When is the memorial service?"

"We're not sure," I said and went on to explain about Tony Greene. A text from Dad earlier had said that there hadn't been any change in his condition: *ICU–critical*.

"Damn. That's awful," Robinson said, shaking his head sadly.

They were both standing at the end of our booth. Pete and I had scooted to the edge of our seats before they came over with the purpose of not giving them room to sit down. Now I felt a little guilty. Thin blue line and all of that.

"You want to join us?" I said, but without too much enthusiasm. I managed not to flinch when Pete kicked me under the table.

Ten minutes later, I was regretting my momentary weakness. I think it was the third stupid video they showed me on their phones that had me ready to leave. Pete had rolled his eyes at least five times, so I was about to make up a meeting that we had to go to when I saw Gordon make the same sour-milk face that Pete had. I looked out to the parking lot again and saw a woman in her fifties standing by their police cars. Then she looked up and stared directly at us.

"Oh, crap, not her again," Gordon grumbled.

Robinson looked up. "That woman with the drug addict

son?"

"Yes, damn it! She bent my ear for half an hour last Friday. Oh, hell, she's coming in. Geez." He stuffed most of his barbeque wrap in his mouth.

"I'm not here to eat. I've just got to talk to that cop," we heard from the front door. The woman made a beeline for the table, pinning Gordon down with her eyes.

His face had transformed into a perfect likeness of an Easter Island statue and he held up his hand to stop her before she'd even gotten to our table.

"Ms. Craig, I put in the missing person report like you requested, but that's all I can do."

"Officer Gordon, I told you he wouldn't have just left. He was doing his twelve-step program. I went to the Narcotics Anonymous meeting at the church. They said he hadn't been to a meeting in over a week. No one has seen him."

I had the uncharitable thought that if he was missing, then you wouldn't expect to find him at his NA meeting.

"You just need to give him some time. I hate to say it, but people fall off of the wagon," Gordon said.

"He didn't fall off of the wagon." The woman was grimacing at him now. "I know my son. He was doing fine. And why would he get cleaned up and ready for work and then just disappear?"

"I can't explain all the things people do. But let me tell you, after two decades on patrol, I've seen everything. I saw a woman jump off of a bridge down in Tampa once. You know where she was coming from? Her nephew's christening. What kind of sense does that make? If I hadn't seen it with my own eyes, people would have been saying it was murder or something. I'm sorry, but a twenty-five-year-old recovering drug addict going missing for a week ain't that strange. I'm saying this to make you feel better."

I couldn't stop my eyebrows from going up at that last comment. *This is how he comforts a woman with a missing son?* I thought.

"You just don't want to go out and look for him! You want to sit here and eat your sandwich and get fatter!" she said, her voice rising toward hysteria.

Pegged him, I thought.

"Listen here," Gordon said, pulling out his *I'm a cop and I'm in charge* voice. "I've done what I can for you. You need to just calm yourself down before you're told to leave." He said this loud enough that I knew he hoped Mary would come over and say something so he'd have an excuse to kick the woman out.

"So who have you talked to?" she asked in a quieter voice, but with grit.

I was beginning to like this woman. I looked over at Pete, which was a mistake. He was having to bite his tongue to keep from laughing at Gordon. Of course, seeing Pete fighting the laughter bug caused me to catch it. Now I couldn't make eye contact with any of them.

"I've asked around," Gordon said and I had to work hard to keep from shouting out: *Lie!*

"Liar!" she said, as if reading my mind.

"Watch yourself. I've got work to do. I can't be going around chasing every drug addict in town who hasn't called his momma this week."

"What about him? What the hell is he doing?" she said, pointing at Robinson, whose only response was a full-on deer-in-the-headlights look. It was too much. I had to bury my face in both hands just to keep from laughing out loud.

"Lady, you need to calm down," Gordon insisted.

"I'm not leaving until you get off of your ass and start looking for my boy!" She had resorted to a full outdoor voice at this point. Gordon started to get out of the booth, and I suddenly didn't feel like laughing anymore. This could get serious real fast.

I looked up and saw Gordon pulling himself up to his full height, his large belly pushing out against his shirt. Robinson was rising in preparation to back up his buddy.

"I could take a look at it," I said, loud enough to cause

everyone to put the brakes on their collision course.

"Who are you?" Ms. Craig asked, looking around Gordon at me.

"I'm an investigator with the sheriff's office."

"I should have filed the missing person report with you all to begin with," she said, giving Gordon a disgusted look.

No kidding, I thought.

"Of course, it will still be their case since you did file it with them, but I don't mind giving it a look. I know how busy Officer Gordon is, so I don't mind helping out."

Gordon looked at me with squinted eyes, trying to tell if I was being sarcastic. Of course I was, but I kept my tone dead-on neutral.

"I guess. Anything would be better—"

"Let's step outside and talk about it," I interrupted before she could goad Gordon into doing something stupid. "You don't mind picking up my tab, do you?" I said to Gordon, who nodded sternly.

I escorted Ms. Craig out the door.

CHAPTER SIXTEEN

I walked Ms. Craig over to where I'd parked my car in the shade.

"I've got a flyer," she said, pulling a sheet of paper out of her purse. A picture of her son smiling broadly into the camera took up a third of the flyer. Below the picture was the word "missing" in hundred-point type. Below that was Seth Craig's name, followed by his statistics: brown hair, green eyes, 5'11", one-hundred-and-twenty pounds, a tattoo of a cobra on his leg and an iguana on his back. There was a picture of both large, nicely detailed tattoos. He must have spent some serious time in a tattoo parlor.

"He was last seen leaving your house," I read.

"That's right. Like I told that buffoon, my son was going to his job at Express Burgers. He was dressed… And that's the thing, he was wearing those shirts. The striped ones with Express Burgers written across the back. He wouldn't have gone anywhere but to work wearing one of those. He made jokes about how stupid they looked." Now that she didn't have her anger at Gordon to hold her fear in check, Ms. Craig was close to crying.

"How long has he worked there?" If it was a month or less, my vote would've been that he'd just walked away.

"Over a year. He'd tried to find some other work, but… it's not easy. The drug thing scares employers. I get it. He has a felony arrest on his record." She waved her hands as though swatting flies. "But that didn't matter. He was okay with the job. Told me just last month that the repetition helped him. He could sort of go on autopilot, he said, and let the time go by. He said that what he really needed to do was to get some distance from his past, from the time that he was using."

"You said that he hasn't been to any of his recent NA meetings."

"That's right, and I talked to his sponsor. Around here, there aren't that many meetings just for drugs, so he'd go to the AA meetings if there wasn't an NA meeting when he needed it. But Harold said that he hasn't seen or heard from him. He's even gone to some of the other meetings and asked about Seth. No one has seen him for more than a week." Despair was evident in her voice.

"I got to be honest. Being in law enforcement, I've dealt with a lot of addicts, both those in recovery and those who aren't. A lot of the ones who aren't, were. So I have to ask, have you talked to any of his friends from when he was an addict?"

"I don't blame you for thinking he might be using again. As soon as I knew he didn't go to work, that's what I was afraid of. Before I even went to the police, I found a couple of his old drug friends and asked if they'd seen him. One of the guys is pretty burnt out. I don't think he could have lied if he wanted to. Well, not convincingly, anyway. They were all really surprised to see me. That's the thing. If they'd seen him recently, then they would've known I wouldn't be far behind and would've tried to cover for him. But every one of them had that look like, 'Wow, where did she come from?' I knew, *knew* that they weren't expecting to see me." She leaned against my car looking beat.

"Okay. Any other places he might have gone? Did he go down to Panama City or someplace like that when he was doing drugs?"

"Sometimes. I hadn't thought about that. Yeah, it's summer. Maybe." This brought her some hope.

"That's a place to start. When someone backslides after a long recovery, they don't always want their friends and family to see it, so they go someplace farther away to party."

"Oh, please God, I hope you're right," she said. It was sad that, at this point, the idea that her son had slid back into his addiction was less scary than the nightmares she'd been having.

"I'm sure that Officer Gordon has put your son in the national missing persons database, but I'll go ahead and send emails to agencies in all the party towns within two hundred and fifty miles. That can make a difference." I didn't say that I would also make sure that Gordon had done his job in the first place. There was probably a fifty-fifty chance that he had never entered the information. "I'll cover Panama City, Daytona, Gainesville, and even out as far as New Orleans."

"Thank you," she said, reaching out and touching my hand.

"Does your son have a cell phone?"

"No. We talked about it a few times, but he was afraid to get a phone. He thought it might be a trigger for him. When he was taking drugs, his phone was his most important possession. He tried to explain it to me. It was like the phone and all of the kids he got drugs from or partied with were all tied up together. He said that if he just holds a cell phone, then all those feelings come rushing back. He thinks that if he can just press the right buttons, he could be getting high again."

"I understand," I said honestly.

"I guess I can too. Remembering him talking about that, I can see how fragile his sobriety was. Maybe I didn't support him enough," she said meekly.

This time I took her hand. "Ms. Craig, you can't think like that. If Seth were here, he would tell you that his sobriety is his responsibility and his alone."

She nodded. I gave her one of my cards, told her to call me at any time and assured her I would keep in touch. As she walked away, I wondered why I had gotten involved in this. But the truth was that it made me feel better to just step in and do some standard investigative work. This would be something I could turn to when I got frustrated with Matt's case.

"You left me in there with those two goons," I heard Pete say.

I turned around to see him chewing on a toothpick and giving me the evil eye.

"Hey, I'm the one that got stuck with one of their cases."

"Cases. Them? Ha!" Pete said. "The only case those two ever worked on had cans of beer in it."

"Almost makes me feel sorry for Maxwell."

"He could fire them," Pete said.

"They came with the job. Besides, his only real choice is to hire rookies or old codgers."

"I think I'd take my chances with the rookies."

"They'll shoot themselves in the foot if you aren't watching them. Of course, that's why he's running against Dad."

I remembered that I still needed to give Pete a hard time. "Changing the subject: before Frick and Frack interrupted our lunch, I was going to ask you about Sarah's little pep talk with Cara."

"Fine, fine, but let's get in the car and get the air going before I sweat to death," Pete said.

A small shiver went up my back at his words. How long would it be before I'd be able to think about turning the air conditioner on in a car without reliving the explosion? Mentally shaking myself, I got in the car and told myself that I didn't smell burning rubber.

Once we were moving, Pete came clean. "I told Sarah that you had some trauma from the explosion, that's all. She's smart enough to put two and two together. I've had my share of nightmares. After that incident with Matt, you know how depressed I was. Even if no one at the office was actually giving me crap about it, I imagined they were."

Years earlier, Pete had been taking a break from patrol at a coffee shop. He'd turned his radio down so low that he didn't hear Matt's calls for help when a routine traffic stop had gone south fast. Matt had come very close to being killed and had blamed Pete, the closest officer at the time, for not coming to his assistance. Bad blood had existed between them ever since. Even a few other deputies had felt that Pete had gotten off easy with only a couple days' suspension and a note in his file.

"But Matt didn't die on your watch," I said, feeling twinges of guilt.

"He easily could have. But I never told anyone the worst part," Pete said quietly. He took such a long pause that I finally looked over at him. With his eyes focused out the window, he continued, "I had nightmares, but not about Matt dying. In the dreams, I'd hear the call and I'd rush to the scene. Matt wasn't there, but the shooter was and then he'd point the gun at me. I'd see the flash and feel the bullets rip into my body. When I told Sarah, she said she'd been having the same kind of dream, only she was seeing me get shot. It took me a while to get through it. But we agreed that it would be okay as long as we lived every day as if it might be our last together."

"Cara told me that. She appreciated the advice. I do too," I told him and meant it.

When we got back to the office, I gave myself an hour to work on Ms. Craig's missing son. I sent out the promised email alerts and I also pulled up his record. He had the usual drug-related charges, including the obligatory traffic-related incidents. I made a note that his license had been suspended from an incident three years earlier. He'd never gotten his license reinstated. All of it was standard fare.

When my hour was up, I made a note to go by the Express Burgers and talk to the manager the next time I had a chance. Then I put it all aside and turned back to the bombing. I'd looked through all of Matt's online reports, but I hadn't pulled the full case files from records. There were always things down there that never made it online.

I found Beth Miller, our head records clerk, in her office making copies of accident reports.

"There's one double fudge muffin left from this morning. But you better hurry. Pete usually comes around after lunch." Beth was an ardent amateur baker. If Dad ever fired her, he'd be tarred and feathered by the entire department staff.

"Perfect, I didn't get a chance to have dessert." I grabbed the muffin.

"There's a box over there," Beth said.

"Of what?"

"How long have I worked here? I'm pretty sure I could do your job. It's the case files from all the violent crimes that Matt investigated. I'm surprised it took you this long to come for them."

"It's just one lead we're chasing."

"Thompsons first. I get it."

"You really could do my job."

"When I'm bored, I read reports." She shrugged. "I'm not just a good cook. If I wasn't fifteen years your senior, I'd give Cara a run for her money."

"You're a better cook," I said, savoring the different layers of chocolate flavor in the muffin and being mildly amused at her light flirtation.

"I won't tell her you said that," Beth said with a grin.

After cramming the last of the muffin into my mouth, I grabbed the box and headed for my desk.

Going through all the files, I realized just how much work Matt had done. I remembered how Teresa had mentioned his working overtime when he served as her field training officer. I couldn't decide whether it was better or worse that he'd spent so much of his time working. On the one hand, he'd left a legacy of the lives he had touched through his work as an LEO. On the other hand, he'd never had the type of rich personal life that most of us had, or at least tried to have. *There has to be a balance*, I thought, reading report after report.

"I see you're deep into it," Darlene said, stopping by my desk and measuring up the box that was still three quarters full.

"At least some of it's interesting," I said. "How's your suicide coming along?"

She frowned. "I just came from the autopsy."

"And what does the great Dr. Darzi have to say on the matter?"

"Probably suicide. He thought all of my circumstantial evidence was weak at best."

"You still aren't happy."

"No. I'm not. But Darzi couldn't find any defensive wounds or anything else to suggest that Weaver wasn't the one that put the gun in his mouth. But how the hell did the shotgun end up across his legs like that?"

"Have you talked to any of his family?"

"Ex-wife. She wasn't surprised."

"Possible suspect?"

"Great alibi. She was across the country. As soon as they got divorced, she got as far away from the, quote, deranged lunatic as she could. Also, there's no money motive. No life insurance policies, no kids to fight over and, believe me, she was over him."

"When was the last time they talked?"

"A year ago, when the papers were signed. When I asked about the divorce, it was the only time she softened up a little. She said that he was a pretty nice guy when she married him. A bit obsessive compulsive, but he'd always been that way and mostly kept it under control. Then, eight or nine years ago, he had an accident and got depressed. That's when the OCD took over his life. She said you had a choice with him—live with the OCD or live with his severe depression."

"I'm sorry. But it sounds to me like you have your

answer," I said, surprised that Darlene was still fighting it.

"You're probably right, for the first time since I met you." Darlene could never resist the zingers. "But I'm going to keep it active for a few more days at least. See if I can come up with a new angle."

"Let me know if I can help. In theory, we're partners."

"That's the rumor," she said, heading back to her desk.

My phone buzzed with a text from Dad asking me to bring Mauser to the hospital. Before I could recover from that shock, he followed up with another message telling me that Mr. Greene had died, but with still no explanation as to why the hospital needed a visit from the monster dog. But mine was not to question why. I told him I'd be there in an hour.

I called Jamie and asked him to pack Mauser's regular travel bag full of treats, water and other essentials for a trip to Tallahassee. As I headed for the door, Sergeant Dill Kirby asked me what the hurry was.

"Dad wants me to bring Mauser over to the hospital in Tallahassee."

"That makes a lot of sense!" the old veteran shouted ironically as the door shut behind me.

CHAPTER SEVENTEEN

I parked in the visitor lot at the hospital and got the big lunk out of the van, which took some effort. I had to explain to him that the air conditioner was turned off and, as hot as it was outside, it would soon be a lot hotter in the van. He eventually saw the logic in my argument and stumbled out into the heat.

Tallahassee has an elite therapy dog organization, but Mauser was certainly not part of it so he couldn't go inside the building. I texted Dad that we were there and he directed me to a courtyard in the back of the hospital. We'd brought Mauser on one other occasion, when Shantel's niece had needed a little unsanctioned pet therapy.

Mauser and I found Dad and Pam Greene sitting on a bench in the shade. There was a bedpan on the ground by the bench.

"There he is," Dad said in the happy voice he reserved for Mauser. This sent the dog into a frolicking frenzy that almost pulled my arm out of its socket. He hauled me over to Dad, who gave him an exuberant greeting of ear rubs and tummy thumps.

"He's amazing," Pam said. She was holding a handkerchief and her eyes glistened with tears. Mauser moved over to her and let Pam pet him. "Tony was allergic to animal fur, so we never had any pets." Though from her expression and the way she scratched and made over the Dane, it was clear that she'd had experience with animals at some point in her life.

"Did you have animals growing up?" I asked while trying to keep Mauser from wiping too much slobber on her clothes.

"We did. We raised black Labs. My father was a bird hunter. He went all over North and South America with them. They were working dogs, but he always treated them like family." She continued to scratch Mauser. "I think we could have used some animals, Tony and I." The tears started rolling down her cheeks and soon she was crying and clutching Mauser tightly. Miraculously, he didn't swing his head and hurt the poor woman. After a couple of minutes, she got control of her grief. "I'm sorry."

"Nothing to be sorry for," Dad and I said in harmony.

"I can't believe…" She shook her head. "I've got a sister and a brother. That's all I have left." More tears flowed from her eyes.

The heat was getting to Mauser, who was beginning to pant. I saw him focus on the bedpan by the bench. I looked down and could see water in the stainless steel pan.

"A bedpan, really?" I said to Dad.

"It's the only thing I could find on short notice. It's clean!"

It didn't really matter as Mauser already had his head crammed down inside the pan, sloshing water everywhere. His antics managed to get a small smile out of Pam Greene.

"I know that this is an awful time to ask you questions about Matt, but we're trying to move the investigation forward." I got a dirty look from Dad, but Pam locked eyes with me.

"Ask me anything. Tony would never want us to let his death slow down the hunt for the man that killed Matt. He killed Tony too. He really did." She looked away, just managing to hold back the tears. "I spent so many years fighting with that man and now I'm lost…" She hesitated, then went on, "I don't know what impression I gave you earlier. We loved each other. It's just that when Carter died there was so much… anger and pain. We got lost and couldn't find our way back to each other. I think we lost sight of Matt for a while too. I always thought we were so lucky that he didn't drift into drugs or some other trouble while we were wallowing in our grief."

"We need to know if there is anything in Matt's background that might point to a person who could have been involved in the bombing, or who might have information that could lead us to a suspect."

"I understand. I'm just not sure if I can be of much help. It all goes back to losing our first son. The years we lost with Matt created a… distance. Even when he was still a teenager, we all were more like strangers living in the same house. Matt was so mature. Tony and I never had to be parents, if you know what I mean. Looking back, I hate myself for letting us all grow apart."

"Don't be too hard on yourself. My mother died ten years ago." I looked over at Dad, thinking of the days of silence that had dragged on between us. "I'm not sure how well we managed."

"Larry's right. It's very easy to let grief isolate you from the ones you care about." I was surprised that Dad was being so open. Normally, he seldom acknowledged emotions like love and grief. But in the presence of Pam Greene's pain, it would have been a very churlish person who didn't want to reach out to her.

"I've tried to think. Matt and I talked to each other at least every other week. Trouble is, it was mostly about the weather, his job or what was going on in our old neighborhood in Orlando. There just isn't anything I can remember. I didn't want to, but I logged into my Facebook page so I could reach out to some of his old friends." She started to choke up again.

To give her a few moments of privacy, I looked away from her and down at Mauser, who'd rolled over on his side and was trying to get comfortable in the shade.

"There were so many messages from old friends," she said after a minute. "Word about Matt had gotten around to almost everyone. Of course, most of them didn't even know about Tony's attack. I had some people who'd known Matt from years ago, people I barely remembered, messaging me. Even a man from here, who Matt knew when he was a deputy, reached out and told me that he had lost a son and knew how much I must be suffering. Everyone meant well, but it was so overwhelming. Though there was some solace in knowing that Matt had touched so many lives. Now I'm going to have to tell everyone about Tony." The burden on her shoulders was almost a physical presence.

"We'll do anything we can to help," Dad said.

"Thank you. Chief Maxwell and his wife have also been very supportive. I've talked with him a couple of times. I've also got a friend who's driving up today."

We talked for a few more minutes, but Pam was clearly exhausted and Mauser's heat index was topping out. Dad and Pam walked Mauser back to the van with me.

"Thank you," she said to Mauser after we'd gotten him inside the van and started the air conditioner for him. Hanging his head out of the window, he took her admiration and goodbye hug in stride.

"Thank you too," she said to me. "Find the person who did this. Please."

"There are a whole bunch of angry agents and LEOs on the trail. We'll find him," I promised.

Leaving the hospital, I thought about running by the Quarter Moon and looking for a birthday present for Cara, but I couldn't leave Mauser in the car. I decided I'd make some excuse to cut out of work early on Friday so I could go shopping.

I dropped Mauser off at Dad's house, switched cars and

headed back to the office. On the way, I decided to look in on Eddie. I needed to be careful stopping by in daylight. After driving in circles and making sure no one was following me, I parked a block away and cut through a wooded lot. I found the gate to the wooden fence that surrounded Mr. Griffin's property easily enough and slipped through his backyard to the house.

I had to knock for a while before Mr. Griffin answered the door.

"Come in, come in," he said with typical enthusiasm.

"We need to put a lock on your back gate. That way, at least the bad guys would have to climb your fence."

"Okay, sure," he said casually. "Your friend is very entertaining. I think I've just about gotten him able to be in a room with a cat!"

What a great achievement, I thought. *Albert Griffin bringing transvestites and cats together.*

"Where is he?"

"Upstairs. He does sleep a lot."

I headed up the stairs.

"Second door on the right," Mr. Griffin added.

I knocked several times on Eddie's door.

"I'm good, don't want anything more to eat. Thank you," came from the other side of the door.

"Open up."

I was just about ready to knock again when Eddie finally opened the door. "Hey," he said.

"Hey, yourself. I've got a couple of things I want to ask you."

"Sure. Come on in, but don't let any cats in. Though I'm kinda getting used to them. What they call immersion therapy," Eddie said, backing away from the door.

The room was furnished with nice Edwardian antiques— big, heavy stuff. There was a bit of dust, but overall they were very nice accommodations. There were a couple of children's toys in one corner next to a wardrobe. I recognized a box of Lincoln Logs and a toy tomahawk. I wondered if Mr. Griffin had children. For all the stories he liked to tell, I realized he'd never said anything about his personal history.

"What's up?" Eddie asked, sitting down in a wooden rocker by the window.

"Enjoying yourself?"

"It's a lot better than a cargo container. The old guy's all right."

"Great," I said, but Eddie ignored my sarcasm. "Your grandfather sends his hate. Wishes you'd been blown to pieces the other day."

"Good old Gramps. And I hope he burns forever at a very high temperature in hell."

"I'm pretty sure he will."

"And my dear father?"

"Not quite the same degree of venom."

"If he hadn't been such a shit to me, I could feel sorry for him. I mean, look at his father."

"I think Justin is finally beginning to see how evil his father is."

"He's always known it. He was just too weak to get out from under the old man's boot," Eddie said in a more mature tone than I'd ever heard him use. "Why couldn't I have had a grandfather like Mr. Griffin?" he asked the ceiling.

"I've got a question for you. Do you know a kid by the name of Seth Craig? By all accounts, he did drugs but was doing the twelve-steps thing."

Eddie's face scrunched up in thought. "Seth, yeah. Pretty average dude. Quiet. I saw him at meetings a couple of times."

"His mom is looking for him."

"He had an interesting story. His gutter stories weren't that good, but his how-I-got-to-be-a-druggie story was great."

"You go to the meetings for their entertainment value?"

"Nooooo, no… It's a… bonus feature. There are some

folks that are pretty darn fascinating to listen to. Hey, I share too. I get some good laughs with the wearing women's clothes bit."

I just shook my head. "Okay, so what was Seth's story?"

"Let me think." Eddie's eyes darted from the ceiling to the floor as he tried to remember. "Oh, yeah, something about stealing a car. He got chased by a cop, then some way or another a kid was hurt. Come to think of it, the kid might have even died. Seth got a slap on the wrist. The point was that he was depressed and started getting high to forget, blah, blah, blah. He was very compelling. Lot of heart. Some people get up there and either stammer and stutter, or say it like they're reading a menu." Eddie waved his hand dismissively.

"Anything else you can remember? Did he ever talk about anyplace else he liked to go? Maybe someplace he went to get high?"

"I don't remember. Like I said, his woe-is-me story was good, but he didn't hit rock bottom that bad, if you ask me. He never even lived on the street. Boring. Now some people, man, they went low. Doing all kinds of nasty stuff to get their next fix. Wow. Those are the stories you remember and say, 'I don't want to go down that road.' You know what I mean?" Eddie was shaking his head.

"Did Seth seem to have any regular friends?"

"Just his sponsor, but that's not really a friend, right?"

"What's his sponsor's name?"

"Harold. Great guy. Long-timer. He's got some stories from back in the day. He goes all the way back to the disco days. Came down from New York to Daytona."

"Where can I find Harold?"

"Anonymity is in the name," Eddie said self-righteously.

"This a small town. No one really expects to keep their identity secret."

"It's breaking one of the cardinal rules." Eddie stuck his hand out. His morals were frequently for sale. Luckily, I was prepared for these kinds of shenanigans from him. I held out an IOU I'd written for twenty dollars' worth of food.

"What is this?" he asked, looking at the note

"You aren't supposed to leave the house, and giving an addict money when they're in the early stages of recovery isn't a good idea. That's an IOU that I'll redeem for food when this mess is over."

"No way."

"I could charge you for the food and clothes I've already given you. Or I could get Mr. Griffin to make you out a bill for room and board. Would you prefer one of those options?"

"No," he said, sounding like a petulant child. He took out his wallet, carefully folding the note and putting it away. "Harold works at the feed store. Big guy, beard, biker tattoos, over fifty. You can't miss him."

All the talk about AA got me thinking about Eddie's ex-girlfriend, Ella. I thought about telling him that I had gone by and talked to her, but in the end I figured it would just open up a can of worms best left sealed.

Satisfied that Mr. Griffin and Eddie were getting along and with a lead for a case that didn't even belong to our department, I left the way I'd come.

I took the box of Matt's reports home with me and went through them while Cara, Alvin and Ivy watched a movie. I still couldn't find anything that made alarm bells go off. I made note of a couple of people Matt had arrested that had put up a good fight, but that was all. Cara and I called it an early night and I managed to get some much-needed sleep.

CHAPTER EIGHTEEN

On Friday morning, I had just reached the car when my phone rang.

"I think we're golden," Pete said, sounding like a kid watching Fourth of July fireworks. "Just got a call from Captain Bennett. Justin wants to talk to us."

Enough said. I drove straight to the jail where Pete, Padilla and Devlin were already waiting.

"I've got ATF on notice," Padilla said.

"Leon County and FDLE bomb teams are standing by too. If he does give us an actionable lead to our bomb maker, we're going to need a lot of expertise," Pete said.

"If he's connected to the cartels, then the suspect might be anywhere, including Central or South America," Devlin said.

"No pessimists allowed," I joked, though of course he was right.

"We roll the same way as last time?" Padilla asked. I was impressed that she was deferring a decision to us.

"Yep. Larry and me face-to-face while you all watch and listen on a monitor. The only difference is that we'll also have Mike Peterson from the State Attorney's office with us. He's been granted authority to agree to a deal on the state charges," Pete said and got nods all around.

Justin looked glad to see us, which just made the situation seem surreal.

"Your lawyer's not joining us?" Pete asked.

"I think I'm in the market for a new lawyer," Justin said with a smirk. He wasn't stupid. "Right now I think I'm safer without one."

The four of us pounded out an agreement which resulted in a number of his charges being dropped. He also left the door open to testifying against his father.

"With him, you're either on his side or one of the enemy. This is going to make me one of the enemy, so I might as well go all the way," Justin responded when Pete asked if he'd be willing to turn state's evidence.

There were several charges that Peterson refused to drop or reduce, but even with those, Justin had the chance of walking out of prison in twenty years.

"The man's name is Al McCoy. At least, that's how I know him. We were asked to let him hide out on our place about a year ago. He's ex-military and did some explosive work as a mercenary in Central America. The guys we bought from wanted him close at hand if they needed him. Nice enough guy. A hard worker, but he has some strange ideas. A bit paranoid for my taste. I gave him a little work around the farm but, honestly, he scared the crap out of me. Mostly, I just let him live in an old house back on some of our hunting land."

Pete handed Justin a piece of paper and a pencil. I looked at the map he drew and had a vague idea where he was talking about. There was a sizeable chunk of wooded land in the south part of the county. This particular area was bottom land. Good for hunting, but too swampy for much of anything else.

"There's also an old tobacco barn," Justin added.

"What should we expect to find at the property. Guns? Explosives? What vehicles does he have?" I asked.

"You've had me locked up here for months, so how the

hell am I supposed to know?"

"What did he have before you got locked up?" Pete pressed.

"He was paranoid to an extreme. This guy didn't even let us in the place once he moved in. I complained to Dad about this jerk coming in and thinking he owned the place, and I was told that, per our supplier's orders, he was to be left alone.

"As far as weapons, he had the balls to point a shotgun at me one day, so there's that. A Mossberg. I'm sure he had handguns and rifles. He showed up in a cargo van with the name of some electrical contractor on the side of it. You're smart enough to figure out that, if you want to drive around the country with all the wires and switches to make detonating devices, an electrician's van would be pretty good cover."

"What color is the van?"

"Standard white."

"And you don't remember the name on the side of it?"

"No, but it's going to be the only van on this property," Justin said, sounding annoyed at the question.

"He might be driving it around town. Could be useful to give out a description," I tossed back.

"I guess. Though like I said, the guy lived like a hermit."

"Would anyone be delivering food to him since you've been locked up?" Pete asked.

"You got a point there. I don't know. Jack had been, but you all pulled him in too."

"He's out now," I said. Jack Thompson was one of Justin's many cousins. We'd pulled him in originally, but he'd made bail a week later. After Matt's death, he'd been brought in for questioning, but there wasn't any reason we could find to revoke his bail.

Justin was introduced to Devlin, who would be his contact with the DEA going forward. I thought Eddie would find it interesting that his father had flipped on his grandfather.

Once we were done with Justin, we headed back to the office and met in the large conference room to develop a strategy for bringing in Al McCoy. Running his name through the NCIC brought up nothing, which wasn't a surprise. He probably had several aliases.

"We can provide a SWAT team and ATF has agreed to provide a bomb squad to accompany them," Padilla said.

"The first thing we need to do is recon the area," Dad said. Things were now far above Pete's and my pay grades. With a major law enforcement operation about to go down in his county, Dad had to be on top of it.

"We have a drone we can use," Devlin offered. "We use them quite a bit these days to look for pot fields. Has a regular and a FLIR thermal imaging camera."

"We could pull in Jack Thompson. Since Jack has brought him supplies in the past, Al might let him get close to the cabin," I suggested.

"Put out a call to have him picked up and brought in," Dad said.

"Timeframe?" Padilla asked.

"The sooner the better," Dad said. If McCoy was allowed to run loose and citizens were killed, it would look very bad when word got out that law enforcement had known about him.

At Dad's request, Lionel West, our newest and best IT guy, came into the room and pulled up a satellite view of the Thompson property onto a large screen on the wall.

Dad pointed to a corner of the property. "There is only one road into the area. The nearest crossroad is half a mile from the house. Assuming that McCoy is on the property, I plan to have this road blocked off as soon as this meeting is over. That will contain him. There are a couple of trails leading away from the house and barn. I'll position a couple of our best snipers on these trails with orders to stop anyone fleeing the property."

"Shoot to kill could be problematic if we haven't identified him or established that he's a threat. We are basing all of this on the word of mid-level drug dealer," Devlin said.

"Agreed. I won't give the kill order to the snipers until we've established that he is fleeing capture and/or poses a threat," Dad allowed.

An hour later, all of the teams and equipment were on the way, with two hours established before kickoff time. Dad received permission from the county's road department to use their biggest bulldozer to block the road onto the property. The huge piece of machinery would take up the entire width of the narrow road. A semi could ram the bulldozer and it wouldn't budge, so once it was in place no vehicle would be getting off that property without Dad's permission.

Pete was our best sniper and would be stationed on the larger of the two hunting trails that led away from the property. The other was covered by a sniper from FDLE. The operation had quickly turned into a major multi-jurisdictional pig pile.

"I just hope the governor doesn't show up for a photo op," Dad muttered.

"Afraid he'll get between you and the cameras?" I joked.

He glared at me. "Don't think I'm having fun. This has the potential to turn into a huge shitstorm," Dad said seriously. "Besides, let's hope everyone can keep their mouths shut until we make our move."

That was a tall order in today's media-intensive environment. Every agency had pledged themselves and their employees to a media blackout until we had at least moved onto the property and had the road blocked off.

By four o'clock, everybody was staged in their assigned locations on the road and trails leading to the house and barn. Dad had the local warrants in hand and Padilla had pulled a couple of federal warrants. We'd been unable to locate Jack Thompson, so we were going in on our own with the drone.

"Ready when you are," Dad said, standing with half a dozen people and staring at a monitor set up on a folding table beside a DEA van. Sitting at the table with his hands on a joystick was a man who looked like he could've been a freshman in college.

"We just want to surveil the clearing with the house and barn. Stay clear of the buildings," Devlin told the man.

There was an insectoid buzzing sound as the drone took off. The image on the screen was slightly disorienting until the drone got high enough to give us a good panoramic view of the woods.

"You want the regular image or the FLIR camera?"

"Regular first, then make a pass with the thermal imagining camera. Are you recording?" Devlin asked.

"Yep." The young man maintained his focus on the screen. His hand barely moved on the joystick as he flew the drone toward the clearing.

When the drone was in place, it stayed high and near the edge of the woods. Every so often it would stop, turn and hover, giving us a clear image of the buildings. We couldn't see any sign of the van.

"There are tire tracks going into the barn," Dad pointed out.

"Makes sense for him to park it inside out of sight of helicopters," I said.

"Or drones," Padilla put in.

"It's possible he's not there," Devlin said, and I could feel the tension rise with those words. No one wanted to think that a man with the tools, the skills and history required to make a bomb was out on the loose.

"There," I said, having seen movement in the house. "Something's at the window."

The flash of white happened again.

"I think that's part of a curtain. The windows are open," Padilla said.

I heard Dad's phone buzz and he looked down at the text. "Damn!" he said, causing everyone to glance at him. "One of my deputies at the roadblock says that a news van just showed up wanting to know what's going on."

"Switch to the FLIR," Devlin told the drone pilot.

"The current temperature is over ninety-five, and with the house being in the sun, there could be parts that are hotter than a human body," the pilot said. He didn't really need to tell us how hot it was. All of us were soaking wet from the heat and humidity.

"Understood. Let's see what we can see," Devlin said.

The thermal imaging camera clearly showed movement inside the house. From the top of the tree line, though, the camera was too far away to get a good fix on the movement. The hot tin roof also made it hard to discern the shape of the moving object.

"Can't tell if it's just one person or more," Dad said.

"Or even an animal," Padilla said, leaning toward the monitor to get a better look.

"It's human," said the drone pilot. No doubt he'd seen hundreds of blurry human forms moving about in distant houses. "I can move in and down a little."

The image shifted until we were looking across the clearing at the house instead of down at it from the treetops. From this viewpoint, it was clear that a person was pacing around inside.

"He looks agitated," Devlin muttered.

"We need to—" Dad started, then it became clear that the moving image was headed toward the front of the house.

"Switch back to the regular image," Devlin said excitedly. The pilot flipped a switch on the joystick and we saw the front door of the old farmhouse open. "Don't move," he told the pilot. "Just hover." Any movement back toward the treetops could have attracted the man's attention.

The man standing on the steps was lean, with broad shoulders and hair cropped close to his scalp. The drone was almost a hundred and fifty feet away, so details weren't clear. However, he appeared to be angry and suspicious as he swiveled his head right and left. Then he stopped and tilted his head. Everyone watching knew that he was listening for any sound that might be out of place. Maybe he had heard the buzzing of the drone. Even though it would have been impossible for him to hear us, we all held our breath.

"Try zooming in," Devlin instructed and the young man nodded. The image closed in, but even the small movement of the drone caused the man to flit in and out of the computer image. "Okay, zoom out. We might have something we can use." By looking at the images one by one, they might've been able to isolate a decent image of his face.

Dad's phone buzzed again. "There's something on the news. I think we're going to have to tighten the noose around Mr. McCoy.

"Are we sure we're looking at McCoy?" Padilla asked.

"He matches the description that Justin Thompson gave us of the person calling himself Al McCoy," Dad said, and I could hear the first signs of impatience in his voice.

"Waiting until we have more information would be safer," Devlin said. "If we have a good image of his face, then we might be able to confirm his identity."

"That would be great, but it's heading toward five o'clock. If we wait much longer, he could use the cover of darkness to slip away."

"He might not hear the news reports."

"Someone from the Thompson clan is liable to call and warn him. I don't want this man loose in my county," Dad said.

"What do you want me to do?" the pilot asked.

"Stay in place. We'll use the drone to keep our people aware of what McCoy is doing," Dad said.

The pilot looked to Devlin for confirmation and got a nod.

"Hey, he's outside the house and he's got a rifle or a shotgun," Padilla said.

Everyone's attention went back to the screen. The man was striding across the yard toward the barn. His head constantly swiveled back and forth until he entered the barn.

"Damn it!" Dad growled. Assuming the van was in the garage, this was a bad development. A man in a vehicle was a lot more dangerous than one on foot. "We've got to move."

Padilla nodded. She put on a radio headset and handed one to Dad. The SWAT team had already moved down the road to within striking distance. There had been an animated discussion about the use of a sniper close to the house. However, with the roads blocked, Dad hadn't thought it was necessary. The odds of our quarry getting out of those woods was pretty slim.

"That looks like smoke," I said, pointing to the monitor. Grey and white wisps were coming out of the eaves of the barn.

Padilla gave the go-ahead and a second monitor lit up with body-cam footage from the SWAT team's leader. They entered the clearing in just a few minutes. The SWAT team asked for intel and Padilla asked the drone pilot to use the FLIR to get the location of the suspect inside the barn.

"He's right inside the front door, not in the van," Padilla said. "Can't tell if he has a weapon or not. There's a hotspot in the middle of the barn." The hotspot must have been the origin of the smoke.

"Roger that. Moving men to the back of the barn," replied the team leader.

Then the FLIR picked up the heat signatures of two men approaching the back of the barn. Before they reached the barn, the front door opened and McCoy stepped out.

"Stand firm," was Padilla's order to the team.

"We want him alive," Dad said.

"He's yelling something," the SWAT team leader said, then yelled, "Pull back! Squad A, pull back!"

The drone pilot switched to regular view and we could see the suspect holding a small object in his right hand. Both hands were raised above his head. His mouth was moving and a garbled shout could be heard in the background over the radio.

"Shit!" the team leader said and his camera flashed an image of the ground before going dark.

We watched the monitor in horror as McCoy was

enveloped in a ball of red fire. The explosion was loud enough that we could hear it and feel the concussion through the ground, even from our command post half a mile down the road. My stomach knotted and an image of a burning car passed through my mind.

After a moment of stunned silence, Dad pushed back from the table.

"I guess that was predictable," he said in disgust. "We'll need the ATF and the bomb squads to clear the two buildings before we can start picking up the pieces of Al McCoy, or whoever the hell he was." I thought for a minute that Dad was going to throw the radio headset as he took it off, but instead he carefully handed it back to Padilla.

We used the drone to go around all the buildings and look through the windows. Wherever the smoke was coming from, the fire must have been contained, because it never spread to the barn itself.

"Luckily this ground is too swampy for him to have buried any landmines," I said.

"Small favors," Dad muttered, still grinding his teeth over the now pear-shaped operation.

"I don't see how you could have done anything else," I said.

"Cutting him off from the barn might have helped. We could have sent someone in as a decoy to lure him out."

"You had to cut off his exit. That required a large operation and the news agencies were sure to catch wind of it. When that happened, well, here we are."

"I don't like having you talk me down off the cliff," he grumbled, pacing back and forth as we waited for the bomb squad and their robot to move in and check out the grounds.

It was dark by nine o'clock and klieg lights had been set up in the yard. The bomb squad had cleared the house, but not the barn. They *had* determined that there wasn't anything big enough inside the barn to explode and endanger people near the house, so the FBI and ATF forensic teams were allowed to move up to the house and begin searching it.

I called Cara and told her I was going to be camping out.

"Better you than me," she said. "Need me to bring you anything? Do you have something for the bugs?"

"The Feds brought in a bunch of supplies and catering. Mind you, the spray they gave us appears to be mosquito food rather than repellant," I said, slapping at the buzzing around my ears.

"Was this the man that killed Matt?"

"I think it's a safe bet that he made the bomb. Who paid him to do it, and who might have assisted him, are the questions we still need to answer. Pete and I are going to walk through the house in a few minutes."

"Is it safe?"

"The house is. They found a number of devices and different explosives in the barn and van. I don't think everything will be clear until sometime tomorrow. We're playing it safe," I assured her.

"None of you are going 'Hold my beer and watch this'?" she asked with a gentle laugh.

I smiled, glad to hear the humor in her voice. "No," I said emphatically.

Pete tapped me on the shoulder and I said goodnight to Cara.

We got a ride up to the house on the back of a four-wheeler. The forensic teams had marked a narrow path across the yard to the house. They wanted daylight before they went over the rest of the yard one more time. We walked straight to the house on the marked path after donning several items of protective gear designed to keep from contaminating the scene. Hot and miserable doesn't even come close to describing it. I looked at Pete, whose goggles were already fogged up as he huffed and puffed his way into the house.

"I'd wait until we could skip the protective wear if I didn't want to go ahead and get on the trail of any accomplices," I apologized, and Pete nodded in reluctant agreement.

Inside, the house had the look of a hunting cabin, with bare pine flooring and old couches and chairs. The kitchen was tidy. There were boxes of generic cereal and stacks of ramen noodle packets in the cupboard.

We looked carefully through the room where McCoy had been sleeping. There were two duffle bags full of clothes, mostly of the plain working variety. There was no paper of any type. No books, no writing paper, no receipts, no letters, no bills, nothing.

"This doesn't look good," I said.

"I think we have a professional," Pete agreed.

"Definitely not our usual country fare. But surely there'll be fingerprints," I said hopefully.

"I don't see a lot of dust," Pete said, looking around. He was right. There weren't any dirty dishes in the kitchen either.

"Can a man live in a house for months and not leave any fingerprints?"

"Look on the bright side. He sure left a lot of DNA spread all over the yard."

"True that."

The forensic team was right behind us and began dusting the house for prints, vacuuming it for trace evidence and tearing it apart to look for anything hidden in the walls or furniture.

CHAPTER NINETEEN

I got a couple uncomfortable hours of sleep in the back of my car, but there was a nice spread of coffee and pastries set up on tables along the road when I woke up.

"At least the Feds eat well," I said to Pete when he walked up.

"They even brought in a trailer with bathrooms," Pete said, sounding almost cheerful. "I'm trying to convince myself that this case is rolling to a close."

"We have to connect the dots to anyone else involved," I reminded him.

"We have Justin, who'll testify why this McCoy guy was staying here. And there'll be plenty of evidence that the Thompsons knew that he was here and were allowing him to stay."

"But that still leaves a lot of holes for a defense attorney to exploit in a case against Daniel Thompson. Not the least of which is the fact that Matt was killed and not Eddie. The prosecutor will have to prove that Eddie was the intended victim to really pin it on the Thompsons." I felt bad crushing Pete's optimism, but I couldn't help thinking that we still had a long way to go.

By mid-morning we were able to go through the barn and

173

look over the van. The bomb squad had moved almost everything in the barn from its original location in their thorough search for anything explosive. However, they had taken extensive video before and during the operation so we were able to see what it had looked like before it was disturbed.

"Here's where the smoke was coming from," Pete said, pointing to an old metal oil drum that had clearly been used as a burn barrel.

"They haven't found a wallet or a cell phone. What you want to bet he burned them?" I couldn't keep the frustration out of my voice.

"We're lucky he didn't burn everything down."

"I think he left the buildings just to taunt us." I was irritated that the bomber seemed to be keeping a few steps ahead of us even after he'd scattered himself over more than an acre of grass.

"We reviewed the tapes from the SWAT team and enhanced the sound," Padilla said, having followed us into the barn. "When McCoy, or whoever he was, came out of the barn, he shouted, 'I could have killed all of you!' right before he blew himself up."

"From what the bomb squad found, I think he was telling the truth," Pete said.

"Strange man. There wasn't an obvious accent on the recording, so he was either an American or spoke English fluently."

"We knew that from Justin. We need to press him for any other details he can remember about McCoy," I said.

"We've rounded up the Thompsons' known associates. Anyone that might have had contact with our bomber," Padilla told us.

"This guy was cautious in the extreme. But anyone can make a mistake," I said.

"Could be. We'll have DNA to compare in a couple of days," Padilla said. "Maybe we'll get lucky and he'll pop up in one of the databases. We've made him a top priority with the labs."

Agent Harvey from the ATF was up to his elbows in a mass of wires, batteries and electronics in the van when we walked over to him.

"Looking at the components in here, I'd say it's probable that he also made the bomb that killed Agent Greene. We'll probably find enough matches for wire, casings and explosives to make it conclusive," he said, looking up from the mess in the van.

"At least that's some good news. What bugs the hell out of me is that there have to be other people involved."

"We'll put pressure on Thompson's people and see if we can get any of them to crack," Pete assured me.

"What about Daniel's lawyer? He's the one most likely to have carried messages from Daniel Thompson to our bomber, or to someone else in the operation who then got in contact with McCoy."

"We're tracking him, but we couldn't get a judge to sign off on a warrant to pull his phone records or to tape his phone conversations. Judges aren't going to make it easy to tap into a criminal attorney's conversations. It sets a bad precedent. But if we can tie him to our bomber, that would make the difference," Padilla said.

"Any luck with tracing a phone number back to the bomber?" I asked.

"Our best bet there is Justin. If he can remember a number or show us a number on his past phone records where they called this McCoy character, then we could start pulling phone records."

"Likely he used a pay-as-you-go burner."

"In which case there may not be a record of the calls or texts he made, but if we had the number we could at least cross-reference it on other people's phone records."

"Like the lawyer's," I said.

"Exactly. And that would give us probable cause for a warrant. Of course, that's a chicken-and-egg situation. Without the bomber's phone records, and if we aren't able to pull the lawyer's…" Padilla shrugged. "This isn't going to fall into our laps. We're going to have to pound some pavement.

"Our forensic teams are bagging and tagging. You all should look at the items they're pulling from the house and barn and see if anything looks like it could tie back to the Thompsons. You all know them as well as anyone," she suggested.

We spent the next five hours looking over every plastic bag that the forensics team brought out from the two buildings. Like most of the evidence taken when there wasn't a clear suspect, it was random and most of it would prove useless.

"Didn't this guy have anything personal?" I asked as we looked at another piece of cutlery.

"I'm thinking some of the tools in the van were probably his personal tools. Someone who does precision work is bound to have tools that he needs and is attached to," Pete said.

"And everyone says you don't do anything but text your family," I said and, as if on cue, the text alert chimed on his phone.

"Pure coincidence," he said and paused to text his daughter back.

"I'm going to talk to one of the ATF agents."

Agent Harvey put me in touch with one of their guys who could build and disarm bombs.

"Would you go through the van with me?" I asked him. "This man built bombs. Maybe you could point out the tools that he would have used, particularly if any of them are specialty tools and look well taken care of."

"I get it. Sure."

A jumble of tools and parts were still inside the van. Anyone would've recognized a lot of them from simple household maintenance—sockets, socket plates, safety tabs for wires, wire cutters, screwdrivers and such. I was convinced that most of it was stage dressing. If McCoy had been stopped by law enforcement, they'd look at all this junk and think nothing of it.

"Can I shift stuff around?" the ATF guy asked me.

"Sure." I pulled out a pair of plastic gloves and handed them to him.

There were a number of rusted sliding metal drawers attached to the inside of the van. He opened each one and poked and prodded inside. From the last one, he pulled out a leather kit with a number of tools inside. They didn't look that different from all the rest, though they appeared to be better taken care of than most of the others.

"Here. These are precision tools for working on clocks or bombs. I'd bet you these were his personal tools." The man stared at them and I saw his face grow dark.

"What's wrong?"

"This guy was in the military. I learned a lot on a bomb squad in Iraq. Different experts take different approaches to defusing bombs. Different methods, different tools. This looks like an Army kit. Or at least like a kit that started out Army and got personalized." He paused and looked like he wanted to hit something. Instead he went on, "Pisses me off when we run into one of our own that's gone bad. It's tough enough dealing with all the foreign nuts."

He pointed out several tools in the kit that would've been hard to find at a hardware store. I found a member of the FBI's forensic team and together we photographed all the tools and the maker's marks that were on them. Maybe we could identify the bomber through the tools he used.

"Did you find anything?" Pete asked, and I explained about the tools. "Good. With a little luck, we'll get this guy's real ID and be able to tie him back to the Thompsons in short order."

"I don't know. Something's not right about this," I said, feeling uncertain. There was an echo in my mind. I realized that I had heard Darlene say almost the exact same thing about her probable suicide. In real life, pieces didn't always fit together and lots of cases had loose ends that were never tied up. I just didn't want this case to be one of them.

With nothing else left for us to do onsite, Pete and I trudged back to our cars. I saw Dad talking with a reporter. He'd done half a dozen news spots since our suspect blew himself up.

My phone rang just as I reached the car. The ring tone was Cara's and I realized that I was totally screwed. We were going to miss tonight's dinner reservations for her birthday, and my plan to shop for a gift had gone out the window when all hell had broken loose yesterday.

"I'm sorry," I said as soon as I answered the phone.

"I know." I was amazed that she didn't sound upset.

"You aren't too mad at me?"

"Of course not. I might be a little disappointed but, on the other hand, I'm glad you all got this guy. He sounds like he was pretty dangerous. I just saw your dad on the news."

"He definitely could have done a lot more damage than he did," I agreed.

"How much longer are you going to have to stay out there?"

"I was just about ready to head home. There's still another day or two of work out here for the forensic guys, but luckily we don't have to be here for that. They'll have to search out to a thousand yards or more around the house just to make sure he didn't hide anything in the woods."

"Wow."

"He was here for months."

"Are the Thompsons involved?"

"Yes. How much we can prove, I don't know."

"But you'll be home soon?"

"Yep, and I'll need to take my clothes off outside. The odor would probably chase you and the animals out of the house."

I was only half joking. The only reason all the LEOs and support staff could stand each other was because we all stank from working outside and sleeping in our cars in the middle of July in Florida. There was also the lingering smell of burnt flesh that seemed to pervade the property. Most pieces of the body had been picked up as soon as the bomb squad gave the okay, but there were still small bits hidden in the ankle-deep grass. It would be a week before the birds, forest carnivores and the weather cleaned up the last of the remains.

"I'll shove you straight into the shower," Cara said.

"That would sound like a lot more fun if I wasn't exhausted."

"What do you want for dinner?"

"I'm supposed to be taking *you* out for dinner."

"Don't worry, I'll cancel the reservations. But you'll pay for it," she joked.

"Don't make anything hot. Sandwiches would be great." Hearing thunder in the distance, I said, "I better go. Love you," and hung up.

"Cara?" Dad asked, walking over to me.

"Yep."

"You need a bath," Dad said. He'd gone home and cleaned up last night, wanting to be presentable for the news crews.

"Thanks."

"Didn't you say tomorrow's her birthday?"

"Yes, and I've already managed to screw it up. I was supposed to go into Tallahassee yesterday and find a present. But here I am instead, smelling of burnt flesh and sweat."

Dad pursed his lips and looked thoughtful. "I've got an idea. But it involves coming over to my place."

"What?"

"I have your mother's jewelry. You can pick out something to give to Cara for her birthday. I think your mom would have liked that."

The offer took me by surprise. It went against several things I took for granted. One, Dad wasn't prone to sentiment, though I knew he'd saved some of Mom's jewelry; two, he wasn't normally generous with me; and three, he usually liked to see me squirm on the hook when

I'd gotten myself in a jam. I *had* noticed that some of these traits had tended to soften a bit since he'd been spending time with his girlfriend, Genie Anderson, but I still wouldn't have expected something like this.

"If you're sure."

"Wouldn't have offered if I wasn't. I'm going to be royally ticked off if you screw up this relationship. And, honestly, I figured you'd eventually need some help to hang onto a prize like Cara." He actually smiled. "Besides, I'm in a pretty good mood. I would have liked to have taken this character alive, but the way things worked out isn't the worst outcome. Alive, he could have presented a host of jurisdictional and prosecutorial problems. Dead... not so much. And we get the bonus of him having done it to himself on camera. Both looking guilty and proving that he was a dangerous person."

"I'd feel better if we knew who put him up to it."

"I agree. The FBI got a pretty good still image of his face from the body camera footage. I gave it to the media and have asked for anyone who recognizes him to come forward. We'll know who he is soon enough. As for the rest of it, you and Pete are going to have to do some grunt work. You can have any resources you need."

I called Cara back and told her about the detour to Dad's place without explaining the reason for it. As soon as we got there, Dad sent me out to the barn to strip down and take a shower in the small bathroom he'd built next to the stalls.

He came out with Mauser in tow and brought me some old clothes that I kept at his place. It had rained before we got to the house and, while the air was steamy, it was still fifteen degrees cooler than it had been an hour before.

"What, you stupid dog?" I asked Mauser as he danced around me, sniffing the air and looking interested. I looked down at the bundle of dirty clothes in my hand. "Oh, this is what you want. You're sick, brother, sick."

I held the clothes above my head to keep Mauser from grabbing them out of my hand and tossed them into the washer in the garage while Dad distracted the beast with treats. Once inside, Dad took me to his bedroom and brought a large suitcase out of the closet.

"Your mom was funny about jewelry. She didn't like to buy expensive things. Told me that they made her feel like she was putting on airs. But every once in a while a piece would catch her eye and then she'd be just like a little kid, wanting it so bad. I'd tell her she could get it, then she'd spend another twenty minutes hemming and hawing about whether we could afford it or not." Dad's eyes got a far away look when he talked about Mom. I knew he was seeing her in his mind, his love for her mixed with the pain of loss.

He put the suitcase on the bed and opened it. Inside were half a dozen different jewelry boxes of various sizes. "You can have anything you want," he said with a softness in his voice that I'd seldom heard.

I opened the boxes one by one and looked through all of the necklaces, rings, bracelets and watches. Most of it was silver and quite a few pieces had sapphires, Mom's birthstone. There were also a few strands of pearls.

Finally, I opened a small box and was surprised when I found a heart pendant inside of it. The pendant was on a simple chain like the ones used to hold dog tags, and the heart itself was stainless steel or aluminum. On one side was engraved the word "Love" and on the other, "Always." There were a few flourishes around the words but, for the most part, it was the plainest piece of jewelry that Mom had owned.

"I thought you would have buried it with her," I said in a voice that even I could hardly hear. I had never seen my mother without this necklace unless she was dressed up for a formal occasion.

"I thought about it, but I couldn't—" Dad paused for a minute, swallowing hard and tightening his jaw to keep it from trembling. "Maybe this is why."

Not trusting myself to speak, I read the words again.

"Did she ever tell you the story behind that necklace?"

Dad asked me after a while.

"No... Wait, she did say that you gave it to her when I was born."

"That's right. I wanted to get her something special so, a few days before you were born, I went to a couple jewelry stores and department stores. Nothing seemed right. Like I said, your mom could be a little funny about jewelry... and I wanted it to be perfect. Then, as I was walking out of the old Northwood Mall, I saw a few pieces of jewelry at a small kiosk. It was run by a woman who was about forty who looked pretty hard-worn. She only had a few things for sale—a couple bracelets, some rings and some pendants like this.

"There was also an MIA flag in a display case and, on the counter, she had some flyers about soldiers who were still missing in Vietnam. The whole thing caught my attention. I asked her if she knew someone who was missing and she told me that her husband had been shot down in 1971. Of course, it was 1985 by this time. Even still, she told me that she was selling the jewelry to try and earn enough money to go to Vietnam and look for him."

"And you bought the pendant."

"I did. She had made it herself from pieces of an old B-52, the same type of aircraft that her husband had been in when he was shot down."

I turned the piece of aircraft aluminum over in my hand. "Do you know if she ever went to Vietnam?"

"No, I never saw her after that. But I asked her what she would do if she went over there and couldn't find him. She told me she'd stay. Because even if she couldn't save him or recover his body, at least she'd be closer to him than she was here. I'm not sure I've ever met someone who was so committed to their love for another human being. So I bought it and told your mother the story. She said it was the most beautiful necklace she'd ever seen."

Dad took the necklace from me and turned it from one side to the other. "Not just two words, but a bond." He handed it back. "If you think you can live up to it, then I would like you to give it to Cara."

I held it in my hand. "Thank you," I said, not taking my eyes off of the word "Love."

Dad reached out and flipped the heart in my hand. "That's the one that takes work."

After a moment's hesitation, I put the necklace back in its box and slipped it into my pocket.

CHAPTER TWENTY

The sun was dipping behind the trees as I drove home, conscious of the weight of the box in my pocket. Giving the necklace to Cara seemed even more significant than when I had asked her to move in with me. I wondered if all of the events of the past week were setting me up for making a decision that I'd regret later. My experiences with other women told me no. With all of my other relationships, the best times and the strongest emotions had come at the beginning. But with Cara, my feelings for her were growing stronger the more I was near her.

By the time I got to the house, I felt sure that I was doing the right thing. Cara met me at the door with a hug while Alvin snuffled my feet and legs with his pug nose. Ivy watched from the back of the couch, not happy at the long hours I'd been working.

"You don't smell so bad," she said.

"Dad made me take a shower in the barn before he let me in the house. My clothes are still in his washer."

"I made some chicken salad."

"I really feel bad that you had to make dinner when we were supposed to go out and celebrate your birthday."

"It's okay. It's just nice to have some time together."

"Thank you," I said and kissed her. "I'm starving."

After dinner, we cuddled together on the couch. Cara chose a Loreena McKennitt playlist as background music.

"This is better than going out," she said.

"Do you want your birthday present now or tomorrow?"

"What a ridiculous question," she said playfully.

My pulse quickened as I pulled the box out of my pocket.

"A jewelry box. That's a good start."

"There's a story that goes with it," I said, worried that the necklace might seem cheap, like something out of a gumball machine.

"Gimme," she said, taking the box. After a dramatic pause, she opened it. Slowly, she lifted the pendant out of the box and held it up, looking at both sides of the heart.

I held my breath. "I told you there's a story that goes with it."

"I love it. It doesn't need a story," she said softly, her eyes shining.

"Dad gave it to my mom when I was born."

Cara slipped the necklace over her head as I repeated the story that Dad had told me. Before I was done, Cara's arms were wrapped around me and I could feel her tears against my cheek. We made love that night for the first time since the explosion.

"Happy birthday," I said, leaning over Cara and waking her gently with a kiss.

"Where is everyone?" she asked, referring to the Alvin and Ivy wake-up crew.

"I got up earlier and fed them."

"Now *that* is a nice birthday surprise."

"You were sleeping pretty soundly. I might have even detected some snoring."

"No way."

"Way," I said, which just led to a wrestling match.

Later, as we were getting dressed, I asked, "Do you want to go to the Palmetto?"

"Mary's new place? You said it wasn't bad."

"As long as Heckle and Jeckle the cop brothers don't show up. Seriously, the food was really good. You just have to push the fact that her father is a serial killer out of your mind. Pete says the Sunday brunch is amazing."

"Deal."

We got to the restaurant about the time that most people in Calhoun were starting church services.

"You just missed Pete. They usually come in before church," Mary said as she led us to a table.

"Which means he's sleeping in a back pew right now," I said with a smile.

For a while we sat in companionable silence, enjoying the excellent food.

"How are you doing?" Cara asked as I leaned back to let my Mediterranean omelet settle.

"It was great."

"Not the food. I mean… overall."

"I'm better. You?"

"I'm taking Sarah's advice to heart. I'm good." Cara put her hand on mine and smiled. Then she looked at me more closely. "But you have that look on your face."

"What look?"

"The something-is-bothering-me look."

I sighed. "Trouble is, I don't know what's bothering me. Technically, we're in good shape with the case. We just need to run down the loose ends. But… I don't know."

"You don't think the guy in the woods did it?" she asked incredulously.

"I'm sure that he built the bomb."

"Okay…?"

"Motive is the problem. I just don't see the point in blowing up Eddie."

"To scare anyone else into not talking?" Cara suggested.

"That's a great answer and probably right. But they didn't blow up Eddie. They blew up Matt."

"But it was just luck that you and Eddie escaped."

"That is also true. McCoy just didn't seem like a guy that made a lot of mistakes."

"He *did* just blow himself up," Cara reminded me.

"He wasn't perfect and he got caught." I shook my head. "I'm just letting this case get to me."

"Sometimes you have to accept the easy answer."

I smiled at her then looked over my shoulder, a little surprised yet pleased to see a line forming at the door. "We should probably give up our table. The after-church crowd is beginning to show up."

We paid our bill and left the restaurant. As we were crossing the parking lot, I saw Beth Miller walking toward me with an older woman at her side. After we greeted each other, she introduced her mother.

"Mom and I usually go to church on Sunday by ourselves. I can only get my husband and the kids there at Christmas and Easter. But I get my revenge by not cooking and going out to eat every Sunday. Don't we, Mom?"

Her mother smiled and nodded.

"Funny bumping into you. Can we talk for a minute?" Beth said to me.

We walked a couple feet away, leaving Cara and Beth's mom talking about the brunch.

"This is kind of a long story, but when I was putting together Matt's files for you to look at, I chose to leave one out."

"Why?" I asked, puzzled.

"That's the long part of the story. See, Lionel made us an… What do you call it…? Algorithm or some such thing… Anyway, a program that I can use with our database so that I can see how many files we've had to pull and all the requests that we've filled. I know your Dad's been worried about budgets and I wanted to be able to track how much work we do to justify all the records staff. Anyway, using the program you can pull up information in a bunch of different ways—by officer, by case, by the type of case. Lionel did a great job.

"Well, when I pulled Matt's cases, one of the things I did was to use this program to find the ones that had been most requested. I thought those would be the most important ones for your case." She stopped for breath, or maybe for dramatic effect.

"And those were the files you gave to me?"

"Yes and no. I also pulled all the violent crime cases he worked, and any that involved resisting arrest with violence. But I did include most of the frequently requested ones. Heck, most were on both lists. The violent crime cases were of the most interest to the media and would often go to court, so the State Attorney would need copies as well as all the lawyers and any insurance companies involved."

"That makes sense," I said, wishing that she'd get to the point because I was starting to sweat standing in the parking lot.

"Okay, here's where I made a judgment call that maybe wasn't mine to make. The third most requested case was one for a stolen car that had ended in an automotive accident and a fatality. But I just looked at it as a stolen car and an accident report. I figured it had been requested so often because of all the insurance companies that were probably involved. And on top of that, it was back when Matt had only been on patrol for a year. It just didn't fit in with the rest of the file."

Beth seemed genuinely upset over this, but I couldn't see it as that big of a deal. "You're probably right," I said reassuringly.

"Maybe. But it wasn't really my call. Mine is only to pull and copy. I know you all have the bomber now, but I just didn't want you to think I was over-stepping."

"I would never think that. Seriously, it's no big deal."

Beth took a deep breath and let it out. "Wow, I feel better. I put the copy of the file in your inbox on Friday. Not that you need it now. If you don't want it, just shred it and the others."

"Thanks, Beth. Enjoy your brunch," I said, wanting

nothing more than to get in my air-conditioned car. "It was nice meeting your mother," I said while signaling Cara to head toward the car.

Once we were back on the road with the air blasting, I told Cara what Beth had wanted.

"You want to go by and pick up the file," she said, making it a statement and not a question.

"Do you mind?"

"No, silly."

I picked up the file and resisted the urge to look at it as soon as I was back in the car. Instead, I turned to Cara. "Anything in particular you'd like to do today?"

"Be with you," she said.

"So maybe go home? Read a little. Lounge around a little. Watch Alvin play in the kiddie pool out back."

"All of the above sounds perfect."

When we got home, I tossed the report in the box with the others. Now that I had it, I didn't feel compelled to go over it right away. Besides, this was Cara's birthday. She'd been very tolerant so far of my job taking precedence over our personal life, but I didn't want to push it when there really wasn't a reason. Everyone was right. We had the bomber, so I could relax.

Later that afternoon, I got up off of the couch after the nap that had overwhelmed me as I tried to read a book on the First World War. I found Cara taking her own nap on the bed, so I went to the box and pulled out the file on the car theft and subsequent accident. I sat down at the table with the report and a beer.

Matt had been on patrol on the Fourth of July in 2007 when he noticed an almost-new BMW being driven by someone that he thought might be too young to operate an automobile. He had decided to follow the car, and while he did so, he ran the tag. Even before the tag came back, the car had started to accelerate. Matt had stayed on its bumper as it drove through the business district of Calhoun. Luckily, it was eleven o'clock at night so there hadn't been much traffic downtown.

Of course, with Calhoun being as small as it is, by the time dispatch had notified him that the car was stolen, they'd left downtown behind and were entering a residential neighborhood. Matt had put his lights on and the car sped up, so Matt notified dispatch that he was in pursuit and flipped on his siren.

Chasing a car driven by a young person through a neighborhood, even at eleven at night, wasn't a good idea. Matt had been within protocol, but being correct is not always being right.

A car was backing out of a driveway when the stolen vehicle turned a corner. The car thief, a kid named Seth Fisher, had swerved, lost control and slammed into a third car in another driveway where a young family—father, mother and their six-year-old son—had just gotten home. Only the father had still been wearing his seatbelt. The son was thrown against the rear passenger window with enough force to kill him instantly. The mother had been stepping out of the car when the vehicle was struck and suffered massive damage to her legs and hips. The father had escaped with only bruises. Fisher, with his seatbelt buckled and behind the wheel of solid German engineering, hadn't been hurt at all.

Besides the initial report written by Matt, there was a vehicular homicide report written by Sergeant Ken Webb. Webb had been one of the first black deputies in the county and had retired shortly after the incident. The file also included all the other items that you would expect, including an autopsy report for the son, hospital records for the mother, and a whole ton of memos back and forth between the State Attorney and Webb.

I could understand why the report had been requested so often. There had probably been numerous lawsuits and insurance companies involved, not to mention all the lawyers that would have gone along with them. Everyone would have wanted their own copies.

I was ready to drop it back into the box with the others

when I noticed a name—Hanna Craig—on a plea agreement that had been finalized almost two years after the accident. She was listed as the mother of the suspect, Seth Fisher. Seth Craig. Could that be a coincidence?

I looked through the report again and noticed another name, then I reached for my phone and called both Pete and Darlene, asking them to come out to my place. I spent the next thirty minutes going over everything in the report carefully.

CHAPTER TWENTY-ONE

"What's all the excitement?" Darlene asked when we were all sitting around my kitchen table.

"Sarah was looking forward to a quiet Sunday afternoon. Just her and me and a grill with a couple of two-inch-thick steaks," Pete said wistfully. "The girls are down in Orlando with the grandparents. Do you know how often we get the house to ourselves?"

"I think this warrants ruining your Sunday afternoon," I told him.

"Do you all want anything?" Cara asked. I'd woken her up and warned her that we were going to have company.

Darlene and Pete declined refreshments and stared at me expectantly as Cara wandered off to the couch and a book. I gave them a brief explanation of how Beth had dug up the report and gave it to me. Then I went over the car theft and the accident. They were like a nightclub audience waiting for a particularly long joke to get to the punchline.

"The driver was Seth Fisher, who now goes by his mother's maiden name of Craig."

"The missing guy?" Pete said.

"Apparently. But it gets better. The man who was pulling out of his driveway and caused Seth to swerve was Joel

Weaver," I said with a flourish.

Darlene's mouth fell open. "*My* Joel Weaver?"

Pete was looking back and forth between me and Darlene. "Who's Joel Weaver?"

"My suicide victim," Darlene said, using dramatic air quotes around the word suicide.

"The one you've been obsessing on for days?" Pete said, his jaw hanging a little lower now.

"Exactly," I said.

"So let me get this straight. Some guy who went missing almost two weeks ago, Matt who was killed last week, and a man who was found dead a few days ago, were all involved in the same accident almost a decade ago?" Pete sounded incredulous while I nodded vigorously.

"There's coincidence and then there's coincidence," Darlene said, still looking flustered.

"See why I called you?"

They both leaned back in their chairs with thoughtful expressions.

"I hate to seem slow-witted, but I'm trying to get my mind around this," Pete said thoughtfully. "So there's a possibility that these three cases—Matt's murder, the man's disappearance and Weaver's death—are all related?"

"Hell, I'd say the odds lean toward probability," Darlene said. "It seems hard to believe that this is all random."

"Craig disappeared. Could he be a suspect in Matt's murder and Weaver's death?" Pete asked.

"I don't know. I don't know anything but what I've told you. This is a whole new world for me," I said.

"I *knew* that wasn't a suicide," Darlene said

"Slow down, missy. Your boy could have had something to do with Matt and Craig and then offed himself," Pete said smugly.

"Now… Damn it, that puts me back where I was," Darlene said. "There are circles within circles in this mystery."

"Hold it. We're all over the place. Let's lay out all the

possibilities," I said. "I'll grab a pad and a pen and we'll go old school."

I came back with my pen, ready to write. "We'll go around and each of us name a different scenario. I'll go first. All are unrelated," I said writing it down even though I didn't believe it for a second. Then I pointed to Pete.

"Weaver somehow was involved in both Matt's murder and Craig's disappearance, then was either killed or killed himself."

Darlene went next. "Craig was involved in Matt's death, then killed Weaver and went on the run."

"To be fair, is there any way that Matt could be responsible for Weaver or Craig? Definitely no on Weaver. The timeline doesn't work, but he could have had something to do with Craig's disappearance. According to his mother, he disappeared before Matt was killed," I said and wrote it down, just to be thorough.

"A third party is responsible for Matt, Craig *and* Weaver," Pete said. "With the corollary that our mysterious Al McCoy is the killer of all three?"

"Or he killed Matt and Weaver, then Craig got scared. But that doesn't really work because Craig disappeared first," I said.

"So it's some combination of Weaver, Craig and/or a third party," Darlene summarized.

"Finding Craig would help," Pete offered.

"Doing more research into his case might give us a lead. Maybe even give us some candidates for a third party. I'll be right back." I got up and dug around on the kitchen counter until I found the flyer that Ms. Craig had given me, then I dialed her number.

"Ms. Craig, I'm going to put you on speakerphone," I told her after explaining that there were a couple of other investigators with me who wanted to talk with her about her son's disappearance. Pete and Darlene introduced themselves to her.

"We want to talk to you about the stolen car and the

accident your son was involved in nine years ago," I said and thought I heard a moan from Ms. Craig.

"I don't see how that can have anything to do with this. He put that all behind him. Seth was finally moving on." There was real pain in her voice.

"I know this is painful," Darlene said in her best woman-to-woman voice. "But we think it's important. We're not accusing him of anything. That case was closed years ago."

"If only that were true," Ms. Craig said.

"I take it that your son had a hard time dealing with the fallout from the incident?" I asked.

"You could say that. I think a lot of his drug use and self-hate stemmed from the accident and the death of that poor little boy. For years he just couldn't let it go."

"He wasn't prosecuted for it," Pete said.

"No, my husband at the time… It's so much water under the bridge."

"If you could tell us what happened in your own words, that would be a big help. Start at the beginning," I said. I'd skimmed most of the reports while waiting for Pete and Darlene, so I had the broad outline, but I was still interested in hearing her version. I saw Cara listening discreetly from the couch.

"If you think it will help find him." There was a heavy sigh. "Seth and his father got into an argument. Seth was sixteen and just getting a bit rebellious. Nothing serious, just not wanting to do everything we asked him to do. That day his dad, Lowell, had told him to mow the lawn. It was the Fourth of July and Seth wanted to go to a party and then to the fireworks in Tallahassee. I won't go into all the details, but finally Seth grabbed his father's keys and ran out of the house. He took off in the BMW. Lowell was furious. He had a temper, but never had I seen him get that hot. He said he'd teach the boy a lesson and called the police. I begged him not to, but he always knew better. The long and short of it is, he reported the car as stolen."

"When was this?"

"The fight happened in the morning. We learned later that Seth had picked up his girlfriend and gone over to Tallahassee. He was on his way back when the deputy saw—" She stopped.

"Ms. Craig?"

"That DEA agent who was killed. That… His name was Matt Greene. Was that the same man?"

"Yes, Matt Greene was the deputy who attempted to stop your son."

"I don't understand," she said hesitantly.

"We're trying to understand it ourselves," I told her.

"Your son made a plea agreement with the State Attorney?" Pete asked.

"That's right. My husband claimed that he came out that morning and found the car gone. He lied and said that he didn't know Seth had taken it. Lowell swore that Seth had permission to take the car out any time he wanted to. He made Seth and me lie too. I fought with him about it. I told him that it was wrong. Lowell told me I was a horrible mother for not protecting my son. In the end, Seth and I went along with it. Lowell and I got a divorce less than two years after the accident."

"Seth pleaded to reckless driving," I prompted her.

"That's right. Originally they were going to charge him with vehicular homicide. I didn't want that. I thought maybe something less, but once the stolen car charge was gone so that the death hadn't happened while Seth was committing a felony, the State Attorney didn't want to go to court with a sixteen-year-old defendant and what looked like bad judgment from a deputy. So he agreed to reckless driving and Seth only had to do a year of community service."

"Wow," Darlene said. "Seth didn't handle it well?"

"No. He had nightmares for years. A year later and he was doing drugs. He'd do them right in front of his father and me. He'd just lost faith in everything," Ms. Craig said, and I remembered Eddie talking about Seth's how-I-became-an-addict story.

"Do you remember a man named Joel Weaver?" I asked.

"Weaver?" There was a pause. "The name is familiar, but… wait. He was connected somehow."

"What do you remember about the other people involved in the accident?"

"The boy, Timmy. His poor parents, Terrance and Carrie Robbins. I just ached for them. The poor woman was hurt so bad, months in the hospital. She wasn't even able to go to her son's funeral."

"Do you remember the other man involved?" I asked.

"The other… Oh… Weaver, that's right. I remember now. He just backed out of his driveway that night. I don't think anyone blamed him for what happened. It's so strange, but I can remember that he was going out to get some ice cream. It was all such a nightmare. The Fourth of July. That's why the Robbinses were just coming home. They'd gone to the fireworks up at the high school that night. And, of course, it was a fight over going to the fireworks in Tallahassee that had made Seth take the car."

"You didn't want the plea bargain?" Pete asked.

"I thought it was too little. I think Seth would have done better if he could have gone through a trial. Gotten a chance to explain what had happened and to be punished. His father never wanted to punish him. He'd get mad, but then he'd let Seth get away without any consequences. I don't know what I wanted, but as a mother I knew that Seth needed to work off some of the guilt."

"Did you ever meet Joel Weaver?" Darlene asked.

"Once. I met him about a month after the accident. I was at the nurses' station on the floor where Carrie Robbins's room was. I'd brought a plant and a card. I know it was stupid. I'm sure she didn't want anything from me. I just had to do something. Anyway, I was there and trying to explain to the nurse that I just wanted to leave the plant and the note and go when I noticed a man standing nearby who was staring at us. The nurse took the plant and, when I turned to go, the man stopped me and explained who he was. It was very awkward. He kept repeating that he had only wanted some ice cream. That's why I remember that. He seemed pretty torn up by the experience. I guess I can understand."

"Did you ever meet the Robbinses?" Pete asked.

"Meet? No. I saw Terrance a couple of times when all of this was going on, and then a few times around town afterward. Now I understand he lives in Tallahassee."

"Did he know who you were?"

"I'm sure he did. We were both at the State Attorney's office at the same time while they were negotiating the plea deal."

"How did he seem?"

"I don't know. He seemed... kind of vacant. Emotionless, maybe. I can understand it after all that had happened. All that loss and pain. Some people just shut down. I remember the prosecutor told us we were lucky that Terrance wasn't the vengeful type, or he'd have been pressing harder for at least a manslaughter charge."

"Have you heard from either of the Robbinses since then?"

I saw where Pete was going with this. If anyone would be looking for revenge, it would be the Robbinses.

"Mrs. Robbins died, maybe three years after the accident. I tried to find out if it was related to her injuries. The only thing anyone would tell me was that she died from natural causes, whatever that meant. Lowell was worried for years that Mr. Robbins would sue us. He never did."

"Did your son ever blame anyone else for the accident?" Darlene asked.

"At one point he blamed my husband. Right afterward, he blamed Lowell for reporting the car stolen, and then later he blamed him for not doing something to stop him from taking the car in the first place. It was only after he got clean and sober that he seemed to be at peace with all that had happened."

"Where's his dad now?" I asked.

"Texas. He's remarried."

"Have you talked to him since Seth went missing?"

"I called him two days afterward. They haven't talked in years, but I thought maybe Seth had decided to mend fences with him. That's part of his NA program. Making amends and all of that. Anyway, Lowell was just as hostile as ever. Hadn't seen him and didn't want to," she said, settling that.

I looked around the room and Darlene and Pete seemed satisfied. We thanked Ms. Craig and told her we'd be in touch."

"What do you all think?" I asked after I hung up.

"I want to meet Mr. Robbins," Darlene said.

"Absolutely," Pete agreed.

I Googled his name and got a Tallahassee address. I also called dispatch and asked them to run a records check. Terrance Robbins was clear. A moving violation or two, but that was it.

"Is Webb still alive?" Pete asked.

"Yeah, I saw him at a political fundraiser for Dad six months ago."

I gave Dad a quick call and got Ken Webb's number. "Sergeant Webb?" I said to the deep voice that answered the phone.

"Who is this?" he laughed.

"This is Ted Macklin's son, Larry."

"Little Larry? What you doin', boy? I hear you've been ridin' around town lookin' like a sure 'nough lawman. What you calling this old man for?"

"I'm going to put you on speakerphone, if that's all right. You remember Pete Henley? He's here with me, and Deputy Darlene Marks. We're looking into a couple of cases that might be connected to an old investigation you conducted back in 2007."

"Sure. Glad to help. Hit me with it."

We told him what we were looking into.

"Man, some ghosts won't stay buried. I knew that one would come back some day."

"Why do you say that?" I asked, puzzled.

"Everyone was too reasonable. An accident like that where a young boy is killed and the mother all torn up. A deputy who probably didn't use his best judgment. I expected all kinds of craziness. I figured I'd have to testify a couple of times. Nothin'. Even the State Attorney was soft on the boy who stole that car. They could have pressed the boy and his father a lot harder. But no. I wondered if everyone was on drugs or somethin'."

"Did *you* want to press them harder?" Darlene asked.

"Hey, that was my last year. You make it to your last year and see if you want to push any investigation. Maybe if it had been some child abuse thing, a big-time murder or a missing person case, but they don't give those cases to short-timers anyway."

"Anything seem odd at the time?" I asked.

"Let me think. Like I said, everyone seemed too calm, but other than that, no. Just same ol' crap, different day. Spoiled kid steals daddy's car, young cop gets too excited and people get hurt. Real damn shame it was a little boy and a nice lady who had to suffer."

"What about the boy who stole the car, or the mother and father of the little boy who was killed? Did anything strike you as odd?"

"Nah. The boy was real broken up. You could tell he didn't mean to hurt nobody. One of those cases where you feel bad for the suspect. Of course, the father was just numb. He didn't have a lot of time to grieve for his boy 'cause his wife was so badly injured. I remember him being kind of… disconnected. All the pain. Who could blame him?"

"Do you remember the guy who was backing out of his driveway and caused the stolen vehicle to swerve?"

"Him I remember. One of those OCD types. He kept talking about the ice cream that he was going out to get. Seemed nice enough. Little screwy, though."

"Have you seen or maybe talked to any of them recently?" I asked.

"Do you know where I am, son? I'm in Panama City. I

go fishing whenever I want and the only thing that pisses me off are the hurricanes. So, no. I haven't seen any of them since I retired. I do come up there and see some of my friends and relatives, but I try not to make it a habit. Sorry I won't be able to vote for your old man this fall."

We said our goodbyes and hung up.

"Thoughts?"

"I say we go visit Mr. Robbins," Darlene said energetically.

"*You're* excited," Pete said to her.

"I've been trying to tell you there was more to Weaver than a straight suicide. You all just blew me off," she said with a smile. "Now I've got the bit in my teeth."

"Fair enough. Sarah's probably already locked the door so I can't get back in the house anyway. What about you, Little Larry?" Pete said, smiling. I was afraid that they had caught the nickname.

"Well…" I looked over at Cara.

"Wait!" Pete blurted out. "It's Cara's birthday!" Cara nodded. "What are you doing, letting this twerp run out on you?"

"I'm afraid I'm getting used to it."

"I *am* sorry. We didn't mean to ruin your day," Darlene said to Cara.

"You didn't," she said and gave me a gentle smile that let me know she really meant it.

CHAPTER TWENTY-TWO

We were soon on our way to Tallahassee in Pete's car, since he'd been the last one to pull into my driveway. We'd promised Cara that we'd bring her back a cupcake for her birthday.

We'd discussed the fact that all three of us going was overkill, but none of us wanted to be the one that was left behind. We shouldn't have wasted our time. We found his house in a subdivision north of Tallahassee, but no one was home. The house and yard were well kept, and nothing in the front or backyard indicated that anyone but a single man lived there.

I caught the smell of a grill coming from a neighbor's backyard. Darlene, Pete and I played rock-paper-scissors to see who'd barge in on the neighbor's Sunday evening. I lost.

"Hi, I'm Deputy Larry Macklin with the Adams County Sheriff's Office. Sorry to bother you, but could I ask a few questions?" LEO Rule 103—always be extra polite when you're playing cop in someone else's jurisdiction.

"I guess." The big man was watching his hamburgers on the grill. "I can't leave the grill. Come on through the gate," he said, pointing with a spatula.

"We were looking for your neighbor, Mr. Robbins. Have

you seen him today?" I asked once I'd gotten into the backyard.

"What's he done?" the man asked unoriginally.

"Nothing. We're just hoping that he can give us some information."

"Almost never see him. My wife and I went over when he first moved in, being friendly. Apparently not his thing." The man flipped the burgers.

"When did he move in?"

"Two years ago, something like that."

"And the last time you saw him?"

"A couple weeks ago. He isn't around much."

"He doesn't come home every day?"

"No, not that I see. Of course he parks in the garage, but lots of nights his lights aren't on." You have to appreciate observant neighbors.

"Do you know where he works?"

"Not really. Like I said, he's not very friendly. Which is fine. Some are, some aren't. To each his own. Keeps his yard nice, though." He gave a big shrug and took a couple of the burgers off the grill and put them on a platter.

"He have any visitors?"

"I've never seen any. Maybe a repairman, but that's it."

"Any noise or problems?"

"Pretty neutral experience having him living next door. Not like the witch two houses down on the other side. Wow! Now she's someone I'd like to talk to the cops about." The guy put a few more burgers on the platter.

We'd downloaded Mr. Robbins's driver's license photo to our phones. I pulled it up and showed it to him. "This him?"

The man squinted at the photo. "Yep."

I thanked him and left him to his burgers.

"Average, average, average. Below average on social interaction," I reported to Pete and Darlene.

"We can ask Leon County to watch the house. See if we can catch him at home."

I called dispatch back. "Marti, do you have a phone

number for this guy?"

"I got a cell. He doesn't have a landline," he said and gave me the number.

"What's the consensus? I call, we might be tipping our hand."

"Wait," Pete said.

"Try and find Craig. He has almost as good a motive. He could feel like the crash was Matt's fault for chasing him and Weaver's for pulling out of his driveway," Darlene said.

"I'd feel better if we found someone who's set eyes on Robbins," I said.

"Right now we're flying blind," Pete agreed.

We headed back to Adams County after stopping by a Publix and picking up one of Cara's favorite Boston cream cupcakes.

"I hope you appreciate the fact that we support your personal relationship," Pete said.

"I couldn't stand to be around him if he lost her. I can just imagine him crying and moping about. No, it's worth a little trouble to keep them together," Darlene quipped.

Ignoring them both, I asked, "What time are AA meetings?"

"You're asking us?" Pete said

I told them what Eddie had said, then pulled out my phone and found a listing for AA meetings in Adams County. "We can make the one at the First Presbyterian Church."

"We promised Cara to bring you home after the trip to Tallahassee. We didn't stop for that cupcake for nothing," Pete said.

"We'll just swing by and see if we can talk to Seth's sponsor. A half hour out of our way."

"Okay, but if she hits you with a frying pan, don't come whining to us," Pete said.

"Frying pan? What kind of sexist comment was that?" Darlene joked.

"It's just a saying. I'm sure she'll hit him with something

more politically correct."

I texted Cara and told her about the small change in plans, assuring her that her cupcake was on the way.

There were a dozen cars in the lot when we parked at the church. I didn't know how long the meetings normally ran, but this one had been going on for almost an hour now. I hoped we'd hit it about the time they were wrapping up.

The three of us wandered down the semi-dark hallway of the church's annex until we found the right room. Peering through the window in the door, I could see someone standing in front of a small group of people in a mix of dress, races and ages. From Eddie's description, I was pretty sure that the big guy standing against the wall by a table with a coffee pot and donuts was Harold. He looked like central casting had sent over a badass biker to challenge a film's hero with a swinging chain. Luckily, he didn't have a chain. I didn't see anyone who fit Seth Craig's description.

"We'll wait for a couple minutes," I said, since the guy who was talking seemed to have the audience enraptured.

Five minutes later, we heard the sound of chairs scraping across the floor. When we entered the room, everyone turned and stared. I shouldn't have been surprised when I recognized three of the people in the room as suspects I'd arrested for substance abuse issues. Awkward.

With everyone staring at us anyway, Darlene took the direct approach.

"Hey guys and gals, we're just here to talk to the big fella. But since we've got everyone's attention, you all know Seth, right?"

Almost everyone nodded.

"His mother's been by a couple of times looking for him," said a woman with purple hair.

"And we're helping her look for him," I said, pulling out some of my cards and handing them around. "If any of you see him or learn anything about his whereabouts, give me a call."

"Damn, three cops looking for him. My sister went

missing last year and the police wouldn't even take a report," a young black woman said.

"Has she been found?" Darlene asked.

"Yeah, but that ain't the point," the woman grumbled. Turned out that her sister had gone missing in Jacksonville, not in Adams County, but we still apologized for any disrespect law enforcement had shown to her or her sister.

"How can I help you?" Harold asked after we'd managed to get him alone.

"When was the last time you saw Seth?" I asked.

"Guess about ten days ago."

"Can you narrow it down any?"

"I'll think about it. I keep a journal where I make notes about the couple of folks I sponsor. I'll check that. My mind isn't what it used to be. Of course, back in the day, I was always so lubed up I didn't remember nothin' then either."

"Do you think he went back to using?" Darlene asked.

"Anything's possible. He wasn't showing any obvious signs of stress. He didn't talk about any big changes in his life. But you never know." He shrugged philosophically.

"Did he talk about any enemies? Or any problems?" Pete asked. It was odd seeing Pete next to someone who made him look small.

"No, man. Like I said, he seemed to be cruising."

"What about other friends or significant others?"

"Just his mom. Even after two years, he was staying clear of entanglements. Said he wanted to keep his head clear. I thought that was a little odd, but he'd had some problems, carried around some guilt. His dad pretty much took off at one point. He hadn't talked to him in years. That kind of abandonment can mess you up," Harold said.

"Did he ever mention the Thompsons?" I asked and was surprised to see Harold's expression close down. His open and friendly manner vanished in a flash.

"Why?" he asked.

"We're looking for a person addicted to drugs who's disappeared and you're surprised that we asked about the

Thompsons?"

"You should know that everyone in this room knows about the Thompsons. You'll also appreciate that none of us are interested in talking about them." His face relaxed a little. "Seth never mentioned them. We never even talked about who his main connection was or anything like that. It's not good to start thinking about that crap. Next thing you know, you get all nostalgic about lying in filth and smoking shit."

"Did he have any enemies?" I asked.

"No, he was an easygoing kid. Really still a kid in a lot of ways. He was pretty far down the rabbit hole by the time he was seventeen. I think he's just starting to mature now that he's clean. Look, when his mom came by, I tried to think of anything I could do to help. I even went around and talked to some of the people I know still using. No one would admit seeing him. He hasn't been at work either. In over a year, he's never missed a day. In a town this size, if you're using, everyone knows it. If he's using, he's in Panama City or Jacksonville, someplace like that. And if that's the case, you'll have to wait until he decides to come back."

We were almost to the door when I pulled out my phone and walked back to Harold. "Have you ever seen this man?" I asked, showing him a picture of Terrance Robbins.

"Yeah, he comes to meetings sometimes," Harold said.

Jackpot! I thought. Pete and Darlene moved closer.

"What's his name?"

"Anonymity," Hank reminded me.

"First name is fine."

"Tom."

"Did he and Seth ever talk?"

"Like everyone else. Just coffee and donut talk. I never saw them huddled together or nothin'."

"Tom was an addict?" I could see the frown on Harold's face and knew that he was getting ready to shut down. "This isn't about invading people's privacy. We're worried about both of these guys. One or both could be in danger." I didn't add that one of them might be a killer.

"He was here; he was an addict."

"Give us a little more," I cajoled.

"He talked about being on Oxy. Lost his wife. Life wasn't worth livin'. Nothin' you don't hear a dozen times a month in the program."

"Was he genuine?"

"What kind of question is that?"

"Did he seem to be telling the truth?" I pressed.

"Yeah. He seemed real."

"Did he have a sponsor?"

"Not here. I think he said he usually went to meetings in Tallahassee."

"One of the steps is to go back and make amends to people you've wronged. Right?"

"That's right."

"Do you know if Seth Craig did that with the people who were in the accident he had as a teenager?"

"I know he'd made his list and was working on making amends, but I don't know who was on it. I'd guess the accident would be a big part of it. Of course, you've got to decide if talking to those people would hurt them. That's part of the deal. You aren't working the steps if you're hurting people as you go."

I nodded and thanked Harold for his time.

"Didn't see that coming," Pete said when we were back in his car.

"Me neither. A shot in the dark," I said.

"And you got a bull's-eye. We caught Terrance in a lie," Darlene said.

"Not much of a lie. I'm sure that plenty of other folks don't give their real names."

"I don't think that's part of the twelve steps," Pete said.

"We'll go on the hunt for both Craig and Robbins hard tomorrow," Darlene said. "I'm smelling blood."

"She's crazy," Pete said to me. "Don't you wish you had me back as a regular partner?"

"You're both loony in different ways. Don't ask me to

take sides."

We agreed that Pete would go by Express Burgers in the morning and talk to Seth's boss and fellow employees; I'd visit Ms. Craig and take a look at Seth's room; and Darlene would try to dig up more background on Terrance Robbins, particularly what he'd been doing since the accident.

When we were finally alone again, Cara insisted that I share the cupcake. "You have to eat some of it. That's the way it works."

"Maybe with your hippy parents. In my house, you scarfed up as much as you could before anyone else could get any," I joked.

In answer, she shoved part of the cupcake in my mouth and I tried not to choke on my laughter.

CHAPTER TWENTY-THREE

I called Hanna Craig first thing on Monday morning, and she told me to come on over.

"He threw out most of his stuff when he came back home."

"When was this?"

"A year and a half ago, when he got back from rehab," she said. I could see the worry and pain on her face as we walked into his room. "I haven't moved anything."

The room was sparsely furnished. A monk who'd given up his worldly goods would have felt right at home. There were a couple of books on the nightstand, along with a clock. An old pack of condoms was in the drawer, but only two were missing. The closet held a few work shirts and a small collection of T-shirts. Pants, underwear and socks filled a chest of drawers. On top of the chest was a cup filled with change and other odds and ends like buttons, old screws and keys.

"He doesn't keep any money. He gives me his paycheck and I put it in a checking account with both of our names on it so that he can't get cash without my signature. When he first came back from rehab, he was so scared of using again..." Her voice trailed off.

"You said he threw away a lot of stuff."

"That's right. All of his band posters, old toys and, well, you can see, just about everything. He didn't want any reminders of his old life. I did save a few things, but they're in the attic."

In an odd way, it reminded me of Joel Weaver's house. I looked under the bed, then I ran my hand between the mattress and the box spring. Hoping the paper I felt wasn't his porn collection, I pulled out several yellow legal pads. I flipped through them, reading notes about his drug addiction and twelve-step program. He wrote in messy block lettering that was easy to read.

I found the most recent pad where the notes were about the "making amends" portion of the program. There was a list with dozens of names that I didn't recognize. Toward the end of the list, I finally found Joel Weaver's name. Below that he'd written: *Terrance Robbins. Tom??* Seth must have realized who Terrance was after seeing him at the AA meetings.

"May I take these with me?" I asked Ms. Craig.

"I didn't even know they were there. Since he's been back, Seth has kept his room clean and made his own bed." There was loss in her eyes. "Be honest with me, do you think he's dead?"

"The truth is, I don't know. But we're working to find him now. I'm sorry you didn't get more support when you first went to the police."

"I thought I was going to have to hit one of those lazy bastards with a two-by-four," she said, causing me to smile at the image of her chasing Salt and Pepper around town with a big piece of wood.

"I'll keep you updated. Promise."

I bagged the notepads, figuring I'd better let Shantel or Marcus go over them before I looked through them anymore. Once I'd turned them over, I met Darlene and Pete in the conference room and filled them in on what I'd found.

"If Seth was hiding anything, no one at Express Burgers knows anything about it. Worst thing anyone had to say was some snot-nosed teenager who said Seth was a narc. Apparently he'd turned the kid's friend in for smoking a joint on the job. The day manager and the night manager both said that Seth is the most dependable employee they've ever had. By all accounts, he's been playing it clean," Pete reported.

The reports that Pete and I gave were perfunctory. Our group intuition was telling us that Terrance Robbins should be at the top of our suspect list. So with the boring bit out of the way, we stared at Darlene. She was looking as tired as I'd ever seen her.

"Okay, boys, here's the score. I was up all night digging into this guy's life history. He hasn't left many tracks. I should make you go down all the dead ends and winding roads I had to take, but I'll be nice. Turns out he's a trust-fund baby. Folks were from Miami. He got an MBA from the University of Florida, where he met his wife. She had connections here in Adams County through her mother's family. They got married in 2000 and moved up here. Their son was born in 2001. Terrance dabbled in a few business ventures, then decided to be a land developer. He bought up property and was working on putting his company together when the accident happened."

"So he came from money?"

"His dad was the president of a bank in Miami. He died of pancreatic cancer when Robbins was seventeen. His mother died of an overdose of sleeping pills soon after. I didn't get the exact amount he inherited, but it was substantial. A big portion of it was set up in a trust to pay out to him and to any offspring he had."

"Lucky?"

"At least until the accident. He apparently did have some substance abuse issues. Got caught for trying to pay a doctor to write him prescriptions for OxyContin. Actually, the doctor was glad to do it, but got caught and prosecuted by the state. Robbins was one of almost a hundred patients who were charged along with the doctor. He got two years' probation with the stipulation that he go to rehab and take drug tests for those two years."

"When was this?"

"The charges were in 2013, six years after the accident."

"You said he started a land development company in 2007. That was right before the housing crash, right?" I asked.

"Yep. Between the accident and the crash, he was hit pretty hard. I actually got a hold of someone at the courthouse in Tallahassee where he pled out to the charges. He said that the accident and his wife's three years as an invalid led to him becoming addicted to prescription medication. Between you, me and the wall, I can buy that. A whole bunch of folks become addicts with less reason. Looked like the judge felt kindly toward him. Two years' probation isn't bad considering he'd bought over thirty thousand dollars worth of drugs and had enough in his house when they searched it to be charged as a dealer."

"So what's he do now?" Pete asked.

"Ha! He's a motivational speaker. Gets paid to go to businesses and give pep talks. Apparently it's a thing. Goes by the name of Tom Price. It's like a stage name. Once I knew that, I was able to pull up his webpage. He gets three thousand dollars a day."

"Wait. I'm confused," I said. "This is the same guy whose neighbor said is practically a ghost?"

"Actors can be like that. That's why people don't understand when they seem to beg for the spotlight on the one hand, but desperately want to be left alone on the other," Pete said. "Maybe he's the same way."

"I guess I can see that." A picture of Terrance Robbins, AKA Tom Price, was forming in my head and the image was scary.

"Million-dollar question. Where is he?" Pete asked.

"I tried to book him for a speaking gig online, thinking it

might give me some insight into his schedule. He seems to not have much going on right now. His brag page said he did a big conference in Orlando last year, but that was the last confirmed date that I could find for him."

"The house in Tallahassee seemed pretty small, considering the money he has. Does he own any other property?"

"I pulled his credit record and did what I could with a property search. The trouble is that he has a couple of different corporations that he's created. Remember, the guy has an MBA," Darlene said. "I've been able to track down most of the property he owns in this county, and I asked Beth to do a search of property listed under his corporations here and anywhere else in the country. From what I could tell, he's wasted a lot of money, but then again, he has more than you'd think an ex-addict or someone who's never had any real success should have."

We all just looked at each other for a while. Finally, I said, "So, really, we have nothing on him. Nothing that would suggest he's involved in anything other than his own business."

"We also don't have him to question," Pete said sadly.

"Awesome," I said grumpily.

"He's got two cars registered with the DMV, a black 2007 BMW and a grey 2015 Honda CRV," Darlene mentioned

"We might not have any evidence, but my Spidey senses are sure tingling," I said. "That black BMW could match the description of the car reported lurking outside of Weaver's house."

"I don't think a judge is going to give you a warrant based on your superpowers or a vague car description," Pete said dryly.

"But we'd be within our rights to put out a 'wanted for questioning' BOLO on him for the disappearance of Seth Craig, since we have an eyewitness who saw them together," Darlene said.

"Thin, but we could probably get away with it," Pete agreed. "Of course, we still haven't tried his phone."

"I'm with Little Larry on this one. I'm beginning to think he's our man and, with his money, if he gets wind that we're onto him he could be on a slow boat to China in no time," Darlene said.

"Do you have a list of his local properties?" I asked

"I do. Ten parcels. Three of them are large tracts of land he was going to use for his development company. Five are unoccupied commercial properties. The other two are just residential lots. I'm guessing you want to eyeball all of them."

"Yep," Pete and I said in unison.

"We'll split them up," I suggested.

"I hate to be the nancy pants who says it, but I think we should approach this guy with caution," Darlene said.

"No, I agree. Anyone spots him, call for backup," Pete said.

I just nodded, trying to decide which of the properties would be the most interesting. I picked two of the commercial properties and one of the land tracts.

The first property was an old brick building with its windows boarded up. The door had a rusted lock that didn't look like it had been opened in years. Nothing to see here.

The next one looked more promising—a storefront tucked one street off of Calhoun's main drag. There were trees all around it and the building didn't look abandoned, but there were no signs either.

A van was parked in the lot, so I pulled in and parked next to it. There was a regular glass door with newspapers taped all over the inside, and off to the left was a large roll-up door like a storage unit would have. The building looked like it might have been a repair shop of some sort.

I knocked on the glass door, not expecting much. But after a few minutes I heard the large metal door roll up. A short, middle-aged Hispanic man was staring at me.

"Yes?" he asked.

I showed him my badge and he smiled. "I'm looking for the man who owns this building."

"Mr. Robbins?" He shook his head. "I haven't seen him for a long time."

"You rent this building from him?"

"Yes, yes. I sell cooking pots, pans, glasses, whatever you need for a restaurant."

"But you haven't seen Mr. Robbins."

"I rented it two years ago. I send him a check once a month. I'm paid up a month in advance. Never see him."

"Where do you send the checks?" The man went over to his van and dug around for a bit, coming back with a well-used day planner. He showed me the number of a post office box in Tallahassee. I wrote it down, then thanked him for his help.

Third one's the charm, I thought wistfully as I drove out to the last piece of property on my list. I was hoping for anything that might point us toward Mr. Robbins.

The tract of land was just east of town, a ghost of an unfinished subdivision that I had driven by hundreds of times. A certain amount of money had been spent on the entrance. There was a wall where the subdivision sign would have gone and about a hundred feet of sidewalk went off in either direction from the entrance. But now everything just looked sad.

A chain-link gate had been erected across the entrance to keep people from driving back onto the property. From the gate, I could see the road and sidewalk curving back out of sight. There were even decorative lampposts every fifty feet along the road.

I examined the gate and the lock keeping it closed. The lock looked in good shape—not new, but not rusted shut either. Looking down at the road beyond the gate, I saw something that made the hairs on the back of my neck stand up. There were brush marks across the sand that had drifted across the road, almost but not quite obscuring a set of recent tire tracks.

I thought about my choices. Doing something stupid was the most appealing, but I resisted the urge. Instead I took out my phone and called Darlene.

"What's up, sugar plum?" she asked. She was trying to sound upbeat, but she still sounded tired. I almost regretted calling her.

"I think I've got a situation here. I'm at the tract of land on the east side of town."

"You need me to come there?"

"I think that would be a good idea."

Ten minutes later, she pulled up alongside my car. I let her get out and look around for herself, wanting to see what conclusions she'd come to.

"Somebody doesn't want us to know they drove in there," she said, looking at the spot beyond the gate.

"And they've gone in since it rained on Saturday," I said.

Darlene frowned and walked around, looking at the gate and the lock.

"You know what we need to invest in?" she asked. "A drone with a camera on it, like the one ya'll used the other day. If we had one of those, we could just fly it over the area and see if anyone is back there."

She made a very good point. You didn't need a warrant to fly over a property.

"You know, that's not a bad idea. But we don't have one now."

"The other thing we don't have is a warrant," she reminded me.

"Look at the lock again," I said.

When she did, I pointed out some scratches near the keyhole. I didn't tell her that I'd put them there myself while I was waiting for her to arrive.

"I think someone might have tried to pick this lock." I took out my phone. "And I think that someone deliberately concealed their tracks going back into the property." I took some pictures of both the lock and the spot on the road. "I believe that there is probable cause to think that someone

217

has entered this property illegally and for nefarious purposes," I said with satisfaction.

Darlene rolled her eyes. "Thin, son, thin. How long did it take you to come up with that excuse?"

"Not too long once I decided that I want to see if someone is out there," I said, pointing to the other side of the gate.

"Entering a piece of property is a bit more tolerated than a structure," she said thoughtfully.

"If we enter on foot, we don't even have to cut the lock off. There's a place over there where a tree's fallen on the barbed wire." I pointed about thirty feet from the entrance where a pine tree lay on the ground.

"This tract is, what, twenty acres? Okay, I'm too tired to argue. I'll call Pete. Go get your vest."

She told Pete where we were and what we were planning to do, managing to make it sound more sensible and like we had more cause than we actually did. Then, with our ballistic vests on and sweat already staining our shirts, we climbed over the fence and headed down the road into the property.

We'd walked about a quarter of a mile when we came to a cul-de-sac where there was a house that must have been intended as the model home for the subdivision. The yard had never been landscaped and there was an old yard sign bearing the name of a local construction company that had gone out of business years ago. Despite all of that, the house looked in pretty good shape. It was a standard three-bedroom, two-bath from the look of it and there were even blinds in the windows.

"What do you think?" I asked. Darlene and I were on the ground, pressed into the undergrowth and watching the house.

"I say we approach the house slowly, staying in the tree line, and hope no one sees us. Maybe if we can get closer, we'll be able to tell something."

"We could just walk up to the front door and knock," I suggested.

"Tree line first," she said and began making her way through the underbrush. She was right, of course. The sun was bright and we'd be in the shadows. There was a fair chance that, even if someone looked out a window, they wouldn't see us.

The closest we could get to the house and still be somewhat concealed was seventy-five feet away. When we reached that point, we stopped and watched the house again. Nothing moved, but as we squatted in the palmettos we heard the air conditioner cycle on. We both grinned.

"Doesn't prove a thing," Darlene said, but for the first time that day she looked wide awake.

"I know. We have no evidence of any crime being committed. We don't even know who's in the house. Could be a legal tenant. Even if it's our suspect, and I'm using air quotes around suspect, what's he done?" I puzzled over the problem.

We sat there sweating for another ten minutes.

"Hell with this. I'm going to knock on the door," I said, starting to stand up.

Darlene grabbed my arm and pulled me back down.

"If someone answers, what are you going to say?" she hissed.

"The truth. I'm looking for a young man who's gone missing," I said, sounding more sure of myself than I was.

"Okay. Do you want me to go with you or stay here? If I stay here, we can't both be taken by surprise up by the house. However, if things break bad at the door, I won't be right there to help."

"Stay here. If something happens, then at least you can call for backup. Technically, this is no different than walking up to any house in any neighborhood and knocking on the door. Only difference is that we went around the gate. For all the person in that house knows, someone might have run into the gate…" As soon as I said it, I realized that was a better excuse for why I was there. "I've modified my plan. I'm going to knock on the door, but I'll tell whoever answers that the gate's been tampered with."

"We're going to get in trouble for this, I can tell. I think I want a new partner," Darlene muttered.

"Yes, we probably will get into trouble, and you just might get your wish and end up with a new partner. But here…" I took out my phone and dialed Darlene's number. "We'll have an open line so you can hear what's happening." Then I stood up and headed for the house.

CHAPTER TWENTY-FOUR

How much of a chance am I taking? I wondered. That was the problem with this situation. There were so many variables that it was impossible to know what kind of danger I was putting myself in. Unfortunately, without probable cause, there weren't any good options. This house was so far back on the property that, short of a drone, there was no way we could keep it under passive observation. And I couldn't call for more backup because, if I was being honest, the law wouldn't uphold our right to enter the property on the flimsy excuse I'd manufactured.

Resigned, I walked purposefully toward the front door. There was a post-apocalyptic air about the place—a perfectly normal house surrounded by sidewalks and a cracked driveway half covered by sand, and with thick clumps of grass growing through the cracks. All the other lots were barren, with weeds and vines already overrunning their boundaries.

When I reached the front door, I could hear soft music coming from inside. *Weird*, I thought and rapped on the door. The music stopped. I waited and listened. After a minute, I knocked again and heard footsteps approaching the door. I could feel myself being scrutinized through the peephole.

Finally, the door opened and there stood Terrance Robbins, neat and unruffled. His eyes were locked on the word "Deputy" printed across my ballistic vest.

"Hey, I guess," he said. His eyes were darting left and right, looking behind me. "I don't mean to be rude, but what are you doing on my property?"

"Sorry, there was evidence of a break-in back up at the gate, and I thought I'd better check to see if anyone was trespassing," I said, trying to sound casually officious.

"Again, I don't want to be an asshole, but I think you're the only one trespassing." His tone was heading toward irritated rather fast. "Where's your car?"

"Left it at the gate. Are you Terrance Robbins?" I asked, knowing that he was.

"That's right. Did I mention that this is my property?"

"Sorry, if I could see some ID…" I was playing very fast and loose with Florida's stop-and-frisk law. An officer with reasonable cause could stop, detain and ask for ID. Would what we found at the gate be interpreted as reasonable cause that criminal activity might be taking place? I doubted it, but I wanted to push Robbins and see what happened.

"I'll go get it." His eyes told me everything I needed to know. They had gone dark and cold. He'd obviously made up his mind that I wasn't just some conscientious officer protecting his property.

Robbins started to close the door, but I stuck my foot in the way. Then he did something childish and very, very stupid. He slammed his foot down on mine, giving me full justification to arrest him. Everything that I had done up to that point might have been debatable and may have voided any charges. But now no one could doubt that Robbins had taken an academic question of police procedure and turned it into a case of physical assault on an officer.

I was startled long enough that I wasn't able to grab him before he retreated into the house. I pushed through the door after him, reaching for my gun in the process.

"Going in!" I shouted, hoping that Darlene was already breaking cover and heading toward the house.

The living and dining rooms were clear, but the house had a very strange vibe. It looked like a regular family home, with toys on the floor and family pictures on the wall. Odd for a model home.

I heard a noise from the other side of the kitchen and quickly made my way toward what I figured was a door into the garage. I just caught sight of it closing and threw my weight against it. I was momentarily thrown off by what I found on the other side.

The garage had been turned into a mix of operating room and torture chamber. The walls were covered with soundproof padding like they use in recording studios, and glaring fluorescent lights shone down from the ceiling. Strapped to a reclining table was what might have been a human, but it was hard to tell through the blood and bruises. Standing behind the chair, breathing hard and holding a scalpel to the neck of the person in the chair, was Terrance Robbins. His victim's eyes were open with a wild and frantic look in them. The gag in his mouth prevented him from talking, but the eyes were begging for rescue.

"Don't make another move, or I swear he'll die," Robbins commanded. I had no doubt he was telling the truth. "Put your gun down," he ordered. I hesitated. "Put it down and slide it over here."

"No," I said, trying to concentrate on the front sight and wondering if I could make the headshot that would turn off Robbins's neurological system before he could cut his victim's throat. Robbins was half-crouched behind the chair and I was only four yards away. But whether I made the shot would depend on a lot of variables, mostly involving what kind of control I had over my *own* neurological system. I didn't want to have to try it. However, there was no way I was giving this psycho my gun.

"Three seconds."

"We have a Mexican standoff. If you kill him, then you

will die."

"Put the gun down and slide it over here," he repeated as though he could mesmerize me into doing what he said.

"I'll compromise. I'll put the gun down, but I'll put it on that table," I offered, nodding toward a table that was a couple feet away and closer to me than to him. I wouldn't have a hard time getting to it before he did. Besides, he seemed very possessive of his victim.

"Do it, then!" Robbins barked.

I thought I heard a sound from the front of the house, but I kept my eyes locked on his. Luckily, his focus remained on me, the gun and our psychological struggle for dominance. I put the gun down on the table.

"Move away from the table," he said, and I moved back to where I'd been standing.

"That's Seth Craig."

"Oh, yeah," Robbins gloated.

"Help me to understand this," I said, holding my hand up and out in a non-threatening manner.

"He killed my family," he hissed.

"I thought that's what this was all about, but… now I'm not so sure."

"He killed my son! Crippled my wife. I lost everything. My business collapsed," he ranted. "Now he's finally paying the price for what he did to me."

What he did to me, I thought. Now we were getting down to it.

"And that's why you killed Matt Greene and Joel Weaver?"

"Damn right. All of them caused it. Incompetence and idiocy."

"Where did you get the bomb?" I knew, but wanted the connection spelled out.

"You know," he spat back at me. He'd obviously heard about the incident on the Thompson property.

"We know who made the bomb, but how did you find him?" I asked.

Robbins hesitated. I could see the battle raging in his mind. On the one hand, he wanted to brag about how clever he was, but on the other, he had secrets that he thought should be guarded.

"I knew him," he said, stopping short of a real explanation. That's when I remembered that Terrance Robbins had had an opioid addiction.

"You knew the Thompsons because of your drug addiction."

"My addiction was his fault." He jabbed the scalpel at Seth's throat and I flinched.

"So did you go to the Thompsons and ask for their help with killing Matt?"

I got a look of pity for my stupidity. "I'd been helping to take care of McCoy. I took him supplies a few times over the last couple of months." He couldn't stop himself from explaining it to me. Going into lecture mode made him feel superior.

"So you went directly to McCoy when you wanted to kill Matt."

"That's right. I told McCoy that we were going to take out Eddie for the Thompsons. I couldn't give a shit about Eddie."

I could see now why McCoy had felt suicidal. Not only was he facing the risk of capture and becoming a potential source of a lot of incriminating evidence against a whole bunch of powerful folks, but he must have also realized that he'd been tricked into making the bomb by this psychopath.

"You worked with the Thompsons?"

"I invested in their operations."

"You mean their drug smuggling?"

"Whatever. They needed cash. I needed an investment with a high return."

And being hooked in with drug dealers made your habit easier to feed, I thought. "Then you shot Weaver."

"Ha, wrong! I took Weaver out there and helped him, but he pulled the trigger. He was grateful that I was going to help him die. That man was a pathetic waste of a life," Robbins said in disgust.

"Why now?"

"What?"

"Why start killing them now?" I asked, knowing part of the answer. The DEA and the FBI had seized all of the Thompsons' assets, which would have included all the money that Robbins had invested. No wonder he'd gone off the deep end. Another huge failure in a long line of failures.

"I'm dying. I have pancreatic cancer like my father. When I heard that Greene was going to be back in the county, it seemed like a sign. They owed me."

"About that. Let's be honest with each other." I hoped that the cavalry was on the way. I had to force myself not to look toward the door where I hoped that Darlene was just on the other side. "You're doing all of this because they ruined your life." *Not because they killed your son or crippled your wife, you maniac.*

"Exactly. Before they killed my family, I had everything. I was ready to develop this land into a top-notch subdivision with businesses as well as residences. I had my family living in a home just like this one so that I could see what innovations to make in the layout and design."

I realized that he must have decorated this house to look like the one they'd been living in at the time of the accident. Reliving his glory days.

"So your son is killed, your wife crippled and the business tanks."

"It wouldn't have if I hadn't had to take care of Carrie. I'd have ridden out the housing crisis," he said.

Yeah, sure.

"Taking care of her and the collapse of your business caused you to start taking drugs." I didn't even mention his son. This wasn't about any of them. The only person who'd ever really existed in his world was him.

"They were right there. Carrie was taking them. That was their fault too!" he yelled.

How was it Greene's, Weaver's and Craig's fault that you stole drugs from your crippled wife? I wanted to ask, but bit it back. Instead I said, "So here you are holding Seth hostage, a knife to his throat in this half-ass operating room in your garage," I said, hoping that Darlene was still able to hear through my phone… or from the other side of the door.

"Exactly. I'm making them all pay. He should have gone on trial. I'm just putting him through a trial by fire. They all should have been tried. I tried to sue them. Judge threw out the claim against Greene, and all I got was a pathetic settlement from the Craigs' insurance company."

"You know, you have an opportunity here," I said and got a suspicious stare back from him.

"Don't feed me any crap. You want to kill me or throw me in prison."

"That's very true."

"So?"

"You said you have cancer. You're going to die anyway. But you can still leave a lasting mark."

"I've killed two people."

"That's small change in this day and age…"

"I can make it three." He put the scalpel closer to Seth's neck. He'd passed out, but I could see his chest rising and falling.

"Another one isn't going to move the needle very far," I said in my best used-car salesman voice. I could see the look of interest in his eyes. At least he wanted to know what I was going to propose.

"Look at him." I nodded toward Seth. "Look at the wounds on his face. The damage that you've already done to him."

"So?"

"You went to some of his AA meetings, right?" I asked, and he gave a slight nod. "Seth is a good speaker, sympathetic. How much more so will he be now?" I said, pointing to the poor man who'd been stripped of his dignity, covered in his own blood and scars. How long had Robbins been torturing him? I prayed that it wasn't the whole time he'd been missing.

"Yeah…"

"Think about it. *People Magazine*, talk shows, Facebook, the Discovery Channel. He could be everywhere. And every time he's in the spotlight, you're in the spotlight. A walking, talking advertisement for how badass you were."

"Don't patronize me," he said, but without any bite. I was reaching his dark inner need to be the center of attention.

"You have *accomplished* something. You may be dying, but that doesn't mean your work has to die with you." It was hard to know where the line between selling and overselling was. I shut up so he could mull it over in his head.

"I see…" His eyes had a distant stare.

I'd dangled the carrot. Now I decided a little stick was in order. "Besides, you can't get out of this garage."

His eyes flashed back to mine and I thought that maybe I should have waited to apply the stick. But one look at Seth made me think that he didn't have the luxury of time.

"You're going to stop me?" There was humor in his voice.

"No. The deputy on the other side of that door and the others surrounding the property, *they're* going to stop you."

"Bullshit!" he tossed out, but he knew.

"Darlene!" I yelled.

"I'm here!" came her voice from the other side of the door.

I watched Robbins as he took in this information. My challenge was to monitor his paranoia and to balance it with his desire for recognition. The minute he felt like he'd lost control would be the same time he became unpredictable.

"I'm not telling you anything you don't already know. Time is not your friend here. Right now, you have complete control over the situation and the outcome. That control won't last. Make the most of it by making the choice that will leave a lasting impression. Do what you want. But think about what I've told you. There *is* a win-win option for you."

"I don't see that," he said. "I understand what you're saying with this piece of shit, but how's that a win-win for me?"

"You told me you were dying." I touched my hand to the pocket where my phone was and disconnected the call, then lowered my voice. "Let him go and then kill yourself. You don't go to jail and he reminds people who you were."

Encouraging him to kill himself wouldn't play very well if anyone ever found out, but I needed him to see a way forward for himself. A way where he could be in control until the end.

"Do you have a phone on you?" Robbins asked after a long while.

"Yes."

"Take it out."

I did as he asked.

"Hold it up and turn the video camera on," he instructed in a controlled and steady voice. I did so, knowing what was coming. I didn't want to film him, but I also didn't want anything to interrupt the flow of events.

"Let me see that it's running."

I turned the phone so he could see the screen and then turned it back on him.

Terrance Robbins stood up. With a calm, steady motion he put the knife to his own throat and pulled it across his neck. In less then a second, a red grin formed under his chin and blood began to spurt from the artery on the left side of his neck. I stopped the video. After fifteen long seconds, his body slowly twisted and sank to the floor, spreading an arc of blood around him.

I rushed to Seth and yelled for Darlene to call an ambulance.

Twenty minutes later, they'd stabilized Seth Craig enough to move him to the hospital. At first he'd refused any morphine for the pain, until I'd called his mother. After telling her that Seth had been found, I asked her to encourage him to take the drugs, just to allow the EMTs to get him to the hospital. At last he relented.

Darlene walked up to me as I stood in front of the house, watching the ambulance drive away as a steady stream of Feds, other deputies and crime scene techs arrived.

"Robbins bled out before the paramedics could do anything," she said to me.

"Can't say I'm going to lose any sleep over that."

"Funny thing about the phone cutting out just before things went crazy."

"I must have accidentally hit it with my hand," I said flatly.

"With the suspect dead, we won't have a trial with a pesky defense lawyer asking us why we entered the property in the first place," Darlene said with just a hint of rebuke in her voice.

I turned and looked her in the eye. "The way things went down was the only way I saw them resolving quickly enough to get Seth out of there alive. Nothing else was on my mind."

"I believe you, which is why I didn't hear anything through the door after the phone went dead." Darlene walked away to talk to Agent Padilla, who'd just shown up on the scene.

A mosquito bit me, and I swatted it against my neck. Pulling my hand away, I looked at the splotch of blood on my palm. Thinking how lucky I was that this was the only bit of my own blood that I'd spilled solving this case, I was suddenly overcome with the image of Matt's body lying in the wreckage of the car. My legs felt rubbery. Why had I lived when another man who might have gone on to do great things was dead? I wondered if I would ever be able to come to terms with that.

That afternoon, I was debriefed and given a minor rebuke by Dad and Lt. Johnson for the way we had entered the property. I tried to convince everyone that any poor judgment should reflect back on me and not Darlene. The truth of it was, no one really cared how we got on the property. When you save a hostage, it's hard for anyone to give you too much crap about the method. And, like Darlene had said, without a trial it didn't really matter.

Cara came straight to the office when she got off work and we sat in her car with the air conditioner running.

"It's really nice not to be visiting you in the hospital," she said.

I squeezed her hand and smiled at her. "I always *try* not to get hurt. You know I'm a baby when it comes to pain."

"That poor guy. Is he going to be okay?"

"Remarkably, he's not even in ICU. A blood transfusion and some fluids was what he needed most. Though Dad did tell me that they had to use over two hundred stiches to close all of his wounds. They also pumped him full of antibiotics, though he told them that Robbins would rub salt or pour alcohol on the cuts, so at least the wounds were clean," I said with a shudder. "At any rate, according to the doctors, he'll be able to walk out of the hospital in a week."

"Has anyone told Mrs. Greene?"

"Dad called and filled her in."

"I feel so bad for her."

My phone rang and I looked at the ID. "It's Pam Greene," I said in surprise.

"Deputy Macklin, I will always be grateful that you caught the man who did this to Matt. I know that Matt would appreciate all you've done. Will you come to Orlando for the funeral on Thursday?"

"Of course."

"I'm glad. I've already told the DEA how much I appreciate their support through all of this, but I've asked them to let you present the flag to me at the funeral. Would you do that?"

I choked back tears and told her I'd be honored. Three days later, with Cara, Dad and Lt. Johnson sitting just two rows behind her, I kneeled down and placed the flag in Mrs.

Greene's hands. As I stood up and saluted her, I finally felt myself begin to heal.

The following Tuesday, I met Ms. Craig at the hospital when she went to pick up Seth. His body was on the mend, but how long it would take for the shadow to begin to lift from his mind, I couldn't guess.

"Could I talk to you for a minute?" Ms. Craig asked after Seth had gotten into her car.

"Of course," I said, wondering what she wanted.

She led me a little way from the car.

"An odd young man came by the hospital yesterday. He said he was your assistant or something and knew Seth from AA meetings."

I began to grind my teeth. *What the hell is Eddie up to now?*

Before I could open my mouth to apologize for anything he might have done, she went on. "He asked Seth to be his sponsor in NA." A tear started to roll down her cheek. "That was all Seth could talk about after he left. I'm so grateful to him. It was the first time Seth seemed like his old self."

"I'll tell Eddie."

"There was something strange, though, about his... chest. I just... I don't know, but it looked like he was wearing a bra. Of course, that's silly," she said, looking confused as she got into her car.

I had no words. I could only wave as I walked back to my car. Before I could pull out of the parking spot, my phone rang.

"I just talked with Dr. Darzi," Pete said without preamble.

"Okay, so?" I said, wondering what this was about.

"I don't know whether to laugh or cry. Turns out Terrance Robbins didn't have pancreatic cancer after all. Darzi couldn't find any signs of it. He figures that the kook had a bladder infection and, knowing that his father had died of cancer, reached his own diagnosis."

"Ain't that a kicker," I said noncommittally.

Later that day, I stopped by Albert Griffin's house. I'd let Eddie know when we found the real killer, but between Matt's funeral and all the work to close the investigation, I hadn't yet had time to give him the details.

"My father actually turned on his dad?" Eddie said incredulously after I told him everything that had happened,

"So the pressure isn't going to all be on you as they move forward with the prosecution of your grandfather and his cohorts. Your dad is now the DEA's chief witness. You'll just be backup."

"Wow! Gramps always treated him rough. Dad's favorite story was about when he was thirteen and snuck off to go deer hunting rather then help his dad fix up a barn the week before Christmas. They had a big industrial wood chipper and the old bastard chipped up all of Dad's gifts as punishment. And just so Dad would remember why he didn't have any gifts on Christmas morning, my grandfather put a cardboard box with all the chipped-up presents beside the tree."

"That's hardcore," I said.

"With stories like that, I always sort of understood where my father got his mean streak. But you know what? It didn't make it any easier to take the abuse."

"That was a nice thing you did for Seth," I said, changing the subject.

"Oh, what, me asking him to be my sponsor? I figure if he can go through all that and remain sober, maybe I can too."

Mr. Griffin walked in with the offer of a beer, but I declined.

"Are you ready to get rid of him?" I asked.

"Not at all. Only problem is, he's making Brutus fat."

On cue, Brutus came into the room and rubbed up against Eddie's legs.

"You've overcome your fear of cats?" I asked Eddie, who was reaching down to pet Brutus.

A. E. HOWE

"Brutus is all right," Eddie said, gently running his hand down the cat's back.

"He's been feeding him chicken strips. I warned him that Brutus would get lazy and give up his day job as a mouser," Mr. Griffin said, shaking his head.

"Do you need help finding a place to stay?" I asked Eddie, feeling it only fair that I help Mr. Griffin get his house back.

"No. Albert said I could live above his garage."

"Did he?" I said. "Let's go take a look at it, if Albert doesn't mind."

"I don't mind."

I half dragged Eddie out of the house. Once outside, I poked my finger in his chest.

"Don't you want to see the apartment?"

"I couldn't care less about the apartment. But I want to give you fair warning. Albert Griffin is a nice old guy. He doesn't need any grief. Despite the meetings and the sponsor, you're still an addict. If you do anything that ruffles that old man's feathers, I will find the nearest ball-peen hammer and come looking for you. No, correct that. Seth and I both will come find you. Do you understand?"

"I do, I do. I swear! I like the old guy too. I wouldn't hurt him for the world," Eddie said.

"Just so we understand each other."

I left the house, thinking what an odd world it was and how our lives turned on such small chance events. As a reminder of how lucky my own life was, Cara greeted me at the door when I got home. I pulled her into a long hug and felt the heart pendant between our bodies as I kissed her.

Larry Macklin returns in:

August's Heat
A Larry Macklin Mystery–Book 10

ACKNOWLEDGMENTS

The usual thanks go out to my wife, Melanie, for her editing skills and support; and to H. Y. Hanna for her inspiration, assistance and encouragement.

And to all the fans of the series—thank you!!

Original Cover Concept by H. Y. Hanna
Cover Design by Robin Ludwig Design Inc.
www.gobookcoverdesign.com

ABOUT THE AUTHOR

A. E. Howe lives and writes on a farm in the wilds of north Florida with his wife, horses and more cats than he can count. He received a degree in English Education from the University of Georgia and is a produced screenwriter and playwright. His first published book was *Broken State*; the Larry Macklin Mysteries is his first series and he has plans for more. The first book in the series, *November's Past*, was awarded two silver medals in the 2017 President's Book Awards, presented by the Florida Authors & Publishers Association. A member of the Mystery Writers of America, Howe is also the co-host of the "Guns of Hollywood" podcast, part of the Firearms Radio Network. When not writing or podcasting, Howe enjoys riding, competitive shooting and working on the farm.